ALL THAT'S BRIGHT AND GONE

ALL THAT'S BRIGHT AND GONE

a novel

ELIZA NELLUMS

CROOKED LANE

NEW YORK

Published in the United States by Crooked Lane Books, an imprint of The Quick Brown Fox & Company LLC.

Crooked Lane Books and its logo are trademarks of The Quick Brown Fox & Company LLC.

Library of Congress Catalog-in-Publication data available upon request.

ISBN (hardcover): 978-1-64385-237-9
ISBN (ebook): 978-1-64385-238-6

Cover design by Melanie Sun
Book design by Jennifer Canzone

Printed in the United States.

www.crookedlanebooks.com

Crooked Lane Books
34 West 27th St., 10th Floor
New York, NY 10001

First Edition: December 2019

10 9 8 7 6 5 4 3 2 1

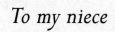

To my niece

Chapter One

I know my brother is dead. I'm not dumb like Hazel Merkowicz from up the street says.

Sometimes Mama just gets confused, is all.

Like every year on the feast of Saint Theodore, his birthday, Mama sets out an extra plate for Theo, with a candle on it instead of food, because I guess Theo isn't hungry. And Mama says, "Isn't this nice? It's like we're all together again."

I guess it's nice.

"Alfie? Uh, Alfie Scott?"

That man with the clipboard probably means me. I stand up. "C'mon, Teddy," I whisper. I cover my mouth with my hand, because Mama always tells me not to talk to Teddy out loud where strangers can hear me.

Teddy gets up when I do, walking on all fours behind me with his big head hanging down. We go over to the clipboard man, who is wearing pale-blue pajamas, and I say, "Here I am."

"Is it Alfie, sweetheart? Did I get that right?"

"It's *Aoife*," I say. *EE-fah*. I have to say it a lot. Grown-ups never get it right.

"Oh, okay. Eva. Why don't you come along with me and we'll go see the doc, okay?"

Teddy growls, but I pretend not to hear him. "Okay," I say.

We walk together down a white hallway that smells like bleach. "That's a real interesting name you've got," says the clipboard man. "The spelling of it, I mean."

"My mama's name is *Sha-VOHN*," I say. "It's spelled S-I-O-B-A—I mean, B-H-A-N."

"Wow, I guess you-all must be Irish, huh?"

"No," I say politely. "We're from Chicago."

The man stops at a white wooden door and knocks. "Come in," someone says from inside.

"Dr. Pearlman, this is Eva Scott," he says, putting a hand on my shoulder and guiding me in. "She's the little girl who was brought in from Westgate Mall."

"Oh yes. Eva. Hello," says Dr. Pearlman. She's a gray-haired lady with a big necklace of yellow glass. There's yellow beads hanging from her ears, too.

Teddy doesn't like her.

"It's with an *f*," I say quietly. "*Ee-fah*."

She looks down at her file. "What an unusual name," she says. "I've never seen it before!"

"It's after my grandmother," I say, because that's what Mama always says. "And my middle name is Joan because my birthday is on her special day." I like that Joan is my saint, because she was brave. Mama says Joan was a warrior and Aoife is a warrior's name, too, back in the old country.

"How lovely." Dr. Pearlman doesn't know it, but Teddy is biting her shoe. He's going to pull it right off her foot if she's not careful.

"How old are you, Ee-fah?"

"Six."

"That's great," she says.

I'm not really sure why it's great, but I nod anyway.

"Well, come on inside. Why don't we sit down over here?"

She was sitting behind a desk, but she gets up to walk over to another table and chairs that are my size, like they have at school. She sits in one of the chairs—I think it's going to topple over, but she's good at balancing on it—and I pull out the other one. Teddy tries to sit in the third chair, but he's fat, and he kind of splodges over the side.

"I think I have some play dough here," she says. "Would you like that?"

I nod. Mama doesn't like me to play with play dough because it makes a mess, but Dr. Pearlman doesn't have to know that.

She hands me a carton with a blue lid. My favorite color is red, but I can be a big girl, so I don't complain. I peel back the lid and stick my nose in, because I like how it smells like melted crayons. Then I dump it out on the table and start to make snakes. I always start by making snakes.

"Would you like to play too?" I ask, because Mama says you should be polite, even when there's not enough clay in one carton for two people to make a lot of snakes.

Dr. Pearlman picks off a little corner. I guess that's okay. She pinches it between her fingers and makes it into a little Frisbee.

"So Aoife, can you tell me about what happened this morning?" she asks. She says my name pretty close to right. I can hear the *f*.

Still, Teddy shakes his head no. He doesn't want me to say.

"I don't know," I say.

Dr. Pearlman sighs. I look down at my hands and flatten one of the snakes.

"Tell me about your mommy," she says.

I don't call her *Mommy*, I call her *Mama*. "Her name's Siobhan," I say. "She's trying to teach me cartwheels. But I can't do them yet."

3

"My mommy and I used to turn cartwheels too," says Dr. Pearlman, smiling.

I try to think of how to describe Mama. If she was an animal, she'd be a horse, because she's pretty and nice and has long hair.

If I could *pick* any animal, I'd be a bear for sure—as big as a house. But if I had to be the animal that is most like me, I'd probably be . . . maybe a squirrel? Or a chipmunk.

But I'd rather be a bear.

"She likes going to church a lot," I say. "And she's going to take me to see the fireworks for the Fourth of July, and I can't wait." We watched the Canada Day ones on TV, but these ones will be even better because we're going to see them *live and in person*. "Mama is the best."

"That sounds really fun!" says Dr. Pearlman. If she was an animal, she'd be one of those birds that deliver babies. She has skinny arms and a big head. "I bet your mommy is the best. But I guess she gets mad sometimes, too, right?"

"I guess," I say. "But not very often." She mostly gets mad at Mac, who she calls *an old cuss* when they are speaking. They are usually not speaking.

"Was your mommy angry this morning?" asks Dr. Pearlman.

"Aoife, I want to talk to you about something important," Mama said. But she never told me what it was.

"She wasn't mad," I say. "But she doesn't like it when I talk to Teddy. And I was talking to him."

"Who's Teddy?" Dr. Pearlman asks, looking around like she expects to see him. Which is dumb, because no one can see Teddy but me.

I motion to the chair where Teddy is sitting. "He's there," I say.

"Ahh." Dr. Pearlman nods wisely. "Hello, Teddy. I apologize, I didn't notice you there."

I giggle. Dr. Pearlman is funny. Mama never, ever talks to Teddy.

"You know, it's interesting, I notice in my papers here that you have a brother named Theodore," says Dr. Pearlman, motioning to the file in front of her. It's full of black boxes and squinty little letters. Even though I can read some things some of the time, I can't read the little words on those pages.

"Yeah," I say, nodding.

She reads a little further and frowns. I figure the papers are telling her Theo died. That's one of the things that makes Mama sad. She goes to visit him every other week, and sometimes I can tell she's been crying when she comes home. One time we went to visit Gramma Aoife, and I was excited, but when we got there it was just a big field full of rocks, so I'm glad I don't have to visit Theo with Mama.

"Did you call your brother Teddy too?" asks Dr. Pearlman, her voice softer now.

I don't know. I shrug. I don't really remember when my brother was around. "Mama always calls him Theo," I say. "But I call my Teddy that because he's a bear."

Right now Teddy is almost as big as the ceiling. That's why he doesn't fit in the chair so good.

I don't really miss Theo at all, because I have Teddy.

"I see," says Dr. Pearlman thoughtfully. "So, your mommy doesn't like it when you talk to Teddy?"

"She tells me not to do it," I say.

"Sometimes mommies have their own opinion about what is good behavior," says Dr. Pearlman.

I know what *opinion* means because Sister Mary Celeste, my teacher at Sacred Heart, told us. An opinion means, *what do you think.*

"It's rude to talk to people when other people can't see them," I explain. "But Mama broke the rule, and that's why she got in trouble."

Dr. Pearlman puts down the file. "She broke the rule?"

"Yeeeah," I say slowly. Teddy is watching me with his arms crossed. He's pouting. But this time he doesn't tell me not to say anything. "She was talking to Theo in the car. She was yelling."

"Your mommy was talking to your brother?"

"Yes. But Theo wasn't there," I say. Because he's *dead*.

Dr. Pearlman has made a heart out of her piece of play dough. "I bet that was scary for you, when your mommy was confused," she says.

"Where is he, Aoife? What happened? What happened to him?"

"She was yelling," I say. "She got in trouble because she wasn't using her indoor voice, and that makes people mad."

In school Sister Mary Celeste tells us to use our indoor voices, and I'm very good at remembering. In fact, I'm the best in the class because I don't like to yell. I like to whisper. But now it's summer, and I won't see Sister Mary Celeste again until the fall.

I start making my snakes into a dog. One snake, folded in half, becomes the front legs, and one becomes the back legs. Then a really fat one becomes the body. That's why it's good to start with snakes. You can build anything out of snakes.

"Sometimes Mama doesn't sleep so well, or she has bad dreams," I say, trying to make a head out of a lump. My fingers are turning blue, and it gets under my nails. I don't like that. "And sometimes she yells and stuff. My friend Hannah says she's scary and she won't come over to our house anymore."

Dr. Pearlman looks sad.

"Hannah wants to be a detective," I say. She's my best friend, even though she's already eight. She reads lots of books about kids who solve crimes, and she's always finding us mysteries, too. She calls regular things like umbrellas or apples *clues*, and she says muddy tire tracks are *evidence*.

When I told Hannah I used to have a brother who died, she asked what killed him. I said I thought there was an accident.

"Maybe it wasn't *really* an accident," Hannah said, looking excited.

"*What happened? What happened to him?*" Mama said.

"Aoife, sometimes even really nice mommies get confused about things, and sometimes they need some help figuring out what's real," says Dr. Pearlman. "I bet there's times when you've been confused and needed someone to help you?"

I nod my head, because there's lots of times I'm confused. But that's why Teddy is here, to tell me what to do. He's really good at that.

"My friends and I here at the hospital want to help your mommy," Dr. Pearlman continues. "Does that sound okay to you?"

I don't know what she means, but I nod my head anyway because that's polite. I look down at my clay doggy. It doesn't look right. I bet Dr. Pearlman can't even tell if it's supposed to be a dog or a horse or a cat. I wish I was better with play dough, like Hannah is. I squish the doggy back into a lump of clay.

"I'm going to make a basket," I tell Dr. Pearlman.

"That sounds like a good idea," she says. She gets up from the table, and I work on making a little bowl out of clay, pushing my thumb in the middle to make the hole.

When Dr. Pearlman comes back, she's carrying a blue purse by the leather strap.

"That's my mama's purse," I say. I'm not supposed to touch Mama's purse without asking. "You shouldn't play with that."

"Well, your mommy said it was okay if I was very, very careful," Dr. Pearlman explains. "Because my friends and I are trying to help her, remember?"

Teddy thinks it would be fun to look in the purse, even though I know I'm not supposed to. But since Dr. Pearlman is opening the top of it anyway, I figure it can't hurt to look inside just once. "Okay."

There's not much in there. Just Mama's pill bottles that I'm not supposed to touch. Although sometimes Teddy likes to rattle them, and they make a lot of noise. That's fun.

Dr. Pearlman puts them to the side, though, and reaches into the bottom of the purse to dig around down there. She pulls out Mama's cell phone and her wallet.

"Do you recognize this phone?" she asks me.

Sure I do. Teddy loves Mama's phone, and sometimes Mama will give it to us to play with. "You can play games on there," I explain. "I like the one with the little candies."

"I like that one too," says Dr. Pearlman. "Do you know how to open the phone?" She shows me the home screen, where you put in the password.

"Yeah!" I say. I take the phone and show her how to slide the bottom so the password window comes up. "You put the code in here," I say, punching it in. 1113. Mama plus me plus Theo equals three. Or as Mama says, one for the Father, one for the Son, and one for the Holy Ghost.

The phone starts up, but Dr. Pearlman takes it back before I can open a game. "Thank you very much, Aoife," she says. "It's a big help to us that you know how to open up your mommy's phone. Your mommy is going to be very proud of you when I tell her how you helped us."

"What are you doing?" I want to know. "Are we going to play a game now?"

"I was hoping you could tell me about some of the people your mommy has in her phone," Dr. Pearlman explains. That doesn't sound like a very fun game to me. "The number we have in this file is disconnected. It would be a big help to your mommy if we could call someone she knows to help us take care of you. Can you tell me if your daddy is in this phone? Or your grandma, maybe?"

"My gramma's dead," I explain. "I don't have a daddy." That's what Mama always says. She says I'm like a Cabbage Patch doll, that she found me growing in a garden and took me home.

"I see," says Dr. Pearlman. "What about this person . . . 'Stephanie'? I see that your mommy called Stephanie this morning. Is that a member of your family?"

"Stephanie babysits for Hannah and me," I say. Stephanie comes almost every day in the summer. My mama and Hannah's mom split the money to pay her, even though Hannah told me once that really she could stay with her cousins and her mom is just doing it to help Mama.

"Ah. How about 'Mac' . . . do you know who Mac is?"

"That's Mama's special friend," I say, although I don't think they're friends right now.

Sometimes Mac is around a lot, but most of the time he's not. Sometimes he goes away for months and months, and Mama says *we're well clear of him this time.*

Dr. Pearlman keeps scrolling. "How about 'Donny'?"

"That's my uncle Donovan. He's nice."

"Oh? Is Donovan your mother's brother?"

I have to think about this. I think he is. I shrug and put my basket upside down on the table so it's a roof.

"Does he live nearby?"

I don't know where Uncle Donny lives. "He comes around a lot," I say. "But not so much lately."

"I'm going to give your uncle Donovan a call. How does that sound?"

"That sounds good," I say. I like Uncle Donny, and so does Teddy.

Dr. Pearlman stands with the phone pressed to her ear. I can hear it ringing. I'm bored of playing with play dough, and I want to play on the phone. "Can I have it back when you're done?" I ask.

Dr. Pearlman puts her finger on her lips. "Hello? Is this Donovan? Yes, hello, this is Dr. Louise Pearlman at Botsford Hospital. Do you know a Siobhan Scott?"

She stands up with the phone squished between her shoulder and her ear. "Aoife, do you think you can play here like a good girl for just a minute while I talk to your uncle?"

I shrug again. Sometimes when grown-ups ask if you can do something, they are really just telling you to do it. I don't think Dr. Pearlman is going to let me play with the phone no matter what I say, so who cares.

"Thank you, sweetheart," says Dr. Pearlman. She picks up the papers on the table and puts them back in the folder. Then she takes the phone and the folder and goes out into the hallway. I can hear her talking, but I can't make out the words.

Teddy leans against the doorframe with his ear pressed up against the door, but he can't hear anything either.

"Teddy, do you think we should look in Mama's purse for some gum?" I say. Because the purse is right there by Dr. Pearlman's chair, even though she hasn't told me it's okay to play with it. I don't like to get in trouble.

But Teddy thinks it would be okay.

"Do you want some?" I ask when I find the pack and open it up. The little pieces spill out of the foil faster than I expected, and some of them fall on the floor. I blow them off like Mama showed me before I put them in my mouth. One, two, three times so it's clean now. Three is Mama's special number. Teddy says he doesn't like gum, so I have to eat all of it myself. For a little while it's fun to chase the pieces around on my hands and knees. The last piece is almost under Dr. Pearlman's desk.

I have a loose tooth, and it squishes between the other teeth when I push the gum against it. I can feel it tugging on the threads that connect it to my head, and it feels good.

"Good news, Aoife," says Dr. Pearlman, coming suddenly back into the room. I am still on the floor, but I stand up and brush myself off when I see she's looking at me.

"I talked to your uncle." I can see she's looking at Mama's purse, which I notice now is spilled all over the table. Her wallet has fallen out on the seat of Teddy's chair, and the empty gum container is torn open on the floor.

"Oops," I say. Bad Teddy.

"Ah. As I was saying . . . I talked to your uncle, and I have good news for you, sweetheart." It sounds funny when she says that. No one calls me that. Sometimes Mama calls me Jumping Bean, but mostly she just calls me Aoife. "Your uncle Donovan is going to come here to the hospital and pick you up. Would you like to go home with him? Just for a little while."

"Is Mama going to be there?" I ask. I haven't seen Mama since the blue men helped her into the back of the van.

Dr. Pearlman's mouth curls down. "Sit down, Aoife," she says, putting her hand on the back of the little chair. So I do.

"Because we want to help your mommy, we want her to stay here at the hospital with us for right now. Okay?"

It's not okay. I look at Teddy, who is chewing on the blue strap of Mama's purse. *Stop that, Teddy*, I think. *You'll get us in trouble.* But I don't say it out loud, and Teddy never listens to me.

"Can I stay too?"

"I'm sorry, dear, but that's not possible. It would be better for you to go back to your house with your uncle, where you can be more comfortable."

When will Mama be home? Teddy wants to know. She promised we'd see the fireworks, so it has to be before then. Right?

"My friend Hannah says that if your parents go away and leave you alone, then men come and take you," I tell Dr. Pearlman. "And she said you might have to live with another family and you might never see your parents again."

"That's not what anybody wants," Dr. Pearlman says. She puts her hand on my shoulder, and it's light but it's hot and big. I don't like it, but I don't make her take it away. "Remember, we want to help your mommy, and you, too."

"And Hannah says if you're bad, you get taken away from your family and have to live in Children's Prison," I say.

"This Hannah sounds like she has a very vivid imagination," says Dr. Pearlman. "Do you think that's going to happen?"

I look at Teddy. He nods his head at me.

"It doesn't seem to me that you have been a bad girl, Aoife," says Dr. Pearlman. "You helped us with your mommy's phone, didn't you?"

That's true.

"I talked to Teddy out loud," I admit. "I make Mama angry when I do that, and sometimes she yells and tells me not to. And today she was yelling, but it was to Theo and he wasn't there, and she didn't make any sense after that."

Dr. Pearlman hugs me. The only people who hug me usually are Mama and one time Sister Mary Celeste at the end of the year, after we had kindergarten graduation.

It feels okay though. Dr. Pearlman smells like oranges.

"Aoife, I know today's trip to the mall was scary," says Dr. Pearlman. "But I really don't think your mommy is angry with you, okay? In fact, I bet she's very proud of you. Now, do you want to go wait for your uncle Donovan?"

Teddy says he's ready to play, so I figure we'd better go before he starts causing trouble.

Chapter Two

It smells funny in the hospital, and it's cold. There's nothing good to look at except a bunch of *Ranger Rick* magazines that have all the puzzles solved already. There is one of those wire-and-bead toys in the corner, but those are for babies.

Teddy tries to make me laugh by making faces. He pulls the yellow beads off the wires and hangs them from his ears like Dr. Pearlman.

"Teddy, put those back!" I whisper. "Those are for little kids to play with. They're not supposed to come off." But I laugh too, so I guess he got his way.

Dr. Pearlman asked the lady nurse at the desk to look in on me, so at first she would come by every once in a while and ask, "How you holding up, honey?"

The nurse had a nice round face and her hair was twisted up in thick, spiky braids like caterpillars.

"I'm fine," I said. "Thank you."

"She's the sweetest little lamb I ever saw," I heard her say to another one of the nurses. "Don't hardly make a peep." Teddy hadn't pulled the beads off the wires then, or she wouldn't have said that.

But then the caterpillar lady went away from the desk, and a different lady came instead, and she hasn't asked me how I'm holding up at all, or anything. And I've been sitting here so long already.

I tried to ask the new desk lady if my uncle Donny was still coming, but a big man came up behind me, and even though I was there first, she talked right over my head to him instead of me. He put his big square body in front of me and I had to step back. Then they talked for a long time. So I decided to go sit back down.

Now I'm sitting in the plastic chair watching the people walk by. There is a woman on the phone talking Spanish. I know Spanish too. I know *por favor* and *gracias* and *madre de Dios*. There are kids at my school that speak only Spanish in their houses and English only at school, but Father Paul says Latin is the universal language for us all to worship the Lord in one voice.

There is a woman who is crying in the corner, real quiet. I don't like it when grown-ups cry. Most of all I don't like it when Mama cries.

If nobody ever comes, will I live here at the hospital forever? There are beds here. I heard the blue men talking about them.

"Aoife!" Uncle Donny is coming down the hallway, and I jump out of my chair to run to him. He's got Mama's purse slung over one shoulder, and Dr. Pearlman is behind him.

"Uncle Donny!"

He picks me up and spins me around in the air, and I laugh and laugh although I also want to cry. Uncle Donny has hair just exactly like my mama's, thick and wavy. I think he's the most beautiful man in the world, and Teddy likes him, too. He's running circles around Uncle Donny's feet.

If Uncle Donny was an animal, he'd be a penguin. He is funny and smart and wears suits.

"How you doing, kiddo?"

"I'm fine!" It's fun to be so high up. From Uncle Donny's arms I am almost as tall as Teddy, who can be any size and right now almost reaches the ceiling.

"You are, huh? Well okay, then!" Uncle Donny bounces me in his arms, and I throw my arms around his neck and hold on.

Uncle Donny is my favorite person except for Mama, who has to be my most favorite because she's my mother. But after her is Uncle Donny.

"Are you ready to hit the road, midget? Or you wanna hang around here a little longer?"

"No, I'm ready, I'm ready! And Teddy's ready, too!"

"Ooh yeah. I forgot about good ol' Teddy." Uncle Donny tries to put me down, but I don't put my feet down, no matter how far he bends over. So eventually he has to straighten up again and I go back up. "Uncle Donny's not a pony, you know," he teases, but he doesn't make me let go. Instead he bounces me up and walks us over to the desk.

"Dr. Pearlman says Mama can't come home with us," I whisper, looking over to where she's talking to the desk lady. "Is that true?"

"Uh, yeah. Aoife, your ma needs to stay here to work on feeling better. So I'm going to stay with you at your house. That'll be fun, huh? We're going to have a great time together!"

"But when will she be back?" I ask.

Uncle Donny doesn't answer. He leans over the desk to wait for Dr. Pearlman to be done talking.

It's true that Uncle Donny is really fun. He plays the best make-believe games with me, and we dress up dollies with funny hats made of leaves and things. Last Thanksgiving, Uncle

Donny and I mixed potions on the back porch out of rainwater and special bubbles and dried-up flowers, and Uncle Donny said it was *real magic.*

I put my cheek up against his scratchy one and rest my head in the crook of his neck. "I want to go home," I say.

Uncle Donny hears me this time. "Well then you're in luck, kiddo, because your uncle Donny is getting us sprung from this joint."

But he talks with the ladies for a long time after that. He talks to the desk lady, and the caterpillar lady and Dr. Pearlman. Although I was wide awake before, now that Uncle Donny is here I'm too sleepy to listen to all the talking. They're not talking about me anyway.

Uncle Donny's shoulder is safe and smells good. I close my eyes and hide my face in it. I want to be a big girl, but I also really want to go home to my own house to see my stuffed animals. I don't want to think about this morning. I just want to lie down in my own bed and go to sleep. Maybe when I wake up, it will turn out that none of today even happened at all and Mama will be there.

"There's going to have to be an investigation," says Dr. Pearlman. "You can expect to receive a call scheduling a visit."

Uncle Donny sighs. "Yeah, I figured."

"If you don't mind, I have just a few more questions for Aoife," says Dr. Pearlman, and Uncle Donny nudges his shoulder to make me sit up.

"Sweetheart, do you remember telling me about your friend Teddy?"

"I'm not supposed to talk about Teddy," I say. Teddy sticks his tongue out, because he doesn't like pretending not to be real.

"I just want to ask you a couple questions about him," she says. "Is that okay?"

I don't know if that would be okay. I look up at Uncle Donny to check, but he's looking down at his phone. Teddy just shrugs when I ask him.

"Can your uncle Donny see Teddy?" asks Dr. Pearlman.

"Of course not," I say, forgetting that maybe I wasn't supposed to answer. But the question is very silly. "Nobody can see Teddy but me, and one time Hannah pretended she could see him but she couldn't."

"Hannah is her friend from next door," says Uncle Donny. "Her real-live, flesh-and-blood friend."

"Don't worry, a lot of children have imaginary friends when they're young," says Dr. Pearlman. "Aoife's right at the age for it."

Teddy doesn't like it when people call him that. He blows a raspberry at Dr. Pearlman.

"Teddy has *always* been my friend," I say. "Ever since I can remember."

"She started talking about him maybe a year or so ago," says Uncle Donny.

But he was still my friend before that. I just didn't used to talk about him.

"And when did the incident with her brother occur?" asks Dr. Pearlman, taking notes.

"Almost three years back."

"Hannah says it wasn't an accident," I say.

"Enough, Aoife," says Uncle Donny. "Okay? Enough."

"I'm just saying what Hannah said!"

"Aoife, talking about Theo is something that might make more sense when you're a little older, okay?" says Dr. Pearlman kindly.

"Thank you," says Uncle Donny, resting his hip against the desk. "I'm sorry, but you understand—it's upsetting for all of us to talk about Theo."

"I do understand," says Dr. Pearlman. "Just a couple more questions, okay, Aoife?"

I shrug.

"Now, what does Teddy like to do?"

That's easy. "He likes all the things I like. We do everything together."

Dr. Pearlman nods. "Do you and Teddy ever disagree?" she asks.

"Sometimes. He likes to get me in trouble," I explain. Bad ol' Teddy.

"What do you think would happen if you didn't want to do what Teddy wanted?" she asks.

"He would be mad," I say.

"All right, what kinds of questions are these?" says Uncle Donovan.

But Dr. Pearlman asks me, "And then what would happen?"

"I think that's probably about enough for one day, huh?" says Uncle Donny. "I think we're about done up here."

Dr. Pearlman clears her throat. "I'd like to follow up with Eva," she says. She has slipped back into saying it wrong again, but I don't bother to correct her this time. "I think it might be good to have another conversation after CPS files their report."

"Yeah, I'm sure we'll look forward to *that*," says Uncle Donny. I don't know what *sea-pee-ess* means, but he doesn't sound very happy. I put my head back down on his shoulder. "Look, if we're all done here, I'd like to take my niece home. She's obviously had a pretty stressful day."

"Absolutely," says Dr. Pearlman. "Goodbye, Eva. You were a very brave girl."

I don't think I was very brave. "Bye-bye," I say, without lifting my head.

Uncle Donny boosts me up in his arms. "C'mon, babe, let's get out of here," he says. He carries me down the white hall and back to the front part of the hospital, where Officer Tom brought me first. Uncle Donny hurries through, past the coughing women and crying babies. An old man shuffles by on crutches, and Uncle Donny turns sideways to get past him. We go out through the glass doors and into the sunshine.

"It's still light out," I say in surprise. It felt like I was sitting in the white room of the hospital for days and days, but now we're standing in the parking lot and the birds are singing.

"It's only six PM," says Uncle Donny. "There's hours of light left." He carries me over to a shiny silver car. "Thank God that's over with. Let's get the hell out of here, huh?"

"You said a bad word," I tell him, giggling.

He laughs too. "Sometimes your uncle Donny likes to say bad words. But don't tell anyone, okay?" He tugs on a curl of my hair. "Now, I don't have a special seat for you in my car . . . do you usually ride in a car seat?"

"There's a booster seat in Mama's van," I say.

"Yeah, well, we're going to have to pick up the van from the mall later. Right now, how about we just try to make it home real quick, okay? You can be the lookout and keep an eye out for the fuzz."

The fuzz means *police*, it turns out.

"Maybe we'll see Officer Tom again," I say, waiting for Uncle Donny to find his keys. "Teddy liked him."

"Oh yeah? Is that who—uh, did you meet Officer Tom at the mall?"

"Yeah. He drove me to the hospital in his police car while Mama went in the special van," I say.

"*The special van*, Christ," says Uncle Donny.

Father Paul says you should never say *Jesus* or *Christ* unless you're really praying, but I still laugh.

"So, did Officer Tom at least put on the sirens for you?" He gets the door open without putting me down.

"No," I say. He stands me up on the seat, and I drop down to sit. "He said the sirens are only for when somebody could die right away. But he showed me the computer thingy in his car, and he showed me his badge, and he let me wear his police hat."

"Well, he sounds like a very nice, uh, cop," says Uncle Donny. "But let's just try to keep an eye out for his buddies until we get home, okay?"

So I get to ride in the front seat of the car like a grown-up. Teddy sits in the back, taking up the whole seat like always.

I don't say anything, but my heart beats faster and my stomach hurts when Uncle Donny starts the car. I have to say a special, secret prayer to blessed Saint Joan that she won't let the other cars hit us and smush us like a pancake. I don't want to go right through the intersection like Mama did and have everyone honk at us.

I feel a little better after I say the prayer. We drive in a slow circle around the parking lot and out onto the main street. Uncle Donny pulls out at the right time, and we go through the light when it's our turn.

Asking Saint Joan for help always works.

"Aoife, can you tell me what happened today?" he asks me.

"I don't remember," I say. It's wrong to lie, but sometimes no matter what you say, it's not going to come out right. And I already know this is going to be one of those times.

Uncle Donny sighs.

The truth is, Mama got a phone call. We were going to go to the mall because I needed shoes again and there was a big

21

sale. Mama was already having one of her bad days. She was too tired to make breakfast, so I put some chicken nuggets in the microwave and we split them, but we didn't have any more ketchup. Mama said the store doesn't sell ketchup anymore. I said ketchup isn't really for breakfast anyway, so it was okay. But I wanted ketchup. It's my favorite food.

Mama got the phone call on the way to the car, and I didn't like how her face looked, like a piece of paper. When she got into the seat, she said, "Aoife, I want to talk to you about something important."

"Okay," I said. "After this song."

We were playing the Disney soundtrack CD and I was singing along. Mama is a good singer. She can make up her own harmony right alongside Princess Jasmine. I've tried to do it, but it's too hard, because when Princess Jasmine is singing you want to sing right along with her. Mama didn't sing along this time. But it sounded pretty: me, Princess Jasmine, and the turn signal tick-tick-ticking. Teddy said I was on the wrong verse, and I said no I wasn't, I was just one line ahead. And then I remembered I wasn't supposed to talk to Teddy out loud, and I looked at Mama to see if she'd noticed.

She was looking at her lap.

Somebody honked at us.

The light to turn into the mall had gone green, but Mama just sat there. The whole song ended and the turn signal was still tick-ticking.

"Mama?" I said.

People were honking and honking now.

She glanced back at me, but not to where my eyes were. It was like she was looking just over my shoulder instead of at my face.

"It's no good, Theo," said Mama.

I was scared then, because Theo wasn't there. Theo was dead. Teddy didn't like it either. He curled up in a ball next to me and put his head under his tail.

"Mama, it's our turn," I said. "We're supposed to go now."

"I've been trying and trying to tell you, Aoife," she said. "I need you to understand what happened."

Somebody shouted something rude.

"He's waiting for us," said Mama. *"Theo, stop it!"*

And then she swung the wheel around *hard*, and we rolled into the intersection just as the light changed and the other cars started coming toward us. I screamed, because they were going to come right through the glass and hit us. Everybody was honking and Mama shrieked, and I put my head down because I didn't want to see. It was so loud it was like standing right next to the organ at church, how the sound goes right through you into your bones. Then the van stopped dead, right in the middle of the mall entrance, blocking the street.

"Theo, you can't," said Mama, in the quiet. But there was nobody around but me and Teddy.

"You're not supposed to talk to yourself out loud," I told Mama, because she always tells me that. But she didn't answer.

She unbuckled her seat belt and got out of the car. We were still in the middle of the road. She didn't even wait for me. She left the door wide open behind her.

"Mama?" I said. Teddy was growling and barking like a dog. "Mama, don't go without me."

I unbuckled myself too, but the back door was locked from the outside. I had to climb up between the seats and go out the front, and by then Mama was standing in the road, and all the cars were stopped around her with the van still sideways across the street. We had almost hit the sign, WELCOME TO WESTGATE

MALL, right between GATE and MALL, and crushed it like a potato chip.

"Stop it, Theo!" yelled Mama. She was pulling on her clothes, and then she grabbed her face with her fingernails.

Nobody was honking anymore. They were all stopped in the street, and everybody was looking at us.

"Mama!" I said. "Mama, quit it!" I ran into the street after her, even though I was afraid of the cars. I knew Saint Joan would watch over me, and Teddy was with me holding my hand, so it was okay.

A man rolled down his window when I went past him. "Hey, honey, are you guys all right? You should probably stay out of the road."

But I'm not supposed to talk to strangers, so I didn't say anything. Teddy bared his teeth.

"Go away!" Mama yelled, bending over so she was scrunched up around herself. "Leave me alone!"

The man was still leaning out the window. "Is that your mom?" he called to me, and I nodded, but I didn't talk to him, so I was still following the rule.

Other people were getting out of their cars, too.

"Somebody call mall security," said the first man.

"Call 911," said someone else.

"Theo, I'm here," said Mama. Her hair had come out of her ponytail, and it was all in her face. "Theo, I'm sorry."

I finally got right up to her and pulled on her shirt. "Mama?"

"Where is he, Aoife?" said Mama, looking right at me. "What happened? What happened to him?" She put her hands over her ears and started to sob.

A lady in a pretty dress got out of her car and came over to take my hand, pulling me away to stand on the sidewalk. I could still hear Mama crying. Her face was shiny and wet.

"You stand over here by me while we wait for the police, okay?" said the lady in the pretty dress.

"Okay," I said. I didn't know what else to do.

Mama was crying and I wanted to tell her to stop, but that never helps me when I'm crying, so I just stood there with the lady and Teddy, waiting until the blue men came.

* * *

I wish I could tell all that to Uncle Donny just like it happened, but I won't be able to tell it right. So I just watch Teddy, who has his face smushed up against the glass, making faces and trying to scare the people driving past us.

"Listen," says Uncle Donny, "I know today was rough."

"Uh-huh," I say.

"Do you . . . do you understand what happened?"

"Officer Tom said that Mama was sick, so they had to take her to the hospital," I say.

"Well, that's one way of putting it, yeah."

"But she didn't say that her tummy hurt, and she didn't close her eyes and lie down like when she has a headache," I say. "Does she have the flu again?" I don't know why the flu would make you stand in the middle of the road yelling like that.

Uncle Donny blows out his breath. "Um, what did the lady at the hospital say?"

"Dr. Pearlman?"

"Yeah. You talked to Dr. Pearlman for a while, right?"

"We played with play dough," I say. "She made a heart."

"That sounds great. But uh, what did she say about your ma?"

I frown, trying to remember. I mostly remember the play dough. "She said sometimes mommies get confused."

"Okay, yeah, that's—your ma was confused again, like she gets sometimes. So she's going to stay at the hospital and they're going to, ah, help get her straightened out."

"And then she's going to come back home?" I want to ask Uncle Donny *when*, but if I ask, he might say that it won't be for a long, long time—and then it will be true. "It's . . . not like Theo, right?"

"*What?* No, baby, not like Theo. Definitely not like Theo, okay? This is a whole different, uh, kettle of fish here. All right? I promise."

"Okay."

"You believe me, right?"

"Yes, because it's wrong to lie."

"That's right! Uncle Donny doesn't lie about the important things, does he?"

We drive a little further until we get to my favorite road, Telegraph. "Almost home now," says Uncle Donny.

"Mama is going to be home in time for the fireworks," I say. Because she said she'd take me, and Teddy and I have been waiting and waiting.

"That's next week, huh?"

I don't know. It's further away than tomorrow, I know that. We'll go to bed and wake up and go to bed and wake up, and at some point, it'll be fireworks. "We're going to go see them at the lake." Mama said they make a reflection in the water. "Mama promised."

"You don't happen to know which lake? All right, well, try not to panic. Uncle Donny's a problem-solver; he'll figure it out. We will go see fireworks, okay? I guess you like those a lot, huh."

I don't want to go with Uncle Donny and not Mama. He can come too, but I want to watch them with her.

I put my head down on the side of the car. It's soft, not like Mama's car, where the inside of the door is plastic. That's 'cuz Uncle Donny's got more money than us. "They already did the Canada ones downtown, and we didn't go."

"Well, we'll get to see them in living color this time, okay? Pinkie swear."

I nod, and I want to say it's okay, but like a baby, I feel my face getting hotter and my eyes start to burn.

Uncle Donny parks the car in front of our house.

"It was because I was talking to Teddy, wasn't it?" I say. "Mama told me not to talk to him where people could hear, and I did. But it was Teddy's fault!"

He puts his arm around my shoulder and squeezes. "It wasn't because of Teddy," he says. "Okay? Your Mama is just . . . sad about Theo sometimes, and it makes . . . it makes it hard for her to—to concentrate, okay?"

"She really misses him," I say. Nobody told me that. I just know it.

"Yeah, that's true," says Uncle Donny, rubbing a hand over his face. "What happened with Theo is, you know, it's very sad. For, uh, everyone. So it makes your ma sad that he can't be with you guys anymore."

When I try to remember Theo, I remember a day on the beach when I got lost, and then someone found me. I remember his swimsuit. It was red. I was crying, and he found me. And that's pretty much all I remember.

"I don't think I really miss Theo," I say. Teddy is better anyway, because he can change sizes and he tells me secrets.

"That's okay too," says Uncle Donny, ruffling my hair. "Now, it's probably a good idea not to talk any more about Theo today, okay? Can we do that?"

"Okay," I say.

Nobody ever wants to talk about Theo. Except Mama, and she can't stop.

*   *   *

Uncle Donny has to dig through Mama's purse to find her house keys. I giggle, because boys don't carry purses, which are for *ladies*. But finally he finds the right key to fit in the lock and manages to get the door open.

"Aoife," he says when we step inside. "What *happened*?"

I don't understand what he means. We're at the beginning of the obstacle course, but instead of making his way through the trials, he's just standing in the doorway with the door open, letting in the bugs.

"You go like this," I explain, showing him how to squeeze around the wardrobe and down the hallway, jumping over the laundry basket without tipping over the stack of boxes inside. If you get to the pizza box at the end, Mama says that's home plate, which means you're safe.

"What the hell," he says. Uncle Donny says a lot of bad words.

Mama is always careful to close the door real fast, because otherwise someone could see in the house and make fun of our obstacle course. Neighbors can be nosy.

Uncle Donny is frowning at the boxes of detergent that are stacked in the laundry basket. "Aoife, how long has the house looked this way?" He crouches down so we're the same height, so I know he must be asking something really important.

"We built the hallway part last month," I say. "When Mama couldn't sleep."

Uncle Donny takes my hand and walks with me into the kitchen.

"Why are the dishes piled up in the sink?" he says. "Did Siobhan stop washing up?"

"We don't need dishes," I say. "Tater Tots taste just as good right out of the package."

"That's what you've been eating? Tater Tots?"

"Yeah, because you can make them in the microwave," I say. Sometimes Mama isn't hungry because of her pills, but she'll usually eat something from the microwave. "Tater Tots and chicken nuggets and fish sticks." When we have them. "And I know how to make them! It's three minutes. Three-oh-oh. Do you want to see?"

"No, that's okay. I'm sure you do a real good job." Uncle Donny looks at the piles of laundry on the kitchen table.

He looks mad, so I try to explain. "We like to eat on the couch, in front of the tent." I take him to the living room.

"What tent?"

"Mama and I built it. It's a safe place, see?" The tent is made out of sheets and pillows, with the floor lamp as the pole that holds it up. Mama and I put it up after she had a bad dream, and we sat inside it and read *The Illustrated Volume of the Saints* by flashlight.

I hold up the sheet so Uncle Donny can bend to see inside. There are candles in there, but we don't light them because that wouldn't be safe. Uncle Donny sits down under the sheet and puts his head in his hands. I climb in next to him and sit, too. It's warm under the tent and smells like baby-powder Febreze.

"Christ, Siobhan," says Uncle Donny.

It's always funny when Uncle Donny says naughty words, but this time he looks sad when I laugh.

I've been trying and trying to tell you, Aoife.

You can't imagine, the sight of those loose limbs—that slack, rounded face turning blue. He wanted to be an astronaut, and instead we buried him underground, in the rain.

I try to visit him there, walking past the rows of graves, and I remember him begging for a cookie or talking about the stars. I can't even get to the right stone; I just end up back at the car, shaking.

I wake up at night, screaming that it was murder - it was murder. But I couldn't stop it, and nobody believes me.

Chapter Three

～

Uncle Donny starts walking around the living room, picking up the paper plates and the plastic cups from the floor. He takes the empty two-liter off the desk where the computer used to be. Mama took the computer away because the spirits can get out of it.

"Is it time to play clean-up?" I ask. Mama and I play clean-up sometimes, too.

"Yeah," he says. He still sounds mad. "It's time to play clean-up now."

So we take down the tent and put the sheets in the laundry hamper. We pick up all the dirty clothes from off the stairs. We clean out the refrigerator, where everything is starting to smell bad.

"Do you know if your ma has been taking her pills?" he asks. But I don't know. He takes his phone into the other room while Teddy and I are playing with the laundry bags and calls someone. If I'm very quiet, I can hear.

"The place is a fire hazard," he says. "God knows what they've been living off of. Aoife says she's been making micro-wave dinners."

I stick my tongue out at the door. I *like* microwave dinners. Although they're better when there's ketchup.

"I don't understand it; I was here a few months ago and everything was *fine* . . . No, I don't know if she stopped taking them or they stopped working. I guess we'll find out. Christ, I don't even know if any of the bills are paid."

He moves farther from the door after that.

"Is Stephanie coming inside tomorrow?" I ask when he gets back. If Stephanie is going to come in the house, maybe that's why we're cleaning up.

"Who's Stephanie?" asks Uncle Donny.

I make a frowny face. "The *babysitter*," I say, and I'm angry because Uncle Donny should know these things already, I shouldn't have to tell him. He should know where the fireworks are, and how to get through the obstacle course, and who Stephanie is. "So Mama can do work or go visit Theo."

Uncle Donny doesn't answer right away. He goes to the calendar in the kitchen and looks at it. "Does she come on Sundays?" he asks.

"She comes almost every day in the summer." Either to our house or to Hannah's house, but lately always to Hannah's house. And lately Hannah's boy cousins are usually there too, because their mom really needs a break from them. They are very wild. Hannah's mom says she can't wait for school to start. I can't wait for school to start either.

Uncle Donny nods and starts looking through the pantry. "I guess I'd better give her a call, huh. Well, we got . . . a stick of butter in the fridge that isn't spoiled. You want, uh, mac and cheese for dinner?"

"Yeah!" I'm not allowed to make that myself because I'm not supposed to use the stove, and the microwave kind costs more. So it's a special treat.

"We don't have any milk. I'll have to make it with water," he says.

"There's box milk in the cupboard."

He goes and finds it. "Why is your ma buying boxed milk?" he asks.

"She doesn't buy it. The church gives it to us. The first Tuesday of the month."

Uncle Donny's whole face pinches up, and he doesn't say anything else, just makes the mac and cheese. I watch him closely to make sure he doesn't skimp on the butter. He doesn't, in fact he puts more in than Mama does, so it's going to be even better.

I climb up on the stool at the counter, which has one short leg so that you can rock it back and forth on the tile. It makes a rattly rocking noise, and I bite my lip because there's been so many nights with Mama sitting at the table while I rock myself on this stool, and now I'm here rocking and rocking but she's gone.

"Now, where could I find Stephanie's number?" Uncle Donny sets a bowl down in front of me, and it's so salty and good that I want to put my whole face in it.

"Mama's phone," I say with my mouth full.

He snaps his fingers at me. "Good thinking, kid. Eat your noodles." So I eat the macaronis, salty and full of butter. They're so hot that I have to use my teeth to take them off the fork without letting them touch my tongue until they cool down. The loose tooth in front makes it extra tricky. But it'll be worth it when it falls out and I get a quarter.

Uncle Donny comes back with Mama's purse in one hand and her phone in another.

"Is it good?" He takes a forkful out of my bowl. "Wow. Okay. That is entirely made of sugar and fat, isn't it? Great,

Donny, feed the kid cheesy carbs. I promise, Aoife, the next meal will feature vegetables."

"It's good," I say. I don't care about vegetables. Unless it's ketchup.

"Glad you're happy, anyway. Now, let me call Miss Stephanie."

"She's just Stephanie," I say.

"Drink your water, hmm?" Uncle Donny already knows the code on Mama's phone, so he doesn't need my help. He goes back into the kitchen and I hear him talking. Teddy wants to eat some of the mac and cheese, too, so I let him lick the bowl when I'm finished.

"If you could just take her for a couple of hours tomorrow, that would really be a big help," Uncle Donny is saying when he comes back into the room.

If Stephanie comes over, then Hannah will come too and we can solve mysteries. Hannah also wants to play detective ever since she read *Harriet the Spy*. She also likes to write down things you say. She has a whole notebook full of times and what I said. 10:55, AOIFE SAYS CALIFORNIA DREAMIN' BARBIES ARE STUPID. She says it's good practice, but I don't know what for.

"Time? Uh, what time. Maybe like eleven?"

"We have to go to church first," I say.

He covers the phone with one hand. "I think we can give church a miss this week, bud."

"We *can't* miss church! Because if we miss it, Father Paul will tell God and we'll get in *trouble*."

"I think God will forgive us, this one time," says Uncle Donny. "And Father Paul is just going to have to understand."

But I'm mad. Every Sunday we go to our church, the Sacred Heart of Mary. Then Mama talks to Father Paul afterwards, and then we get ice cream on the way home.

"No!" I say. "We *have* to go!" I feel so bad, I want to throw the empty bowl right on the tile floor. And I hope it shatters everywhere and makes a big mess!

"Uh, Stephanie, let me call you back." Uncle Donny takes the water glass off the table like he knows what I'm thinking. "Aoife. Calm down."

"*No!*" It's not fair. I can't even hide in the tent, because Uncle Donny made us take it down.

Uncle Donny sighs. "How about we go for a walk. It's still light outside. We could take a little stroll around the neighborhood."

"No!"

"C'mon, let's take a walk." Uncle Donny takes my arm and walks me to the front door, stopping to hook Mama's purse over one shoulder as he goes. He shuts the door before Teddy can get out, so Teddy has to climb out the window to join us.

I'm so mad I can't even see where we're going. If Mama was here, we wouldn't be talking about skipping church tomorrow. And she would never throw away the home-base pizza box. How are we going to be safe now?

"Walk, Aoife." Uncle Donny nudges my shoulder, and I walk.

For a while we are quiet. The shadows are just starting to come over the lawn from the fence between our house and Hannah's. As we pass the house next door on the left, the neighbor's gray cat comes out to sit on the sidewalk.

"That's a nice cat," says Uncle Donny.

"It doesn't like me," I say. Those neighbors are gone a lot, and sometimes in the winter Mama puts out food for it, so it likes her better. But if I go near it, it runs away. Maybe it's scared because of Teddy, who's usually right behind me. I don't think cats like bears.

"What a pretty night," says Uncle Donny.

Maybe it is kind of pretty. I look around to make sure. I once heard Mac tell Mama that the neighborhood is going downhill, and there is a big hill from Midland Road to our house. It's good for sledding.

Every house in my neighborhood is little and square, packed together on top of one another so you can see in every window from every yard. In the big neighborhood on the other side of the street, the houses are spaced so far apart that Mama says it looks like a golf course.

We like our neighborhood better because each yard is different here. Some of them are full of bushes and trees, and some are just lawn. Some have dandelions, or the grass is so long it looks like a jungle. Some have a little stone path through the middle of the yard. Those ones look like a fairy-tale cottage.

Mama says our house is a *four-on-four*—it's square like a monopoly house. I think it is the best house of all. And from the window in Mama's room, you can see the lights of Detroit.

"Look," says Uncle Donny. "There's a doggy."

I look. "That's the mean neighbor's dog," I say. "We should go the other way." It's a kind of a poodle, I guess. It's little and white with curly fur. Its name is Roo, but Mama calls it *Rheumy* because that means *sickly*. It's on a long leash, but Mr. Rutledge hasn't come around the corner yet.

"We're just walking. I think it's okay," says Uncle Donny.

"No, we should go this way." I pull on Uncle Donny's arm, but he doesn't come with me. Suddenly there's Mr. Rutledge behind the dog and he sees us. I look down at my feet. Teddy pulls on my hand, wanting to go play with Roo, but I don't let him.

"Good evening," says Uncle Donny as we walk past.

I already know Mr. Rutledge isn't going to answer. One time when Hannah and I were playing on the sidewalk, we didn't see him coming until it was too late. He spat right in the middle of our chalk picture and it made an ugly swirl of purple, right where the door of the magic princess castle was supposed to be. We didn't want to draw any more after that.

Because I'm looking down, I only see Mr. Rutledge's shoes and Roo, who looks up at Teddy with pink, cloudy eyes. Mama says he's blind and that's why his eyes are that way. He comes close enough to sniff my leg, but Mr. Rutledge jerks the leash and pulls him back.

I don't look up.

"Okay then," says Uncle Donny, as the feet move further away. "You have a good night."

I wait until I hear the jingle of the dog's leash get quieter and quieter until I know they're gone. Then I pull on Uncle Donny's sleeve. "You shouldn't have talked to him," I say fiercely. "Mama says we should never, *ever* talk to Mr. Rutledge, and if he says something to us we should go home and tell her right away."

"Rutledge?" asks Uncle Donny. His voice sounds funny. "That was Mr. Rutledge?"

I nod my head yes. Uncle Donny puts his hand on my shoulder and squeezes tight. "Okay," he says. His face looks just like Mama's before she throws up. "Okay. Let's go this way." He nudges me to keep walking ahead of him. "We won't run into him again. Now, why is it so important that we go to church, huh?"

I'd forgotten about that. I don't feel so mad about it anymore. "We go on Sundays," I say. "That's what we always do on Sundays."

"Your uncle Donovan is not a huge fan of church. Uh, is there like a carpool or anything?"

I don't know what that word means, *carpool*. I shrug my shoulder. "Mama and I walk there, and then we get ice cream afterwards."

"We can still get ice cream," he says.

"It doesn't count unless we go to church first!" I'm getting mad again. I would stomp my feet, except we're walking, and it's hard to do that and still keep up without tripping.

"Okay, okay. Sheesh. Fine, we'll go. All right?"

"*And* we'll get ice cream," I say.

"I already said we could get ice cream."

So then I'm happy. When we get back to our street, I even try to pet the gray neighbor cat. Teddy is chasing fireflies—he loves fireflies—so I hope the kitty will let me get close.

"Here, kitty," I say, in my very sweetest, highest voice. But that stupid cat just waits until I start to get close, its eyes all big and bugged out, and puts its ears back. And when I take another step, it turns around and runs into the bushes.

Teddy snaps a firefly right between his teeth, and it makes him glow like a lightbulb from the inside.

"Better luck next time, champ," says Uncle Donny.

When we get home, Hannah is waiting for us on the front step.

"Aoife, do you want to play dollies?" she asks. She has the big plastic tub of Barbies under her arm.

"Who's this, Aoife?" says Uncle Donny.

"This is Hannah from next door," I say.

Hannah has been my best friend since she stopped Hazel Merkowicz from stealing my pączki on Pączki Day. I got the last raspberry one, and Hazel, who is a year older than me, had to take a lemon one. And she said if I didn't give her mine, she'd knock my teeth in. But Hannah heard her and told her to get lost or she'd tell on her. And Hazel said, *Who are you going to tell*, and Hannah said, *My dad, who's a cop*.

I remember how much I wished I had a dad when Hannah said that. I don't know if Hannah's dad would have really arrested Hazel Merkowicz for knocking my teeth in (or for stealing my raspberry pączki?), but he might have. Mama would probably have told me to turn the other cheek and try to get along.

"Aha, Hannah from next door! Hi Hannah from next door; I've heard a lot about you. I'm Aoife's uncle Donovan. Any friend of Aoife's is a friend of mine." Uncle Donny puts his hand out for Hannah to shake, and she does, her round face all pink. It's funny, because he's talking to her like she's a real grown-up. Hannah's older than me, but she's still only eight.

"Can Aoife play tonight?" she asks.

I realize then that Hannah doesn't know anything that happened. As far as she knows, today is the same as any other day. It doesn't seem right that while Mama and I were going to the hospital, Hannah was just sitting around in the yard at home like normal, and now she wants to know if I'll play dollies.

"I guess there's a little daylight left," says Uncle Donny. He looks at me. "Whattaya say, Aoife, you wanna play for a little while?"

I do want to play. Hannah has much better Barbies than I do. I only have three and one of them is Pocahontas, who's not even that good. And Hannah has real-size Princess Barbie dress-up clothes, even though they're mostly too big for me.

But Hannah's mom never gets confused. And I don't want to tell her what happened. In fact, I don't want to tell anybody, ever. And I know she'll probably figure it out. Hannah is much cleverer than I am, and she's really good at solving mysteries.

But sometimes Hannah can explain stuff, too, and I want to talk to someone about Theo.

Where is he, Aoife? What happened? What happened to him?

So I say okay, I do want to play.

"Just until it gets dark, all right? And stay nearby."

"We're not allowed to go as far as the corner anyway," I say. That's what Mama always tells us, because that's the street where Mr. Rutledge lives.

"Sounds good."

Teddy is making faces. He hates to play Barbies.

Hannah takes my hand and pulls me over to her yard. She takes out Marine Biologist Barbie, who looks regular right now because she's wearing regular clothes. She hands her to me and keeps Totally Rad Barbie for herself.

"Hannah, how do you find out how somebody died?" I ask, after checking that Uncle Donny won't hear.

"You investigate," she says at once. "You write down all the facts, and then you make a list of suspects, and then you interview the witnesses, and then you solve the case."

I knew Hannah would know.

"Why?" she says. "Whose death are you investigating?"

I don't answer. I watch Teddy where he's chasing fireflies in the grass. Uncle Donny walks down to his silver car and starts unloading the trunk. It looks funny at the end of our driveway where our minivan belongs. But we left the van in the parking lot at the mall. It's probably still sitting there waiting for us to come back for it.

"I bet I know who," says Hannah. "I bet it's Theo." She is brushing Totally Rad Barbie's pink hair with a plastic brush. One pink hair catches in the bristles and pulls right out of her head.

Teddy comes over to listen too.

"How did you guess?" I ask.

"Easy. Nobody else has even died."

That's true. Except one time Mama and I found a dead bird, a starling, under the little crab apple tree. Mama said it must have been trying to leave the nest but it couldn't fly right. And it fell.

"Okay," I admit. "You're right. It is Theo."

"I knew it! You know, I had a dream about Theo once," says Hannah.

Hannah has a lot of dreams. Not me. Sometimes I dream that Teddy and I are playing in the park, or that Mama and I are in the grocery story, but I don't usually remember my dreams like Hannah does. Maybe it's because she's eight and I'm only six.

Mama says dreams aren't real. They are only in your mind. But when Mama has bad dreams, she wakes herself up screaming. Then the two of us sit together on the couch with all the lights on and watch TV until we fall back to sleep. I heard Mama tell Mac once that she dreams about demons, that they've taken Theo. She doesn't know that I heard her say that.

"Aoife, I'm trying to tell you my dream, and you're not listening," says Hannah, and Teddy bumps my shoulder to pay attention.

"I'm sorry. Okay, tell me," I say, even though I don't really care.

"I was right here in the yard, and his ghost came to talk to me. He was all blue and cold-looking. And he told me that we have to *solve his murder*."

I shiver. Hannah likes to read ghost stories, but Mama doesn't ever let me read them because they're too scary. Mama and I only like stories about animals or princesses. Or *The Illustrated Volume of the Saints*.

I don't tell her this, but I don't think I believe in ghosts. After they die, people go to heaven to watch over us, and God wouldn't let them come back and scare people. Hannah probably doesn't know that because her family doesn't go to church except at Christmas.

"Even if he was murdered, why he would he come talk to you about it?" Hannah's family moved here after Theo died, so she never knew him.

I am trying to make a braid in Marine Barbie's hair, but it's slippery. Hannah can do it better. Mine always fall out.

"Be-*cause*," says Hannah, getting mad. "That's what ghosts *do*. They haunt people because they're trying to tell you something, and they won't go away until you figure it out."

Teddy nods. Maybe everybody knows that about ghosts.

"Do you really think Theo was murdered?" I ask.

Hannah nods her head. "He told me he was," she says, "and when a ghost tells you something, it has to be true, because they can't tell a lie."

That does make sense, I guess.

Hannah takes her Barbie out of my hand. "Aoife, are you really going to tell your dead brother that you won't try to find his killer?"

"I didn't say that! It's just that—I'm not even supposed to *talk* about Theo."

"That's probably why his ghost is so angry. Everyone is forgetting about him, and nobody is trying to solve his murder."

But I don't think anybody has forgotten about Theo. Sometimes it seems like he's just as real to Mama as I am. All along the staircase there are pictures of Theo as a baby, Theo at three, Theo at six, Theo at ten. We couldn't forget Theo if we tried.

At the top of the stairs is the last picture, when he was thirteen. Every time I go upstairs to go to the bathroom, I have to pass Theo. He's looking straight into the camera, his face all pointy like Mama's. He has dark hair, cut straight across his forehead.

When I look at his face, I feel like I almost do remember him, a little bit. I remember that day at the beach, his hand reaching out. His red swimsuit. And I remember how his hand was so much bigger than mine.

But now I am remembering how Mama was calling out to Theo when the blue men came, like he was standing right there.

Is Theo haunting Mama because we haven't solved his murder?

I can hear the phone ringing inside. But Uncle Donny sticks his head out instead of answering. "Five more minutes, ladies," he says.

"I'm going to do more digging," says Hannah, trying to fix what I did to Marine Barbie's hair while Teddy watches closely. "My dad showed me how to look up child molesters on the Internet, so maybe we can find some clues."

Mama says it's because Hannah's dad shows her stuff like that that he doesn't get to see her more often.

"What are you going to do?" she asks.

"I don't know," I say. Thinking about Theo being murdered makes me feel funny. It sounds like something that comes on the TV late at night, after Mama has fallen asleep and I'm still watching. A murder happening to my own brother is like seeing the dragon in the end of *Sleeping Beauty* for real, or the giant octopus at the end of *The Little Mermaid*. I don't think stuff like that is real life.

But Theo was real. His picture is real, hanging next to mine.

If Hannah's right—and she usually is—then someone out there killed my brother.

43

"Okay, it's getting dark," calls Uncle Donny. "Time to go inside."

"Okay, Mr. Donovan," Hannah calls back. She gets up and brushes off her skirt. She raises her eyebrows in the way that means she's trying to be sly. "We can talk later, Aoife. We need to make a plan."

"Do you think we can solve a mystery without getting in trouble? I don't want to go to Children's Prison," I say.

"Well, you *probably* won't," says Hannah. "Maybe people will thank us for catching the murderer and sending him to jail!"

Uncle Donny comes out to stand in the grass. "Say good-night, girls," he says.

"It's okay, we can talk when there's no grown-ups around," Hannah tells me, and she scrunches up her whole face to wink.

"Oh yeah," says Uncle Donny, "that didn't look suspicious at all." But he's smiling when he says it. He puts his hand on my shoulder and holds open the front door.

I wish I could tell Uncle Donny about Hannah's dream. But he already told me not to talk about Theo any more today.

"Hey Mr. Donovan?" Hannah has one hand on the railing, but she isn't going up the front steps to her house. "Where's Mrs. Scott?"

I look up at Uncle Donny, afraid he'll say something about how Mama started yelling and had to go to the hospital. Or he'll ask why Hannah said *Mrs.* Scott (which she always does) when Mama isn't married.

"She's got something important to take care of, so I'm going to be staying with Aoife for a while," he says instead.

"Because she works so hard," I say. I don't actually know what that has to do with anything, but it's what Mama always says about Uncle Donny when he can't come over.

Hannah nods, so maybe it works. "Okay," she says. "Goodnight."

But I know she likes to investigate *everything*, and she'll just ask me again later.

Uncle Donny leads me inside. "Did you have fun, Aoife?"

"I guess I did," I say, although I'm not so sure. I still feel creepy after talking about ghosts and murders and Children's Prison. I wish Hannah had never told me her dream.

Teddy doesn't seem scared, though. He's bouncing around just like always.

The phone starts ringing, but Uncle Donny looks at it on the counter and doesn't answer. After a few rings, it hangs up. I don't ask who it is. In a few minutes it starts ringing again. Uncle Donny takes it off the hook after that. I can hear the dial tone.

"Almost time for bed," he tells me.

I watch Uncle Donny drag the bags of garbage out to the curb even though it's not Tuesday. He doesn't sing the garbage song like Mama does, but he says I can sing it if I want. So Teddy and I sing it together, real quietly, and then Uncle Donny says it's time to go upstairs and brush teeth.

It feels like it's been the longest day ever, like this morning was years and years ago. Walking up the stairs, it's hard to put one foot in front of the other. I'm afraid I will fall asleep on the toilet.

"Wash your hands first," says Uncle Donny, so I do, and then we read a story in bed for a little while.

Mama usually reads me stories from *The Illustrated Volume of the Saints*. It's got pretty pictures on each page, with a paragraph about how each saint lived or was martyred. Mama's favorite is Saint Catherine, who was almost beaten to death on a wheel but got to have her head cut off instead. I already know that when I go to catechism, I'm going to pick Saint Joan as my saint. I was born on May thirtieth, which is her special day.

Theo was born on November ninth, the Feast Day of Saint Theodore. He set a pagan temple on fire and then was martyred by being thrown into a furnace. I'm glad I was born on Saint Joan's day instead.

Uncle Donny does not read from *The Illustrated Volume of the Saints*. He reads *The Berenstain Bears Go on a Diet*. Mama does not like the Berenstain Bears, but Uncle Donny doesn't seem to mind them so much. He even does voices, so I make him read it twice.

"All right, that's all she wrote," he says, the second time. It's still not all the way one hundred percent dark outside, because it's summer and it seems like it's light almost all the time. "Sweet dreams," he says, and then he leaves.

It's hard to sleep knowing Mama isn't in the house. Usually when I'm trying to fall asleep, I lie in bed and listen to the sound of her movies playing in the living room, which is right below my bedroom. Until we had to get rid of the TV, anyway. Uncle Donny washes dishes downstairs instead, which isn't nearly as much fun to listen to.

I use my tongue to push my loose tooth back and forth. One time men broke into a house in our neighborhood. I heard Hannah's mom tell Mama about it. They broke in during the night while the family was asleep upstairs, and they took the TV and the computer from the living room, and they broke a window. And Hannah's mom said it was bad men from the city that did it. She said the family could have all been murdered in their beds.

I try not to think about any murders of anyone.

Teddy goes downstairs and checks that there are no murderers breaking into the house. If there were, he would be bigger than them, so he would eat them up. But he comes back after checking every window and door. No murderers, he says.

Sometimes when I'm scared at night, Mama will sing "Ave Maria" with me. But she's not here. I try singing it to myself, but it's not as good.

I finally manage to fall asleep, but even then I keep waking up because Uncle Donny is making lots of noise on the stairs. He gets to the top of the staircase—*creak, creak*—and then goes back down—*thump, thump, thump*. There's a pause at the bottom and then he comes back up again. Up and down, up and down.

Teddy thinks it's funny, and he laughs. But I don't know why he's doing it, and I wish he would stop because I'm trying to sleep. Finally I put a pillow over my head, even though it's hot under there, so it's quiet enough that I think I can ignore him.

* * *

I am dreaming that Teddy and I are catching fish in the creek. Teddy is using his bear paws like giant spoons to scoop the fish out onto the bank, and I'm catching them in a net. But then Teddy growls at me, and he's right next to me pushing his nose against my arm the way he does when he wants my attention.

Watch, says Teddy.

I open my eyes.

It's still dark outside. It must be very late, because there's not even the sound of any cars on the road. Instead I can hear footsteps—*creak, creak, creak*—in the hallway. Someone is walking outside my door.

Keep watching, Teddy says.

Then I see the shape of feet under the door, just standing there. The door opens very slowly. I peek through my eyelashes, but the light from the hallway is too bright, so for a second I can't see. I decide to lie very still and pretend to be asleep, because maybe it's bad men from the city, and if they think I'm asleep they might go away. Or even if they don't go away, if it's bad men, I don't want to see them.

But after a second I have to peek again.

It's Uncle Donny, dressed in his boxers and a white tank top. His hair is all messed up and sticking out, not like he usually looks. He just stands in the doorway and stares at me.

See? says Teddy.

Uncle Donny comes into the room, but he doesn't say anything. He's just looking at me.

"What is it?" I ask, forgetting that I was pretending to be asleep. "Uncle Donny, what do you want?"

Uncle Donny walks across the carpet and sits down on the side of the bed. I pull my legs away before he can sit on them, but now he's squashing me.

"I'm sleepy, Uncle Donny. Why did you wake me up?"

He doesn't answer, just sits on the bed and looks at me. I don't like it. I want to go back to sleep.

"Leave me *alone*," I say, even though Mama says you should never sass grown-ups.

His face screws up, and without a word, he gets up and walks out, leaving the door wide open so the room is too lit-up for me to sleep.

I can hear him on the stairs, walking up and down. To the top of the staircase, then back down. Then up again. A little while later, the door pulls closed and it's dark.

Grown-ups are weird, says Teddy. I agree.

I lie back down and go to sleep, and this time it's me and Teddy chasing flying fish in a field. I don't wake up again until morning.

All That's Bright and Gone

My Dear Aoife,

They say I may be able to call home soon. Or maybe I already did. I hope I didn't scare you. I scare myself, to be honest with you. Just now I looked down at my hands and my fingers were all puffed up like bread dough. Something in one of the medicines, I guess.

This is my second attempt at trying to write. The first time the lines came out like Theo's pictures when he was a little boy, holding the crayon clenched in his fat fist, making snakes. I don't think I'll be able to put this letter in the mail either, but I'll write it anyway.

Time has gone off again. Sometimes the pause between words is longer than the next hour. I think I'm talking normally, but they tell me it comes out in a blur—too fast. The nurses say I've been here less than a day, and I would swear it was weeks ago that I took you to buy shoes at the mall.

What happened to Theo—it feels like it is happening right now, and all the time.

I don't know if you will have children of your own, but I recommend against it. Propagating the faith, I think—while important work—is best left to a family other than ours. Anyway, children are a trap. Don't you think I would have moved away, after Theo, if I could have? But you, my sweet snare, you held me here in this town, because you loved your preschool and because we had free babysitting at the neighbors' and because I couldn't take the risk of going without work while I had your little potbelly to feed. I was as trapped as my ma, who was never able to earn her own money, who spent her days ironing my father's shirts and trying to soak other people's blood from his cuffs, and his own spittle from the collar.

I thought about Father when I woke up at the hospital and they explained what I had done. They tell me that I was screaming—shrieking, *was the word the doctor used to describe it*—*and not making any sense. They were asking me about you, baby, but I couldn't understand, partly because Aoife was also my mother's name and partly because they were saying it wrong. Thank the sweet Lord I didn't hurt you worse.*

It was like standing inside a thunderstorm, it was so loud inside my head, and if I was screaming, well, it was only because I was trying to let some of it out.

They tried to tell me I had been skipping my pills, but I was pretty sure I hadn't. Not all the way sure, but I didn't think I would do that to you, baby. Even when we ran short of food, I always filled my prescription first, may God forgive me. But that's what this disease does to you, Aoife: you can be sure and still wrong.

Do you remember, the two of us went into the city and there was a man in dirty clothes, standing on the corner? He followed us all the way to Fisher Theatre, talking first in an ordinary voice and then more and more loudly, saying that we were sitting on the bench of judgment. I should have been more compassionate than anybody, but instead I looked into his red, sweaty face—*and he stank, Aoife, he smelled like shit and sweat*—*and I was fright-ened. I picked you up, and you couldn't understand why he was talking to us, you kept asking who he was. And he was only what I have been, and what I became, again and again, baby.*

You don't remember, but we've been homeless before. We left Chicago with nothing except whatever Ma could carry in her bag. Donny didn't even have his shoes. You were only one egg out of multitudes at the time, but since the Blessed Father must have already had you in His sight, in a way you were there as well.

When we were still living in the old apartment, I remember being paralyzed by the garbage chute. We were supposed to take the bag of garbage to a room in the hallway and put it into this

vent, and let it go. But I couldn't do it. I couldn't open my hand
and let it fall down the chute, because I knew that the minute I
did, the garbage was going to turn into my keys or my mother's
rosary.

I would stand out in the hallway with the sack of trash on my
lap, weeping.

And that's what children are, Aoife. You can't hold on to them
and you can't let them go.

All my best wishes,
Mama

Chapter Four

❧

The next time I open my eyes, it's light again. Uncle Donny is standing in the doorway, telling me to wake up.

"Are you going to sleep all day?" he asks me. "We still need to eat before church!"

I sit up in bed and he's right—the sun is up and I'm hungry for breakfast. It's kind of mean for Uncle Donny to make fun of me for sleeping in when he's the one who woke me up last night, but Mama always feels bad after she has a bad night, especially if I have to go to school, and I don't want to make Uncle Donny feel bad. So I get up and get dressed in my church dress.

I'm glad we're going to church, where God and his Blessed Saints will protect us from any ghosts except the Holy Ghost, who does not haunt children in their dreams.

He's waiting for us, said Mama. Why did she say that?

"Uncle Donny, can you fix my hair?" I ask as I come downstairs. Mama always does it fancy for church.

"Uhh . . . you know, Uncle Donny has a lot of skills, but fixing little girls' hair is not one of them."

"But you have to do it," I explain. "I don't know how."

"All right, all right." He sits behind me and takes the comb out of my hand. "So, uh, what am I aiming for here?"

"Mama likes to pull it back." I say. I wiggle in the chair until he touches my head with the comb.

"Okay," he says. "How hard can it be, right?" He gathers up all the hair in his fist and kind of tugs on it.

"Did you take a shower, Aoife?" he asks.

"No." Mama tells me when it's time to take a bath.

"Okay. Well, let's just . . . uh, put it up here, uh, kind of like this, maybe?" He tries to wrap an elastic band around the bunch of hair, but the curly pieces go everywhere. "Uh. Yeah, that looks good, I think. How about some little clips, maybe?"

It takes probably five or six clips to get all the hair flat against my head, but we get it done. "This is cool," I say, looking at myself in the mirror. I look like a gymnast in the Olympics. "Mama never does it like this."

Teddy thinks it looks really good, too. He combs his hair next, but since he's hairy all over, it takes a long time.

"It looks awesome," Uncle Donny agrees. "Go find a cardigan." Mama always says that too, because even though it's hot outside, every place has air conditioning so you get cold if you just wear a dress. I can't find a cardigan, but I find a raincoat, so that's just as good.

"Okay," says Uncle Donny, "Are you ready for breakfast? I don't think we have time to eat out; we'll have to make do. I'm going to pick up some groceries this afternoon so we have something for lunch. Your uncle Donny is sick of mac and cheese."

I don't see how anybody can be sick of mac and cheese.

"I don't need to go out for breakfast," I say. Mama says eating out isn't worth the money when we're on a budget, and we're always on a budget, ever since I can remember. Hannah's family goes out to eat all the time. They go to the Cheesecake Factory at the mall and Hannah brings home cheesecake slices in a box and sometimes she shares them with me.

Uncle Donny sits down with two bowls of cereal and we both start to eat. "You know, Aoife, I'm really glad that you knew to tell the doctors to call me," he says. "That makes me very happy."

I don't tell Uncle Donny that it wasn't exactly my idea, because I don't want him to be sad. I nod instead. "Dr. Pearlman wanted to call my father," I say. "But I told her that Mama found me in a cabbage patch."

"Your grandmother used to say that," says Uncle Donny. His voice sounds strange. "Did Siobhan teach you that?"

"Uh-huh."

"Aoife," Uncle Donny starts to say, "you know, everybody *has* a father—"

Just then the phone rings again. Uncle Donny glances at the number, picks it up, and then hangs up.

"Is someone trying to call us?" I ask.

"No. Just a wrong number. Look, Aoife, I need to swing by work this afternoon, so I'm going to ask the neighbors if you can play there."

"Can I come to work with you?" I've been to Uncle Donny's office once, in a place called Southfield. It's all shiny gray—gray halls, gray carpet, even the music is gray.

"Sorry, bud, not this time."

"Are you going to do math problems?" I ask. "That's what Mama does."

Uncle Donny is stacking up the bowls. "Yup. I'm a tax lawyer, she's a bookkeeper. That's because this family is good with numbers. And that's a skill you can take to the bank, kid."

Someday maybe I can work in a shiny gray office like his, instead of in our study like Mama.

"Did Mama ever work in an office?" I ask.

Uncle Donny is standing at the sink. "A long time ago," he says. "But now she . . . now it's better for her to stay close to home. But that's fun, huh? This way she's around to play with you more."

"Yeah," I say. That's fun. But he doesn't sound very happy.

"I can count really good," I say. "Do you want to hear? I can count all the way to a hundred and I never get confused."

"Uh, sure. But finish getting ready first, okay? We've got to get going here."

Just then the phone rings again, and this time when Uncle Donny checks it, he puts down the dish towel and answers. "Hello? Yes, this is he . . . what, now? Um, okay, sure." He covers the receiver with one hand. "Aoife, can you go play upstairs for a minute? I need to take this, and it's nothing you need to hear."

That kind of makes me want to listen to it, but when Uncle Donny scrunches up his forehead, I guess I'd better go. I drag my feet on the stairs so I can still hear.

"Everything is fine here, of course," says Uncle Donny. "I mean, obviously my niece misses her mother, but we're, you know, holding it together."

I want to know who Uncle Donny is talking about me to.

"Yes, Aoife is asking when she can come home."

Then I do a bad thing. I know I shouldn't do it, but I go upstairs and use the trick Hannah taught me: I sneak into Mama's bedroom to pick up the phone there so I can hear what Uncle Donny's talking about. But I only do it because he said my name!

And Teddy says it's okay, so I don't feel bad.

I have to be very careful picking up the phone, or Uncle Donny will hear me and know I'm listening, and then we'll be in big trouble. I hold my breath.

The woman talking to Uncle Donny doesn't sound familiar. "We've stabilized her condition so far," she's saying, "but she's not going to be ready to be released for a while. We're not able to provide an estimate at this point. But even when she is stabilized, I want to warn you now that she's going to require a lot of follow-up care."

Boring, says Teddy. *This is boring.*

"Whatever she needs, we'll find a way to make it happen," says Uncle Donny.

"She's able to talk for a few minutes today, if you're ready. But try to remain calm and keep the conversation low-stress, okay?"

"Uh, listen, I've been trying to track down the status of her lease here, uh, I don't know if she's paid up on the rent . . . can I ask her about that? I mean, it's going to be a lot more stressful for her if she loses her home when she gets out, you know?"

I have to cover my mouth so I don't gasp into the phone. Oh no! I don't want our house to get lost! I'm so upset about it that I miss what the lady says back to Uncle Donny. The next thing I know, the phone clicks over and somebody else starts speaking.

"Donny?"

"*Mama!*" I say out loud. "Mama, I'm here on the phone, too!"

"Aoife?"

"Wait, who is that?" asks the first lady.

"Aoife, you're not supposed to be on the phone," says Uncle Donny, and he sounds *really mad*. But I'm so happy to hear Mama that I don't care. "That's her daughter," Uncle Donny says. "I apologize, I didn't realize she was on the line."

"Mama, I miss you!" I say.

"I miss you too, baby," says Mama. She doesn't sound so confused to me. I don't know why the hospital people are making her stay somewhere else. They're probably just mean and stupid.

"Mama, hi!"

"Aoife, you need to hang up now."

"No, no," says Mama, "she can stay. It's okay. But Donny, you didn't tell Theo I'm having my troubles again, did you? Don't tell him, Donny, please. You know how upset he gets."

"Oh jeez," says Uncle Donny quietly. "Siobhan, Aoife's on, remember? Let's not talk about this now. Just—you listen to the doctors and get better, all right? We miss you here, but we're doing all right. Everything's fine at the house. I'm—I'm taking care of everything."

"You were always such a good boy, Donny," says Mama.

"Mama, are you coming home soon?"

"Soon, baby, real soon."

That means in time for the fireworks, right?

"Aoife, you hang up the phone right now," says Donny. "I don't know where you are, but I'm going to find you, and you're going to be in big trouble if you don't hang up."

"But I want to talk to Mama!" I say. It's not fair. Mama's already been gone *forever*, and even now that she's on the phone, Uncle Donny wants to hide her from me.

She's your mama, not Uncle Donny's, Teddy agrees.

"I think it's better for Siobhan to get off the phone now," says the lady.

"Uh, yeah, I could see that," says Uncle Donny. "Aoife, say goodbye to your ma, okay? She has to go now."

But I don't want to say goodbye to Mama. I can already feel my eyes filling up with tears, because what if I hang up the phone and I never talk to her again? She said she'd be home *soon*, but grown-ups say things like that sometimes—like when Mama says that Christmas is *soon*, or that we'll see the movies in the theater *soon* when they come out on DVD. But by the time that happens, I won't even remember them, or I'll be too old to want to watch. And it's still only July, it isn't even *almost* Christmas.

"Aoife, hang up." Uncle Donny has found me. He must have walked through all the rooms. I didn't even hear him on the stairs. I guess all his practice climbing up and down them really paid off.

He kneels down next to me on the carpet and picks me up. I'm still trying to be a big girl and not cry loud enough for Mama to hear me. He takes the phone out of my hand and holds it up. "Say bye, Aoife," he says quietly.

"Bye-bye," I whisper.

"Bye sis," he says, into the other phone in his hands. "I love you. We all love you. Take care of yourself and get better, okay?"

He puts his phone on speaker so I can hear Mama. "I love you both, too," she says, sounding little and far away. "See you later."

Then Uncle Donny puts his thumb on the power button, and all we can hear is the dial tone.

* * *

I thought Uncle Donny would be mad at me for sneaking around on the phone, but for a long time he doesn't say anything, just sways back and forth with me while I cry. He puts his hand on my back, and I can feel his heartbeat through his palm. He doesn't even yell at me.

The tears dry up and then I'm just tired, leaning on his shoulder.

"You know I would have called you when your ma got on," he tells me. "I just wanted to make sure it was okay first."

"Teddy told me to do it," I mumble. Which isn't all the way true, because I got the idea from Hannah. But it's the sort of thing he would say.

"Someday you're going to have to explain to Teddy that he's getting you into big trouble, telling you to do things you know you shouldn't do," says Uncle Donny. "You ought to know better than to listen to him."

I don't say anything. Teddy sticks his tongue out at us.

"Do you still want to go to church?" asks Uncle Donny. I nod against his shirt. "Okay. I'm going to change clothes and then we'll go."

He puts me down, squeezing my shoulder. I listen to the familiar sound of him walking away down the hallway.

"You know, we could just stay here and watch cartoons," he suggests, from the guest room while he's changing.

"We don't have a TV anymore," I say when he comes back. "Mama says that the TV is how Satan gets into your mind." But sometimes we watch it at Hannah's house—and I just try not to listen too much.

Uncle Donny looks squish-faced when I say that. He goes into the living room to open the cabinet where the TV used to be. But it hasn't been there since Mama put up a plastic crucifix and a picture of Mary of the Immaculate Heart instead.

"Huh," he says. He closes the cabinet again.

*　*　*

We walk to church, which is just at the other end of the neighborhood. We're running late by the time we walk up the steps. There's nobody handing out programs at the door and saying, "Good morning," but that's okay, because lots of times Mama and I are late, too, when she has a bad night. So I'm used to it.

I like the inside of the church. It looks like a princess castle. There's lamps hanging from the ceiling and pillars between the pews. Mrs. Hannigan is sitting at the piano in front playing gentle music. It's never very full but it's never empty.

Mama says that church is a good place to think. I have a lot to think about today.

Usually Mama gives me the program and I color in all the *O*s with a ballpoint pen, and by the time I've gotten to the last *O* it's almost time to go downstairs and drink apple juice. Then we go get ice cream, and if Mac is around he might meet us there. Sometimes it is better to get ice cream without him, if he is being *an old cuss* again. But Uncle Donny didn't take a program, and now there's nothing to do but watch everybody else while we're sitting in the pew waiting for apple juice time.

Teddy is curled up underneath the pew, sound asleep. He likes to sleep where it's quiet.

My favorite part of church is when people are praying. I like to look at people's faces when they don't know I'm watching. All the grown-ups are bent over, and sometimes they cover their heads with their hands, but sometimes I can see them and I like how serious they look. Usually adults are more careful with their expressions.

I look over at Uncle Donny, but he isn't praying. He's checking his phone. He winks at me when he sees me watching.

Uncle Donny is silly. He didn't remember to kneel and cross himself when we walked past the tabernacle. He doesn't hold his hands up when Father Paul says, "We lift them up to the lord." He doesn't know when to sit and when to stand. He doesn't sing along with the hymns. He doesn't say the creed. When it's time to hold hands, he doesn't realize until Mrs. Czapla waves her hand in front of him.

I'm happy that Uncle Donny and I are here, because after we die I want us all to go to heaven and sit on the clouds with Theo and Gramma Aoife, playing harps like the pictures in the stained-glass windows. I never say that to Mama, though, because it would make her sad.

Everything about Theo makes Mama sad.

I wonder if Hannah will get to meet Theo in heaven. They don't go to church very much, so I'm worried that she won't, and she's the one who's so interested in him. I'm busy thinking about Hannah in the Lake of Fire, so I'm not really listening to Father Paul when he starts talking. He talks for a long time while I look around. The statue in the front of the church is actually Blessed Mary, but sometimes I pretend it's Joan of Arc. Instead of being dressed up in armor, she's wearing a flowing dress and her hair is down. She looks very pretty.

Mama always says we should pray to Saint Joan and ask her to help us be courageous. Saint Joan was brave because she trusted the voices of Saint Catherine and the archangel Michael when they spoke to her. Mama hears voices too sometimes—she told me she does.

Saints are like ghosts, maybe, but nicer.

Hannah said Theo is haunting my mother. Is that why she was screaming? *He's waiting for us*, she said, like he was sitting in the food court at the mall. Is that what saints do?

Father Paul is reading from the Bible again. "In order to receive the blessings we seek from the Lord, we have to be willing to do the Lord's work," he tells us. "Ask yourself what the mission of the Lord is for you, and when He calls on you, take up his mantle and be not afraid."

"What's a mantle?" I whisper to Uncle Donny.

"It goes over a fireplace," he tells me.

I don't always understand Father Paul so good.

"Trust in the word of God, and there will be no need for fear," says Father Paul. "The might of the Lord will hold you up."

"Uncle Donny, how do you know what the word of God is?" I whisper. Is it a special, secret word, like cursing?

Uncle Donny is reading on his phone. "What? Aoife, shh."

Teddy starts to snore under the pew. He's so loud that the pew rattles just a little.

Father Paul leads the grown-ups in a prayer, but I have my own prayer: *Please let Mama come home in time for the fireworks.* Mama says it's wrong to ask God for favors. She says we should only pray for other people. But hopefully it's okay if it's for me *and* Mama, because I'm sure Mama wants to see the fireworks, too.

Then the collection people come down the aisle and the time for prayers is over. Mama and I always put three dollars in the collection plate: one for the Father, one for the Son, and one for the Holy Ghost. But Uncle Donny drops a whole twenty-dollar bill in the plate and then hands it on to Mrs. Czapla without looking.

I think if Uncle Donny put that much money in the collection plate, God ought to look pretty hard at my prayer to see the fireworks with Mama.

We sing some pretty songs, but without Mama I don't want to sing anything, and Uncle Donny doesn't make me. I just look at my shoes and wait for the music to stop, and that's what he does, too. Maybe he's missing Mama just like me.

When it's time for communion, Uncle Donny doesn't go up to the front even though he's old enough. I don't go because I haven't had my confirmation yet. So both me and Uncle Donny stay in the pew as we watch Mrs. Czapla go slowly up the aisle. Teddy climbs up next to me to watch too.

She opens her mouth and has Father Paul put the bread right on her tongue, instead of holding out her hand like Mama does. When the juice person gives her the little cup of grape juice, she bows her head over it before she takes it from him. Then she drinks.

Mac says drinking from a little cup like that is called taking shots.

The church is quiet because people are taking the Communion, and I'm sleepy from how Uncle Donny woke me up last night. The sanctuary is warm and it smells dusty, which Mama says is incense. Incense is a fancy smoke that Jesus likes. Mac likes to smoke, too. I guess it's a grown-up thing.

Sometimes it's hard to sit quietly at school when I'm tired after Mama has a bad night, and sometimes Sister Mary Celeste lets me put my head down on my desk, but she doesn't look happy when I do that so I don't like to ask.

I try to fix my eyes on the altar, which is where the Holy Ghost lives. *Dear Blessed Saints*, I say, but quietly, in my mind, the way I talk to Teddy. *Please tell me: did somebody murder my brother?*

The candles in the front of the church go out, one by one.

I gasp. It's a sign! I look around, but nobody else is watching except Teddy, who winks at me. The grown-ups are all looking down. I think it is a message.

Dear Blessed Saints, if I find out who killed him, will my mama come home in time to watch the fireworks?

Overhead, very slowly—and then louder—the bell in the steeple begins to ring. The only time we hear the bells usually is at Christmas or when somebody gets married. Now it is getting louder and louder, as if Teddy climbed right up into the tower and he's riding the bell up there like a swing, back and forth, faster and faster. It sounds like there's more than one bell, even. It sounds like a whole bunch of them now.

But Uncle Donny doesn't even look over, and in fact nobody else is paying any attention, not even Father Paul, who starts talking right over the sound of the bells. I think they are beautiful, even better than when Mrs. Hannigan plays the "Ave Maria" and Mama hums along. Then, between one blink and the next, the whole church is lit up, like someone has turned on all the lights, and it's so bright that my eyes start stinging, but I don't close them.

Then I hear my name, pronounced just right, the way only Mama says it. *Aoife*. And now the bells are ringing it: *Eee-fah, Eee-fah*.

Yes! I say. *Yes, that's me!*

Aoife, say the bells. *Aoife*.

I realize that I must be hearing the voices of the saints, just like when Saint Catherine and the archangel Michael started speaking to Joan of Arc. And I think the word of the Lord must be *Aoife*, because that's all I hear.

Okay, I say to the saints. *I will do it, I promise*. And just like Father Paul said, I'm not afraid. Because I want Mama to come home, and I don't want her to be haunted anymore. I promise that I will be very brave, just like Joan of Arc. I will take up the whatever-a-mantle-is. I will solve my brother's murder and bring my mother home.

Then the lights start to go dim and I can feel my eyes filling up with tears, because I don't want the voices of the saints to go away. They're so beautiful. The tears are spilling over my cheeks when the bells stop ringing and the lights slowly go out.

And then I'm sitting in church again, and Father Paul is only just wrapping up the prayer. And I'm not even crying for real on the outside.

Uncle Donny looks over and makes a face at me. It's a funny face and I laugh out loud, and everybody looks over. So then we have to duck our heads and pretend to be serious again.

When it's all over and Father Paul has said, "The Lord bless you and keep you, the Lord make his countenance to shine upon you, amen," Uncle Donny gets up and takes me by the hand to lead me down the pew.

"All right, let's jet," he says.

Teddy squeezes behind us, almost too fat to fit.

Uncle Donny is leading us to the side exit. "After service we get cookies and juice and talk to people," I explain, pointing towards the Fellowship Room where the cookies are. Teddy really likes cookies, and so do I.

"Yes well, I think we've had enough of the Lord for today," says Uncle Donny, still heading for the door. "Okay?"

"But we have to walk past Father Paul and shake his hand." I point to where all the church people are lining up in the aisle.

"True, that does sound fun, but this way takes us out to the street faster. And Uncle Donny wants his ice cream sooner rather than later. Doesn't that sound good?"

It does sound pretty nice, I guess. "Maybe we can shake Father Paul's hand *twice* tomorrow," I suggest.

"Tomorrow? Why tomorrow?"

Uncle Donny is so silly. "Tomorrow is Family Bible Study," I say. "Oh, there's Stephanie!" I run over to give her a hug. She's with her mom and dad—I bet they're going to get juice.

Stephanie is in high school and rides a bike with a wire basket. She lives somewhere in the neighborhood, but I've never seen her house. I think Stephanie's really pretty, even though Hannah makes fun of her pimples sometimes.

"Aoife, don't run off— Hello, Stephanie. You must be the famous babysitter. I hear good things." Uncle Donny shakes her hand. "Say, I don't suppose you're coming back here tomorrow for Bible study, are you? I was thinking, ah, maybe Aoife could come back with you. I'll really make it worth your while."

"Oh, you should come join us," says Stephanie's mom, who is in charge of New Membership. I know because Mama says she's doing a not-so-great job.

"Ooh, sorry, I've got a, uh, very important conflict at that time," says Uncle Donny. "But thank you for thinking of that. Aoife, you don't mind going with Stephanie, do you?"

"No," I say. I like Stephanie, even though Hannah says she only goes to Bible study because Peter Henly from up the street is there.

"I can probably take her," says Stephanie. "I'll just have to check my schedule, but I think it'll be okay."

"You're a *godsend*," says Uncle Donny, and then he laughs and nudges me - *because we're in a church, get it?* I laugh, too. "But seriously, Stephanie, Aoife and I would love to stick around, but we've got to make like a tree and leave. Very important appointment to get to. Ice cream related. Bye now!"

He takes us out the side door, and all the way across the parking lot he holds my hand tight and I have to hurry to keep up. It's sunny and bright outside after how dark the sanctuary was once the saints left.

I want to tell Uncle Donny about how the word of God came to me, but something tells me that wouldn't be a good idea. It's my own special secret, and I don't want to tell anybody about it, not even Father Paul. Even though he would be disappointed to hear that the saints came to visit his own service and he didn't even know about it. I'm going to keep it buried deep in my stomach, where secrets live.

Dear Donny,

I thought maybe I was over the worst of it, but these new pills have some different side effects and I'm not feeling quite myself. They say it may be a while before I come home. It shouldn't be that hard: if I take my meds on schedule, and don't talk to the voices, I could be on my way out in a few days. But nothing is ever as easy as it seems.

There's something important I need to discuss with you. But it's waited this long—I suppose it can wait a while longer.

The nurses took me for a shower today, and it reminded me of when we were little, how I used to wash you in the sink when Ma was shut up in her room again. Of all the things I'm grateful for in my life, I think I'm most thankful for those five years between us. I suppose it might be a sin to be grateful, since there were three babies in those years. One of them was even born, but it was too small and blue already. She named each one of them, you know. The last one, I remember, was Saoirse. The rest had saints' names, I suppose. Do you know I used to see them in my dreams as a child? I dreamed of them dancing above the bed, little blue angel babies, with the faces of the stained glass windows at church.

In those days, I was terrified that the demons would come and take you away, Donny, like they had taken Ma's other children. That was why we had you baptized in the hospital as soon as you were born: Ma wasn't sure you would live, and she wanted you to go straight to heaven and not be trapped in purgatory with the others. When I told her I had dreamed of them in heaven, she cried.

Or maybe it didn't happen like that. I don't know.

How should I know?

Do you remember my saint's name? I encouraged Theo to pick Saint Francis, hoping he would be kind and gentle to God's weak creatures. I think Aoife will pick Saint Joan, and Lord knows she'll probably need that holy courage. But mine was Catherine, for the Blessed Saint who was pulled apart, arms one way and legs another—and it came true. My heart is stretched further and further, and someday I'm afraid it will pull right apart.

All they'll find is the shape of a woman on the carpet, and my empty clothes, and I'll have ascended straight to heaven like a firework.

Throw these letters away, Donny.

Your Loving Sister,
Siobhan

Chapter Five

We walk past the Penguin Palace where we stop for ice cream, and then we walk home the long way eating it. The ice cream drips down the front of my dress, but Uncle Donny doesn't even get mad. He teaches me how to suck it out of the bottom of the cone like a straw.

"What do you want to do this afternoon, kiddo?" he asks. "The world is our oyster. Unless you want to watch television, apparently."

"I want to play outside," I say, because that's what I like to do best of anything. And because I need to ask Hannah to help me start solving Theo's murder.

"Hey, sounds like a party," says Uncle Donny.

Teddy is full of energy because of all the ice cream, so he races around me in circles. Then right as we get close to the house, a loud red rattling truck drives slowly past us—and I know that truck by the American flag painted on the back. It's Mac!

Mac backs up and pulls into the driveway.

"Hi Mac!" I shout.

I used to call him *Uncle Mac*, but Mama says he's not really my uncle and I should stop calling him that. I think it's because he goes away a lot, which is not like a real uncle. Even when Uncle Donny and Mama *have words*, he doesn't go away for long. Mac goes away for months and months until we've almost forgotten him. Plus, Mama told Hannah's mom that he *left her high and dry*. And they both shook their heads, so that's a bad thing, although you'd think being dry would be better than wet.

Mac gets out of the truck, but he seems confused. "Hey, Alfie," he says. He always calls me that, not because he can't pronounce it but because that's his special way of saying it.

"Mac is Mama's special friend," I explain to Uncle Donny, who has come up behind me. Maybe Mac is not going to be *an old cuss* today. "And this is my uncle Donny!"

"Yes, I'm familiar," says Mac, holding out his hand for Uncle Donny to shake. He does, but slowly. "I'm sorry, I was expecting Siobhan. Is she around? I've been calling. Seems like the phones are down."

"She's a little busy at the moment," says Uncle Donny, and his voice sounds different than usual, like when he's in a hurry but he's trying to be polite. "Can I help you?"

Hannah comes out of her house because she sees us standing around in the driveway. "Hello, Mr. Donny," she says. "Hello, Mr. Mac. Can Aoife play now?"

"That sounds like a good idea," says Uncle Donny, and this time he doesn't check with me if I want to or not. "Just stay close, okay, girls?"

Luckily, I'm happy to play with Hannah, because I want to tell her about my mantle. "Maybe we can sit on your steps and talk," I tell her, and I try to give her a special look so that she knows it's about a secret.

"Okay, sounds good," says Uncle Donny, waving me off.

I pull Hannah away by her shoulder.

"Aoife, why does your hair look like that?"

"My uncle Donny did it," I say, smiling. She looks not so impressed. Teddy will pull her hair if she's not careful—he's done it before, but not hard enough for her to notice.

I look back and Uncle Donny is still talking to Mac, who is now leaning against his truck. It's an ugly truck, with the windows taped up, but it looks extra bad next to Uncle Donny's shiny silver car, which is not taped up anywhere.

"Hannah, I thought more about your dream," I say. "I think you're right. Maybe we really do need to solve Theo's murder."

I don't tell her about the saints or how they'll bring back Mama, because I don't think she'll understand those parts.

"Great!" says Hannah. "Let's start right away!"

"We need to make a list of suspects, right? And then interview witnesses?"

"All right, I think it's time for you to leave," says Uncle Donny, and his voice is loud enough that Hannah and I both stop talking and look over. Mac is leaning back against his truck like he doesn't mind being shouted at. But I know he doesn't like it when Mama does it. Mac is scary when the yelling starts. I remember once, a long time ago, Mac threw a plate against the wall and it shattered everywhere. It was Mama's special plate from the Old Country and it belonged to Gramma Aoife. I still remember the sound of it breaking into a million little bits. It makes my stomach hurt to hear him yell, like a fist in my throat, closing. Teddy hides under the porch, even though his big butt sticks out. He hates it when grown-ups fight, too.

"Well maybe I will, for now," says Mac. "Alfie! Goodbye, girlie. See you when I see you."

He always says that. "Bye Mac," I say back.

Uncle Donny just crosses his arms and watches with his stern face as Mac gets into his truck and backs out of the drive. He honks his horn cheerfully, and Hannah and I both wave.

"Your uncle Donovan seems mad," says Hannah thoughtfully.

"Maybe Mac was being grouchy again," I say. I don't tell her that last time I saw Mac, there was more yelling than that. Maybe Uncle Donny is on Mama's side.

"If your uncle Donovan and Mac had a fight, who do you think would win?" Hannah asks. I picture how the two of them looked standing at the bottom of the driveway. Mac is gray and tough and Uncle Donny is skinny and tall.

"Mac," I say, but I'm not a hundred percent sure. Uncle Donny is pretty good at getting people to do what he says. Mama says he has a *lawyer's silver tongue*, but I asked him to show it to me once and it was pink. That's what a *figure of speech* means.

"I think your uncle Donovan would win," says Hannah. "Because he would call the police and the police would see that he's an upstanding citizen and Mac is white trash."

Hannah just thinks that because Mac drives a dirty red truck and wears sweat pants and smells like cigarettes and because her mom tells Mama he's no good. And sometimes Mama also says he's no good. And I don't know one hundred percent if he's any good or not.

"Are you girls okay to play out here a little longer?" Uncle Donny calls over.

"Absolutely, Mr. Donovan," says Hannah sweetly. She's sitting up straighter all of a sudden. "I'll watch out for Aoife, don't worry."

He does not seem very worried.

"You know, I wonder, Aoife," Hannah says to me, stroking her chin like a cartoon character. I know she saw that on TV somewhere. "Did Mac know Theo?"

I don't know the answer to that. I don't always remember Mac being around, but Mama usually introduces him as *an old friend*. Or maybe she just means he's older than her?

"Why?" I ask.

"Because I'd say we already have our first suspect," Hannah says. She takes out a notebook and writes, on the top of the page, MACK. "Do you know his last name?"

"No." I never thought about it before, but I guess he must have one.

"Try to find it out," Hannah tells me. "And ask him if he knew your brother. We know your uncle doesn't like him; maybe that's because he suspects him of killing Theo."

"Mama wouldn't be Mac's friend if he killed Theo," I point out.

Hannah tosses her head. "She's probably *blinded by love*, like on TV," she says.

I hope that's not true, but she does wear glasses sometimes. And it definitely seems like Uncle Donny doesn't like him very much.

Hannah's mom calls her from inside the house. Neither of us answer. She won't find us right away.

Hannah is adding numbers to her list of suspects. "We need at least one more," she says. "There's usually two or three."

That makes sense. If there was only one suspect, the mystery would be too easy to solve.

"We can probably find a few more this afternoon," says Hannah. "I heard my mom say she's going to invite you over. We'll find a good time to sneak away, and then we'll look for clues. Okay?"

I look over at Teddy to check what he thinks. Teddy nods his head real big. I did promise I would be brave. "Okay."

"Hannah!" calls Hannah's mom. "Are you out here?"

"Aoife, is your uncle married?" Hannah starts packing up slowly.

"I don't think so."

"He's very handsome."

I frown. "So?" I don't like Hannah saying it, and Teddy growls.

"So my mother is single, too. Maybe she can marry Mr. Donovan—and then we'd be like sisters!"

"No we wouldn't," I say.

"I said we'd be *like* sisters, not that we'd actually *be* sisters. We'd be cousins, though, I think. Just think, I'd have five cousins instead of four." Hannah looks pleased.

I don't have any cousins.

"I guess," I say. But secretly I don't know if it would be fun for Hannah to be my cousin and my neighbor. What if Uncle Donny started liking her more than me? She's older, and she can do better Barbie hair. And she can make her whole body into the shape of a bridge if she starts off on her back on the grass.

"Hannah, here you are."

We both look up because Hannah's mom has come to the front door. I like Hannah's mom, even though Teddy says she's boring. If she was an animal, she'd be a big groundhog standing up in the grass. She is big and soft and looks good to hug. But I still like my mama more.

"You're supposed to be cleaning up all those toys in the basement before your grandma gets here. And your lunch is sitting out on the kitchen counter."

"Can Aoife eat with us, too?"

"If her uncle says it's okay." So I know Hannah has been talking about us at home, or else her mom wouldn't know about Uncle Donny.

When I ask, Uncle Donny says that will be a huge help because he needs to go run errands. He goes over and introduces himself to Hannah's mom and says they are lifesavers, which is a kind of candy. I am glad he is happy, even though I don't really like to eat with Hannah's family because all the stuff they eat is weird and not like Mama's food (when she used to cook). Mama never made lunchmeat sandwiches on white bread. When Mama is feeling up to cooking, she bakes her own bread out of brown wheat, and we eat it with soup that she cooks in the Crock-Pot all day long so it's extra delicious. And I'm not really hungry right now anyway because we already had ice cream after church, but I know not to argue.

Anyway, these days Mama and I don't have a real lunch either. We just have some water and crackers and Mama says it's just like communion.

"Thanks a million," says Uncle Donny, coming out of Hannah's house. "Aoife, be good, okay?"

"I'm always good," I say. "Teddy's the one who causes trouble."

"Teddy again, hmm," clucks Hannah's mom.

"You know when I was your age, I wanted an imaginary room to myself," says Uncle Donny.

Hannah's mom laughs. Uncle Donny is so funny.

But I don't want them to get married.

Meanwhile, Hannah's mom is smiling at my hair. "I called Stephanie to come over, too," she tells Uncle Donny. I didn't think I'd see Stephanie again so soon, but it's good because she doesn't watch us all that close.

"Sounds like a plan," says Uncle Donny.

"Did Mac make you mad?" I ask, as he hands me a tube of sunscreen and a baseball cap. "Are you going to have a fight?"

"No, we're not going to have a fight. Sometimes, uh, Mr. Mac and I don't get along, but that just means we have to use our words and talk things out."

"But you didn't talk things out. You told him to go away."

"Ah, yes, but that was only so that we could, you know, think about the words we're going to use next time we see each other and talk things out then."

I guess that makes sense.

"Now, put some sunscreen on, Aoife."

I like the smell of sunscreen, so even though it's cold and it makes me greasy, I put it all over. When I am finished, Uncle Donny laughs at me.

"Missed a spot," he says. So he rubs the rest of it in more, all over my shoulders and my neck. Then he uses his thumbs to wipe some off my cheeks and puts it on my ears.

"Have fun playing outside," he says. "I wish I could come with you. Never get old, Aoife! Always stay young and beautiful!"

"Okay," I say.

"Good. Now I won't be long, okay, E-fers? Have a good time." Uncle Donny kisses my head, goes back to his shiny car, and drives away.

As soon as we turn around, Hannah's mom has to go break up a fight between the two boy cousins, who are yelling about the Xbox. Hannah's mom says the boy cousins are *driving their mom to distraction.* I think they're very distracting, too.

Hannah and I are just thinking it might be our chance to start investigating, but Stephanie shows up first.

"Thank God," says Hannah's mom. "Please take this whole rowdy lot out to play." Even though Hannah and I are never rowdy. That's the boy cousins.

"I was thinking of taking them down to the park, if it's okay with you," says Stephanie.

The park! I love the park, although Mama never wants to take me. I only get to go when she visits Theo. But luckily, she goes to visit Theo a lot. Teddy loves the park, too. It's his favorite place to be. In the park, he shrinks down to his smallest bear size, no bigger than I am, and runs through the trees with Hannah and me.

I hope when we get to the park we can sneak away and go to the Secret Place. Teddy is the one who discovered it, and he showed me one day when Stephanie wasn't watching properly. It's all the way at the far end of the park. Now whenever we go, we always try to find a way to go play there.

"That sounds great. Just don't bring them back too soon." Hannah's mom is trying to get the littler cousin, Ethan, to put on sunscreen even though he doesn't want to, and he's hollering over her. Finally she finishes and gives him a shove out the door.

"Aoife, how's your mom doing?" she asks me over her shoulder.

That reminds me all in a burst that Mama isn't next door waiting for me to come back. I forgot for a minute in the excitement of investigating. I don't think I'll be able to answer at all without starting to cry. Teddy rubs around my legs to make me feel better.

"She—she's fine, but she's busy, so my uncle Donny is staying with me," I lie. Even though I know it's wrong to lie.

I get the feeling Hannah's mom knows something is wrong, but I'm glad she doesn't ask anything else. Maybe because Ethan is screaming that he didn't want to wear sunscreen and he shouldn't have to because his mom doesn't make him.

"I don't care what the rules are in your house, Ethan. In this house we all wear sunscreen when we're outside between ten and three. Aoife, I hope she's feeling better soon. Tell your uncle that if he needs anything, I'm here to help, okay? Now out, all of you. I mean it. I need to clean the carpets before Grandma gets here. Stephanie, thank you; you're a national treasure."

Outside, the boys run ahead of us, pushing each other, and Stephanie wheels her bike along between us and them. Hannah and I walk slowly behind, telling secrets.

"We have to figure out Mac's last name so I can check if he's a molester," Hannah whispers. "That's your job. How are you going to find it out?"

"I could just ask him," I say. "He'll probably tell me." I think about the sound of that plate shattering against the wall, and I wonder if that's how Mac killed Theo, too. Maybe he broke him into a thousand tiny pieces that Mama had to sweep up. I don't like to think about that.

"How are we going to find the rest of the suspects?" I ask.

"We'll have to investigate," she says.

"How will we even know it's the murderer when we find him?"

"Because, he *or she* will try to kill us," Hannah whispers back.

Oh.

It's so hot outside that the black street has bubbles, but I don't stop to poke them with a stick even though I want to, because we're on our way to the Secret Place.

"You're too slow," yells the bigger cousin, Liam, to Hannah and me. Stephanie and the boys got too far ahead of us and are standing on the corner, shoving each other. Liam is up on top of the curb and Ethan is trying to step up to stand there, too, except Liam keeps pushing him off. Next thing I know, Liam will start pinching his nose, which is what he always does to make Ethan start crying.

"Go on ahead, we're coming," says Hannah when we're close enough to talk in a normal voice. "We want to go look at the stream."

"The stream is stupid," says Liam, wiping his fingers off on his pants. I don't know what he's touched that leaves a greasy stain like that.

"Well, just go do whatever you want to do, then," says Hannah. "It's not like we care." I think she's brave to talk to the boy cousins like that. Liam is a whole year older than her, and Ethan is a year older than I am, so I never say anything to either of them if I can help it. We don't usually play with the boys unless Hannah's mom says we have to.

"Stupid," says Liam, shoving Ethan so he bumps into Hannah. Ethan starts yelling and trying to hit him back, but he's too little, and Stephanie sighs and nudges them to start walking again.

"All right, keep it moving, we're almost there," she says.

"Maybe we can ask Stephanie if she knew Theo," I say.

"That's a great idea!" Hannah takes my hand and pulls me off to the side. "She could be a *material witness*."

Mama says that sometimes Hannah is not showing off because sometimes she just doesn't realize I'm not understanding what she means. Either way, Mama says I should ask politely and be gracious about the chance to learn something new.

"What's one of those?" I ask, maybe not as gracious as I should be.

"It's somebody that may have seen something very important," she says, excited to explain. "Stephanie is probably old enough to remember Theo, and she may be able to tell us what happened to him."

I'm glad we have one of those around to talk to. "Let's do it," I say.

We've been dragging our feet enough that the boys are already at the park, running around on the grass yelling, and

Stephanie is waiting for us with the bike in the shade. She doesn't mind waiting, though—Stephanie likes to read books while she babysits us, and she doesn't really care what we get up to as long as we come back when she calls us. Her job, she says, is to keep us alive until we get home.

That's how come I know Hannah and I will have a chance to go to the Secret Place.

Sure enough, she takes a blanket out of her basket and spreads it out on the grass, and then sits facing away from us. "Don't play too near the creek," she says. "And stay within earshot, okay?"

"We will," I say.

"Cool." She takes her book out of her bag and flips it open. I can read the title: *The High. Way. Man's. Lady.*

"What's a *high-way-man*?" I ask.

"Go play," says Stephanie without looking up.

Hannah kicks the back of my foot so I know she's about to start the investigation. She stands very straight and plays with the edge of her T-shirt, tugging it down. She's trying to act like an adult, I guess. "Hey Stephanie?"

Stephanie turns a page of her book. "Mm-hmm?"

Hannah bumps me with her elbow. "Um," I say. I look at her and she makes her eyes round, and nods. Teddy is next to me, nodding with his whole body, too.

"I was—" My voice comes out too loud. "I was hoping you could tell us about my brother. About Theo."

Stephanie looks at me over the top of her book. "About Theo," she says.

I swallow. "Yes," I say. "Please. I want to know."

Stephanie frowns, and I don't think she's going to answer. She's going to do exactly what Mama and Uncle Donny always do, and say that it's not a good idea to talk about Theo.

"Did you ever meet him?" I ask.

"Well, obviously I knew who he was," she tells me. "He was a year below me in school."

That doesn't make sense, because Stephanie doesn't go to Sacred Heart. She goes to regular school. Mama says Father Paul got me special money from the diocese. Maybe they didn't know Theo needed it too?

"What was he like?" Hannah says at the same time.

"I've got to be honest, I thought he was kind of a little creep. Him and his nerdy friend always tried to peek into the pool locker room to spy on the girls." She rolls her eyes. "But . . . he was just a twerp. He didn't deserve what happened to him."

"Do you know what did happen to him?" Hannah jumps in. "Nobody else will talk about it!"

I'm too busy trying to understand that Theo was almost the same age as Stephanie, once. But she kept getting older and he didn't. Stephanie is practically a grown-up, but Theo is still thirteen forever, in the photo over the stairs.

"I only know what people said at the time," says Stephanie, picking up her book again. "And that is nothing I'm going to talk to little kids about. I like this job just fine, thanks."

"Just tell us one thing," Hannah begs. "Please, please, please?" She looks over and elbows me, giving me a look and jerking her head towards Stephanie.

"Please, please, please?" I say.

"She's his *grieving sister*," says Hannah, her voice high-pitched. "Can't you please just answer a few tiny little questions? We already know the murder is unsolved so we just want to find out the how and the why!"

She got that from her Junior Detective Guidebook, I know. *Who, What, When, Where, Why.* All we know so far is *Who.*

Stephanie pinches up her mouth like Mama when she hears about someone saying the Lord's name in vain. "No way," she says. "You guys shouldn't even be thinking about murders and stuff. A kid *died*, okay? It's not a game." She holds up her hands in front of her before Hannah can say anything else. "No. I don't know why you want to dig it up now, but you're not going to find out anything you want to know. Trust me."

But I have to know. Because otherwise Mama's never coming home.

"Now, you two—scram," she says, picking up her book again. "And stop messing around with this."

Hannah and I both know she isn't going to say anything more. It's almost impossible to make Stephanie change her mind, which we prove every time we try to get her to buy us ice cream.

She waves her hands like she's shooing off flies. "Am-scray," she says, which means *leave*.

"Let's go, Aoife," says Hannah.

As soon as we are out of Stephanie's earshot, Hannah pulls me down in the grass. "Even though our material witness isn't cooperating, we still confirmed the murder is unsolved," she says, her voice high-pitched with excitement. "I can't believe something like this happened right here in my own neighborhood!"

I'm not as excited as Hannah. It was too weird hearing Stephanie talk about Theo like he was a real person. I kind of got used to thinking of him as a photograph, forever.

"And we learned that Theo had a friend. That's a clue, too. Maybe we can find him and he would know what happened."

She starts a new page on her notebook. On the top she writes, TO FIND OUT. #1. MACK'S LAST NAME. #2. THEO'S FRIEND. "The investigation is under way," she says seriously.

"Great," I say.

"Come on, let's go to the creek and make a plan," says Hannah, taking my hand.

When we're sure Stephanie isn't going to look up from her book (Hannah says a highwayman is like a construction worker), we sneak after Teddy towards the Secret Place. It's all the way at the edge of the park, which is thick with the bushes Mama says are called honeysuckle.

The park is made up mostly of a grassy lawn. There's a playground with a blue metal slide and a set of monkey bars. I used to be able to go all the way across the monkey bars last year, no problem, but this summer I grew an inch and got heavier, and now I can't do it anymore. There's also a painted pony on a big spring so you can ride it and rock back and forth like you're riding a real horse. Then there's a wooded area around the creek. It's a bad place to fly kites because the trees on the hillside grow so tall. But sometimes people have picnics there.

If you go through the brambles and watch out for the poison ivy, you can climb halfway down the hill using the branches to hold on. Then, there's a big flat rock that hangs out of the side of the hill over the water. It's only just big enough for two small people—an adult wouldn't fit.

This is the Secret Place.

We don't tell anyone that we come here, because grown-ups always think that, whatever you're doing, you're going to get hurt. Like when Hannah's mom found out that we were riding down the hill on a car seat balanced on top of a skateboard, and she took it away. And when Mama found the bird's nest I'd been hiding for Teddy to hatch more baby bears in, and she made us put the nest outside, just because there were little tiny bugs coming out of it. That's why Teddy doesn't have any children.

So we don't tell anyone about the Secret Place.

Hannah and I scramble down on our backsides and sit on the big stone together and throw branches down at the creek. It's fun to hear them crack on the rocks. The sun makes the rock warm, and it smells like hot dirt and baking pine needles.

"The girls at school don't even like to solve mysteries," says Hannah. "They're really stupid. They'd rather go to the mall or something." She rolls her eyes and throws another stick.

I am sorry Hannah is sad, so I try not to interrupt her when she explains about how to interrogate a witness, even when Teddy tries to distract me by pushing over a giant rock in the water, and it makes a splash. He's always biggest and brightest in the Secret Place. He likes the sunshine on his fur.

"Did you hear that?" asks Hannah, peering over the edge of the rock. We always have to be careful to stay back from the edge. "I think it was a fish."

She listens for a minute but doesn't hear anything else, because Teddy has curled up and gone to sleep. Hannah takes out her notebook. "So, now we have one suspect and one witness," she says. "This afternoon, we need to find at least one more of each. But I think we're off to a good start."

I nod. That is pretty good.

"Do you think we can interview your uncle as a witness?" asks Hannah.

"I don't know. He's very busy at work. He's trying to figure out how to pay the bills so we don't get the electricity shut off again."

"What are you going to do if he can't make the rent?"

"What's *the rent*?" I ask.

"Well, like my mom owns the house we live in, so we can't get kicked out. But somebody else owns your house, and your mom just pays them to live there."

"That's not true!" I say. Nobody else owns our house but us.

"Yes it is. And if you ever don't pay, even one time, they'll kick you out. My mom explained it to me."

"That doesn't make it true," I say. But Hannah is usually right about things like Children's Prison, and then I remember Uncle Donny saying on the phone before Mama came on that Mama would *lose her home.*

I wonder if we could all live in the Secret Place forever and ever.

For a while we play our favorite game, where we drop sticks into the water and see which one goes downstream faster. Hannah's stick always wins, although one time I'm pretty sure she got the sticks mixed up. Then she tells me the story of her latest Encyclopedia Brown and I pretend to listen. But finally we hear Stephanie calling us. "Hey girls, it's almost dinnertime," she yells. "Hannah, you have to get home to see your grandma."

"We're coming!" Hannah calls. We have to run up the hill, because if we take too long Stephanie will come looking for us and she might find the Secret Place, and then we probably wouldn't be allowed to come anymore.

The Secret Place is just for us—and Teddy.

Chapter Six

Summer is the best time of year.

It's still not even close to dark as we head back. We walk all the way to Hannah's house, but her grandmother hasn't come yet, so Hannah says that means we still have time to look for clues before dinner. The boy cousins go down in the basement to argue over the Xbox and Hannah runs up to her room while I stand on the front porch and watch the waves of heat coming up from the street.

I don't understand what you're seeing when you see heat waves like that, because there's nothing there, but still you can see it. That's like Teddy, or like the saints in the church—they're still real, even if they don't quite make sense. I'm not wrong about seeing the heat come up from the sidewalk just because it's invisible.

"Aoife wants to play in the backyard, Mom," says Hannah, coming back downstairs. "Is that okay?"

The nice thing about playing with Hannah is that she's old enough to play outside all by herself. I wouldn't be allowed to unless I was with her.

"Just until Grandma comes," says Hannah's mom. "Dinner's almost ready. Stay within sight of the house—and *don't* go down to Mr. Rutledge's corner."

"We won't!" says Hannah. "C'mon, Aoife." She takes my hand and leads me out through the side yard as Teddy clomps after us on all fours. I notice she's got a backpack with her, but I don't have time to ask her what's in it.

"Okay," says Hannah. "Your uncle's car is still gone, so this is our chance to look for clues. C'mon."

We run together to the bushes and climb under the fence, which has the bottom pieces broken off. Now that we're in my backyard, we sneak around to get in the side door, which is never locked during the day.

Hannah runs straight to the stairs, faster than I can keep up because her legs are longer than mine. "Come on, we don't have a lot of time."

She leads the way into Mama's room, and I follow more slowly with Teddy nudging against my legs. Even he knows we're not supposed to go in here without asking permission.

The room looks just like it always does, which is a surprise somehow. I think it should look different since Mama didn't come home. But everything looks like she'll be right back. Mama's shirts are still hanging up in her closet. The morning we went to the mall, she was trying to choose between two cardigans, and the one she didn't wear is still hanging over the back of her chair. She hasn't come back and put it away yet.

"I don't think we should be in here," I say, but what I really mean is that I'm afraid I'm going to start crying like a baby. I miss Mama. The room still smells like her, but she's not here. Those are her earrings, and her watch, and that's her bed that she made the morning we left—the pillows are still crooked— but she's not here.

"Come on," says Hannah, opening the closet door. "Help me look."

Mama's jewelry box is on the dresser next to the lamp. I open it, even though I know everything there by heart. Sometimes, if I promise to be careful, Mama will let me play with her earrings and wear her necklaces. There's a strand of pearls Mama says are graduation day pearls, and she says that one day she will give them to me. And there's a sparkly stone in a gold ring, and a silver bangle.

"People always hide things under the bed," says Hannah, getting down on her knees to look.

Teddy is rolling over and over on top of the sheets the way he does when something is too tidy. He likes beds to be rumpled, so you can climb right in there and snuggle up.

The Illustrated Volume of the Saints is sitting on the dresser with a candle and Gramma Aoife's rosary. Both the book and the rosary are very special.

I have to move the rosary to pick up the book, so I do it carefully with both hands. Mama taught me to say the Hail Mary and the Our Father on this rosary, and she said that it protects our house from evil spirits. But I'm not interested in that today. I want to look at the book.

There's a bookmark at Mama's favorite, Saint Catherine. That's Mama's confirmation name, and the saint she prays to the most. I turn the pages through the paintings of people being burned and stuck with spears and crushed under piles of rocks to get to Saint Joan.

My saint is wearing armor and riding a horse. They could have painted her burning at the stake, but they didn't. They put her leading the armies of France instead. The text on the other page says that Joan was a maid who led a holy war against the wicked soldiers of England. She trusted the voices of the saints when they appeared to her in her visions.

"Aoife, stop messing around," says Hannah. "We're supposed to be looking for clues."

"I'm not messing around," I say. But I put the book down and put Gramma Aoife's rosary carefully, carefully on top of it.

"What's this?" Hannah is halfway under the bed, her butt sticking out and legs wiggling in her denim shorts as she reaches for something underneath.

"What's what?" I say. I've hidden under that bed before, and there's nothing but a bunch of boxes.

Hannah is dragging out a big box and pulling off the lid. "Maybe there's a diary!" she says, sounding excited. "In books, there's always a diary full of clues, and it ends the day someone died."

"Then we need to look for Theo's diary, not Mama's," I say. I come over and look anyway.

But it's just a bunch of papers in the box. I thought we were looking for clues. On TV, clues are usually footprints or a dropped handkerchief or something. If Hannah just wants to look at papers, that's not even where Mama keeps the really important ones. Those are in the box in the linen closet. But I don't say that, because Hannah doesn't like it when I interrupt her in the middle of investigating.

"Start looking, Aoife," says Hannah, sounding excited. She has spread the papers across the carpet and is digging through them.

I sit cross-legged next to her. Most of the papers are boring, but there's a stack of birthday cards with pictures of cats or butterflies. One of them is tucked into an envelope written in Mama's beautiful handwriting. Mama loves to write letters.

I guess she didn't send these. Most of them are pretty pictures, one of flowers, one of birds. I'm planning to look at each of them one by one when a photograph falls out of the stack, and then I'm looking at a picture of Mama and a man in a tan uniform.

"What's this?" I say. He's a dark-haired, handsome man, with thick plastic glasses. He's standing behind Mama with his arms around her, and she's smiling at the camera.

Hannah crawls around behind me. "Do you know who that is?" she asks.

The only people who put their arms around Mama like that are her special friends, and that's not Mac in the picture, or anyone else I remember. "No," I say. "I've never seen him before."

"I bet I know," says Hannah, sounding excited. "Maybe it's your father!"

"No, because Mama found me in a cabbage patch," I explain. But Hannah just rolls her eyes and flips over the picture.

ME AND BEN, AUGUST 1998, says the back in Mama's beautiful handwriting.

"It could be a clue," says Hannah. "Add it to the list." Sometimes Hannah tells me what to do even though she's already doing it herself, like right now.

She takes out her notebook, and under SUSPECTS, right under MACK, she writes BEN, 1998?

"Okay, that's the most important clue. Let's check Theo's room next," she says. She brushes off her knees and runs across the hall.

I can't believe I found a clue, all by myself. I just picked up a birthday card, and there it was. Maybe I'm a great detective. I hope so, because I want to bring Mama home as soon as possible.

I stay behind to put the papers back in the box and then push the box back under the bed. I don't want Mama to find her stuff all moved when she gets back. When everything looks exactly the way it should, I follow Hannah.

Theo's room is just the way he left it—the posters on the walls, the Game Boy that I'm not allowed to put new batteries in. All of his school awards, for spelling and field day and soccer. His remote-control car is in the corner where he left it. His bed is still made with *Avatar* sheets. Even most of his clothes are still in the closet.

Hannah is going through his drawers. "I can't find a diary here either," she complains.

"I don't think boys keep diaries," I tell her, watching her push the drawer shut. Hannah keeps one, I know—I saw it once, all pink and tied up with pink ribbon.

Hannah goes over to the bookshelves, looking at Theo's Star Wars series. "There's nothing good here," she says.

"There's schoolbooks," I say, pointing at the bottom shelves. "Notebooks and stuff." I remember those from when Mama was gathering things to give to a rummage sale at church. She gave away all the clothes I outgrew, but in the end she didn't get rid of one thing of Theo's. "He was really good at school."

"This is useless," says Hannah, pouting. "What we need is a firsthand account."

"An account?"

"That's what they call it when somebody can tell you an important clue that solves the case," Hannah explains. "And I know just who to ask."

Hannah goes back to the top of the stairs and takes the last picture of my brother off the wall.

"You're not supposed to touch that!" I say. Mama would be so angry if she saw Hannah's fat fingers on the glass over Theo's face. That's her favorite picture of Theo, the one she kisses goodnight.

"Don't be a baby, Aoife. We need it," says Hannah. She takes the picture back into Theo's room.

Teddy growls. He thinks that Hannah is bossy, and sometimes he threatens to eat her. But after a minute he goes in after her, and I follow behind him.

Hannah sits down in the middle of the floor and opens the backpack. "Look." She takes out the apple-shaped scented candle that her mom keeps in the bathroom at her house, and the ceramic dish that used to sit on the back of the toilet. She puts it in front of the picture in the middle of the floor. She's also got the notebook where she wrote down her list of suspects.

"What good is that stuff going to do?" I ask.

"Wait. Turn out the lights and pull the curtain."

Nobody has touched the curtains in a long time. They're full of dust, and the folds have been turned lighter by the sun. But between the two of us, we get them closed, and then Hannah shuts the door so no light comes in from the hall.

"What are we doing?" I say again. Teddy doesn't like Theo's room. He wants to go. He's scratching on the door like the cat next door when it's time for Mama to feed it.

"Don't be a baby," says Hannah. She pulls something else out of her backpack, some kind of funny little plastic box. "This is my grandma's," she explains. "She left it at our house." She does something to the end of the box, but nothing happens.

"I don't get it."

"It's harder than I thought." Hannah is pushing a little lever on the end of the box, but slowly, like she's afraid it'll make a loud noise or something. Then all of a sudden there's a little *snick* sound, and the end of the box is on fire.

Hannah shrieks and drops the box.

"Hannah!" I yell. But by the time it hits the carpet, the fire is already out.

"Phew," she says.

I'm thinking this is not such a good idea. "Hannah, I'm not supposed to play with matches."

"This isn't matches," she says. "It's a lighter. It just startled me. Don't worry, I can make it work." But she doesn't sound so sure. This time, when she picks it up, she's even more scared trying to push the button, and for a long time nothing happens.

"We're going to get in trouble. Your mom is going to notice we're gone."

"No she won't. My grandma's always late, and my cousins are really bad." Hannah pushes the button and the lighter makes the *snick* sound again. This time, she manages to keep hold of it, and the fire stays on.

"It's getting hot," she says, nervously. She's trying to light the wick of the candle without putting her fingers in the flame. The wick doesn't catch.

"Put it out," I say.

"I can do it. There!" The candle lights up. The lighter goes out. "Okay, we got it."

"Your mom's going to know we lit that candle," I say.

I'm not scared, even though Hannah's face looks creepy with the candle flickering underneath her chin, and in the dark, Teddy's eyes glow like headlights. The picture of Theo looks funny, too, like all the shadows on his face are long and dark.

"We need to interview Theo about who murdered him," Hannah says. "I saw this in a movie. It's called a séance. You light a candle, and then you summon his departed spirit."

"Is this witchcraft? Because Father Paul says witchcraft is a sin."

"It's not witchcraft, it's just good detective work. Now be quiet." Hannah picks up the candle in her hand again. She's lucky it comes in a little ceramic dish, or that wax would melt over her hands.

"I summon you, Theodore Scott," she says dramatically. "Reveal yourself!"

Teddy starts whining, but that's the only thing that happens. It's creepy sitting in the dark, but other than Hannah's heavy breathing I don't hear my dead brother or anything.

"I don't think it worked," I say.

Hannah closes her eyes and leans closer over the candle. I think her hair is going to catch fire, but she flicks it behind her ears just in time.

"Are you praying?" I ask her suspiciously. Because I don't think she should be praying about this.

"Be *quiet*, Aoife, I'm not praying. I'm just . . . concentrating. Now, Theodore. Tell us who murdered you. Was it Mac? Or was it Ben? Wait . . . *do you hear that?*"

"No, what!"

"Tapping," says Hannah, triumphant. "I can hear him tapping in the walls!"

All the air gets trapped in my throat and I can't breathe. I think I'm going to throw up. I get up and run to the door.

"Aoife, come back," calls Hannah, sounding annoyed. "Aoife, I was just kidding! I don't even hear anything, do you? Huh?"

But I've already thrown open the door and run back out into the hallway, where I'm confronted with the blank wall where Theo's picture is supposed to be.

"I'm sorry!" I say. "Theo, I'm sorry!"

"Aoife, you're being such a baby right now." Hannah comes out of the room. She's blown out the candle already and the hallway is light. I'm not as scared and my stomach feels better.

"Were you really kidding?" I ask.

"I thought I heard something. But maybe I didn't. But, it didn't happen until I asked about Ben and Mac. I think that supports my theory that one of them murdered your brother."

Why would Mama be Mac's special friend if he killed Theo? And Mama was smiling in the picture with Ben, which she wouldn't do if he was a murderer, right?

"I know it's scary," says Hannah, putting her hand on my shoulder. "And you're just a little kid. How can you stop an evil murderer? But I promise, if Mac or Ben killed your brother, we will find the evidence and take them to justice!"

"I think we should go back to your house now," I say, wiping my nose. "Did you get the stuff out of Theo's room?"

Hannah puts the lighter and the ceramic dish back in her backpack, but she hides the apple candle under the bed "for later," and I know she hasn't given up. Except for some places where wax dripped on the carpet, you can hardly tell we were in the room at all. The curtains fold back into exactly the same shape they were in. Then Hannah puts the picture back on the wall, and although it's a little crooked, I don't think anyone will notice.

"I'm sorry you were scared, but we found important evidence," says Hannah as we go back downstairs. Teddy presses close to my legs until we're all the way in the hall.

As I follow her out the front door, I realize that, unlike Joan of Arc, I wasn't very brave. I don't think Joan of Arc ran to the hallway when it was time to fight off the British soldiers. Maybe Theo really was trying to tell me something and I was just too much of a baby to listen to it.

"Hannah, do you really think Mac might have killed Theo?" I ask. Somehow that seems a lot worse than Ben, who I've never even met. I shiver, remembering the sound of that plate breaking against the wall.

Hannah nods her head. "It all fits," she says. "Maybe we don't know for sure yet, but he's definitely one of my top two suspects at the moment." I didn't know there were more than two suspects, but I don't want to ask.

Back over the fence, Hannah was right—her mom hasn't even realized we left the yard.

*　*　*

Uncle Donny picks me up from Hannah's house not too much later. By then I'm practically falling asleep on my feet.

"Stephanie really wore you guys out at the park," says Uncle Donny, sounding impressed. Like Stephanie did *anything*.

"Did you have a good time playing with Hannah?"

"We just went to the playground," I say, because I don't tell anyone about the Secret Place and I definitely don't want to talk about our investigating. "Hannah's boy cousins were there, but they were always fighting. And Liam, the older one, pushed down Ethan and he cried."

"Yeah, boys are the worst, aren't they?" That makes me laugh, because Uncle Donny is a boy.

"I miss Mama," I say.

He stops walking and leans over to pick me up in his arms. "I miss your ma too," he says, carrying me over the yard and through the front door. He's so strong that he can walk and carry me at the same time.

"Can we talk to her on the phone again?"

Uncle Donny sighs. "I'd like that, munchkin, but the doctors say your ma has been—she's extra confused right now, and she won't be able to talk for a little while. I'm sorry. As soon as she's feeling better, we'll make sure to have a call, okay?"

It's not really okay, but I don't say anything. It makes me sad to think that Mama has been confused. I know she isn't going to get any better until I solve the mystery.

Uncle Donny puts me to bed and doesn't even have to read me a story, I'm so sleepy. But just as I start to fall asleep, I hear the front door open and Uncle Donny talking to someone.

I know I'm supposed to be in bed, but I creep out of my room with Teddy right alongside me. I know how to walk real quiet down the stairs. Not like Uncle Donny. I put my feet on the outside of each step between the railings on the stairwell. When I get to the bottom, I sit on the step and peek.

"We've got to keep it down, I'm afraid," Uncle Donny is saying. "My sister's kid is asleep upstairs."

I'm not, but I put my hand over my lips so I won't give myself away. I don't know the man with Uncle Donny. He's dark black all over with a shiny bald head. Father Paul says God makes people different colors but we're all the same on the inside. He says God makes a beautiful rainbow out of all the colors, but I don't know why nobody comes in any fun colors.

Uncle Donny is holding the man's hand like Mama holds mine when we walk to school, and he leads him over to the couch. They watch a movie on his laptop, because we don't have a TV, and I can see the screen from here. It's the kind of movie I don't like, where people just talk and talk and nothing fun ever happens. I like movies where there's animals or princesses or magic. I lean my head against the railing of the stairs and wait.

The stranger puts his arm around Uncle Donny and they huddle up on the sofa just like Mama and I do, his head on Uncle Donny's shoulder. After a while of nothing happening except them hugging more, I creep back upstairs. It's nice that Uncle Donny has a best friend, too, I guess.

I get back into bed, and this time I fall straight to sleep.

At first, I dream about fishes. We're all swimming, me and Teddy, Uncle Donny and Mama. Teddy is still a bear, but underwater, he's sleek like a seal. Maybe seals are just bears that decided to go swimming and never came back out.

But then the dream starts to shift. Like how dreams do, when they don't make sense but you don't notice until you're thinking about it later. I forget that I was ever swimming, and instead it's me and Teddy in the park like always.

Teddy is facing away from me, and although I call out "Hi Teddy!" he doesn't answer and he doesn't turn around.

Teddy starts walking away, and I follow him through the park. Just like Hannah and I do, we go through the bristle bushes, and they grab at us like hands. We see my favorite tree, crooked and white like a lightning bolt. We go around the tree, and there, halfway down the hill, is the Secret Place.

Theo is waiting in the Secret Place.

With a gasp, I wake up. It's not morning yet. It's still dark outside. I can hear the sound of Uncle Donny on the stairs, walking up and down. I know it's him because Teddy goes out in the hallway and checks.

It was just a dream, I tell Teddy. He goes to get Monkey Sock Puppet, which Mama made me and is his favorite stuffed animal, and puts it on the bed to guard us.

And outside the door, Uncle Donny creaks and creaks, up and down the stairs.

Dear Theo,

I know that Father Paul says there is no demon stalking our family. He tells me that the Devil and his servants wage their holy battle far from the sight of mortal eyes. He tells me to listen to the doctors and to take my pills. He has always been a friend to me and to our family, and I believe that he is a good man and the servant of our faithful Father. I believe that he is washed in the blood of Christ.

But he is wrong about the shadow that follows us. It is real, and it lives still, and it is still seeking us. It sends my brother unnatural desires. It appears to my daughter and whispers duplicity. I have seen her talk to creatures that can't be seen, and I know that the demon is awake and following us.

Perhaps it was his cursed hands over my own that turned the wheel of the car into traffic. The sound of my daughter shrieking was only a prelude to the screaming of the souls of the damned in Hell. I pray abjectly that the Blessed Mary will intercede, not on my own behalf, but on behalf of my sweet girl, who needs a mother and has no one else in this world to watch over her except for Her.

But I tell you, it is better that that car should have hit us full on and carried us safely to my Father's Kingdom than that I should lose another child into the hands of Satan.

She talks about you sometimes, but God help me, I have asked her to stop.

I'm sorry, Theo. I did the only thing I could do.

Do you hear me?

I did the only thing I could do.

Yours Ever in Christ,
Ma

Chapter Seven

The next morning, Uncle Donny is already awake when Teddy and I get up. He's sitting in the study looking at the paperwork on Mama's desk, and he's on the phone.

Then he looks up and sees me. "I gotta go," he says. "Yes . . . No, I'll talk to you later. Bye for now." He hangs up. "Morning, midget."

"What are you looking at?" I ask, climbing up on the chair.

"I'm trying to figure out how to pay the bills around here. We don't want them to come shut off the electricity, do we?"

No we don't, because it was really cold last time.

"I'm hungry," I say. "Is there breakfast?"

"There sure is," says Uncle Donny, walking with me into the kitchen. "What does madam prefer this morning?"

When I open the refrigerator, there's so many different kinds of food in there that it kind of makes my stomach hurt. All the drawers and the shelves are full. Are more people going to live here? Who is going to eat all this food before it starts to go bad?

Uncle Donny makes me s'mores Pop-Tarts, which turns out to be Teddy's new favorite food ever, and then he says I need to make sure to take a shower before I get dressed because I'm starting to smell bad. Uncle Donny is funny. Mama always makes me shower at night, because the house gets so hot when we turn the air conditioning off because we're on a budget. If you go to sleep with wet hair, then you won't mind so much.

"Listen, Aoife," says Uncle Donny, and he has the paper in front of him but he isn't reading it, so I know what he's saying must be important.

"Yeah?"

"Do you remember Dr. Pearlman from the hospital saying that some people from CPS wanted to come visit us?"

"Teddy didn't like Dr. Pearlman," I say.

"Great," says Donny. "Well, I think some of her friends would like to come over later; does that sound like fun?"

"What's *sea-pee-ess*?"

"That's the part of the government they're from. They . . . try to help families when they have some difficulties, like ours."

"Oh." The ones who take you to Children's Prison? But I can tell Uncle Donny wants me to say *yes, it sounds like fun*, so I swallow hard and nod my head anyway.

"Okay, good." Now Uncle Donny reaches for the newspaper and unfolds it. He likes the box-game, same as Mama. You put letters in the little boxes and then you win. Teddy climbs up on the chair to look over his shoulder.

"What if Teddy doesn't like Dr. Pearlman's friends either?" I ask.

"You know, I think it would be a good idea if you asked Teddy to wait in the bedroom while you talk to them," says Uncle Donny. "Okay? Just so that he doesn't get upset when they come visit."

"Okay," I say, although Teddy doesn't exactly do what I tell him to. He makes a face, sticking his tongue out.

"In fact, it's probably a good idea to talk about other things with Dr. Pearlman's friends, and *not* Teddy, okay?"

"Mama says it's rude to talk to someone if nobody else can hear them," I say.

"Right, exactly. We wouldn't want to be rude to the CPS ladies, would we. Right?"

"Right," I say. But Teddy won't eat his Pop-Tart now, because he's mad at me.

"Now, this morning you wanted to go to Bible study at the church, right?"

"Yes please." I like to go to church anytime, because Father Paul is nice and there's food and because Mama says the demons can't get you if you're in the church where the angels are watching you—but now I have an even better reason to go to church, because maybe my own special saints will come back again and tell me better about how I'm supposed to solve the mystery of Theo's death.

"Okay, well, Stephanie's coming at ten, so be sure to be dressed and ready for her when she gets here."

So far we have two suspects, Ben and Mac, written down in Hannah's notebook and nothing else. We haven't even found out one thing on the TO FIND OUT list. That's not going to be enough to bring Mama home in time before the fireworks. I need to do better investigating.

I guess I could start right now.

"Uncle Donny?" I ask, making the crumbs from my Pop-Tart into a happy face.

"Yes?"

"Do you know a special friend of Mama's named Ben?"

Uncle Donny's eyebrows go up. "That's a name I haven't heard in a while," he says. So that means yes. "Where did you hear about Ben?"

Teddy doesn't think I should say where it was, so I just shrug. "Was Ben nice or was he scary?"

Uncle Donny looks at me for a minute. "Well, he wasn't scary. Did somebody tell you he was?"

"Was he more nice or less nice than Mac?"

"Boy, hard to choose," says Uncle Donny, rubbing his eyes. It does not sound like he thinks it's hard to choose. "I'd have to say he was nicer than Mac. But a bear with a sore head is nicer than Mac."

This is called *interrogating a witness*.

I want to ask where Ben is now, but Uncle Donny stands up and puts his hand on my shoulder. "I don't want you to worry about old troubles, Aoife," he says. "It's a beautiful summer day, and time is fleeting. How about you go upstairs and take that shower, huh?"

I wish there was a way to explain to Uncle Donny that it may be the old troubles that are keeping Mama from being here and enjoying the day, too.

I'm not supposed to take a shower by myself, but Uncle Donny sits on the toilet seat while I splash around. I'm barely finished getting dried off and dressed when the doorbell rings. I hear Uncle Donny open the door and hurry to get dressed.

"Stephanie, thanks for coming," says Uncle Donny. "Come on inside. We've got, uh, Pop-Tarts."

I come downstairs and Uncle Donny looks me over. I did my hair all on my own, but it still isn't staying in the ponytail, and we haven't done laundry, so I'm out of clean shorts. "Well, I think you look good enough for God, anyway," he says. "Okay, Stephanie, time to hit the road, huh?"

Stephanie didn't bring her bike today, so we walk together with Teddy dragging his feet behind us, and she has to slow down so we can keep up. I'm impressed because she can walk while she's looking at her phone, and she never trips over anything and she doesn't get lost.

"Where's your mom been lately?" asks Stephanie, as we walk.

"She is working very hard right now," I say politely, which is maybe or maybe not a lie.

"At least your uncle seems cool."

I nod, because he is cool, although I wish he wouldn't always wake me up in the middle of the night. I think about Mama, being sad and extra confused and not even able to call us on the telephone. I know I need to help. So I take a deep breath and do a brave thing. "Can I ask you a question, Stephanie?"

She glances over. "Maybe," she says.

I am thinking about Hannah's notebook. "You know my brother's friend that you talked about yesterday?"

"I told you to get over that stuff," she says.

"I know, but I just have a question about his friend. I just want to know his name. I promise I won't ask anything else. Please."

She is quiet for long enough that I think she's not going to answer.

"Please?" I say. "I promise I will keep it a secret."

"Edward," she says at last. She looks so sad. "His name was Edward."

Edward.

A horn honks. We're standing in front of the church, and when I look up I realize there's a familiar truck parked outside— a rusted red pickup with a flag painted on the back.

"Hey, Alfie. You're late!" says Mac, rolling down the windows as we walk up. "I'd almost given up on you . . . Were you just going to keep God waiting?"

Mac gets out of his truck and closes the door. I remember Hannah saying we would know he was the murderer because he would come and try to kill me. I take a giant step backwards, closer to Stephanie.

"Hey there, Stephanie," he says, nodding to her. They've met a few times before. "Listen, I need to talk to Aoife for a little bit. Is that okay?"

My heart is pounding. I want to tell her not to go, but it doesn't come out. Stephanie checks her watch and looks up at church, like she's not a hundred percent sure what to do.

"Go on ahead, I'll take care of her," says Mac, waving her off.

I always thought Stephanie was so grown up. But when Stephanie nods and turns towards the stairs, I think she might have just been pretending all this time. Because she does what the real grown-ups say, just like me.

"So listen, kid, I'm thinking we need to catch up," says Mac, when she's gone. "C'mon, you don't want to go hang out with a bunch of stuffed shirts, do ya?"

I don't know, but I shake my head. "I'm supposed to go to Bible study," I say.

I don't want to get broken into a billion little pieces. But I also told Hannah I would try to find out Mac's last name so she can look him up on the Internet, and this might be my big chance. I remember the bells ringing in the church, and promising to take up the mantle. Joan of Arc would definitely want to interview Mac about my brother.

Teddy is playing mother-may-I on the church steps, ignoring both of us, so he's no help.

"I bet God will understand," Mac says.

"That's exactly what Uncle Donny says!" If Mac was the kind of guy who murdered kids, I bet he wouldn't talk just like Uncle Donny, right?

Mac laughs shortly. "I bet he does. So whattaya say, you ready to blow this popsicle stand?"

He doesn't *seem* like he's trying to kill me. It's scary, but I take a deep breath and climb up into the front seat of the truck, because Mac doesn't have a proper car seat either. And Teddy climbs up right behind me. "Where are we going?" I ask.

"It's a surprise," says Mac. "You like surprises, don't you, Alfie?"

"I think I do," I say.

Mac drives faster than Mama. He turns on the radio and sings along to the songs, and it sounds good even though I don't know any of the music. It's not Taylor Swift like Hannah likes to listen to. It's a man with a low, hissing voice.

I wonder if Mac drove my brother Theo away in this truck before he killed him. Maybe Theo was sitting right where I am now.

Blessed Joan, please don't let Mac be the suspect. But if he is, at least let Mama still come home.

We get on the highway and the truck starts to shake.

"She doesn't take well to these high speeds," says Mac, taking a cigarette out of his pack. Mama doesn't let him smoke inside, but I guess a car isn't really inside.

While he's driving, Mac lights the cigarette with a silver lighter, kind of like the one Hannah stole from her grandmother, but fancier. This time I'm watching more closely, and I see that he pushes down on a little lever to make the fire come out. For a minute I forget to be scared.

"Aren't you afraid it will burn you?" I ask.

"Your buddy Mac has been lighting cigarettes for a long time," he says. He puts the lighter down into the space between the seats, and I can see there's a picture of a bird on it, and there are letters underneath: U-S-M-C. Is that for his name?

Well, I am supposed to be interviewing the suspect. I take a deep breath. "Mac, are these your initials?" I show him the letters on the lighter so he knows what I'm talking about.

Mac glances over but then looks back at the road. "Put that down," he says. So I do. He clears his throat. "That's nobody's name. It's for the Marine Corps. You know what a veteran is?"

"It's a doctor for animals."

Mac frowns. "A veteran is someone who served his country in the military," he says.

This is not what I wanted to talk about. "Is Mac your whole name?" I ask. "Like, is it your first name or your last name?"

He glances over again. "You don't know that?"

I shake my head no.

"John MacMillian Corey, at your service. Mac to my friends."

I can just imagine Hannah writing that down in her notebook, and I know I made the right choice to get into the truck with Mac, even if he might be a murderer.

He clears his throat. "We've always been good buddies, right kiddo?"

Teddy shrugs when I look over at him. "I think so?"

Mac takes an exit off the highway and swings between the lanes to make a turn. "We have, right from the start. So that's why I thought I could ask you the straight story about your mother. You know me and her are good friends, right?"

"You're special friends," I agree.

"Right. So, I tried to ask your uncle Donny about her, but I'm thinking the person I really need to talk to is you. Do you know where she is?"

I'm excited to know something Mac doesn't know. "Mama went to the hospital," I say. "She's confused, but they're going to explain things to her so she can come home."

Mac is quiet for a while after that, smoking his cigarette. He holds it out the window when he's not breathing it in, so it doesn't smell *too* bad. The stink of smoke and old leather seats are what I always think of as Mac smells, even when he hasn't been around in a while.

"What happened?" he asks me. "Can you tell me?"

I play with my hands for a minute, thinking. "Well . . ." *Here is the church.* "We went to the mall," I say. *Here is the steeple.* "Mama was driving the car." *Open it up, and see all the people.* I lift my hands, wiggling my fingers up so that Mac can see the people, too.

"Go on," says Mac.

So I tell him the whole story, and this time I don't get nearly as upset as when I told it to Uncle Donny. I think I've told it enough times now that it's just a thing that happened— plus now I know that if I solve the mystery, Mama can come home again. But I don't tell him that. I know how to keep a secret, just like a grown-up. Mac doesn't say anything when I'm done.

"And I opened the phone!" I add, proud. "I opened it all by myself because Dr. Pearlman didn't know the password."

Mac flicks on his blinky signal and pulls off into an empty parking lot. There's nobody around, and the cement is all broken up with weeds. It's very quiet. If I was going to murder someone, I would think this is the kind of place I'd do it.

"That must have been . . . real scary," says Mac, slowly.

I nod my head.

Mac hits the steering wheel with both hands and says a *really* bad word.

My heart knocks against the inside of my chest, and it hurts. My hands are shaking. They don't stop, even when I fold them together in my lap like I'm praying.

"I'm sorry," I say. "I was talking out loud to Teddy, and it made her upset." Teddy comes to crawl into my lap. He's scared too, but at least we're together.

"It's not that," says Mac.

But I'm still sorry.

"You said she got a phone call?" asks Mac. "Do you know who was calling her?"

That doesn't seem like what a murderer would say right before he murders someone, right? I take a breath. "What phone call?"

"You said right before she flipped—before she started yelling—you said she got a phone call."

I guess it's true that she was on the phone when she came out to the van to drive me to the mall. "I don't know who it was," I say, which is true. "I just know she didn't want to talk to them."

"How do you know that?"

"Because I heard her say she had to go, but she didn't really." We could have waited longer to go get shoes.

Mac clears his throat. "So with your mom . . . gone, for now, I guess it's just you and your uncle, huh?"

And Teddy. I nod.

"And what the hell would have happened to you if your uncle hadn't been around, huh?"

"Hannah says they take away kids and put them in Children's Prison," I say.

"Ex-act-ly," says Mac. "Children's prison, just so. It's not a good state of affairs, Alf. Didn't anyone in the hospital ask about your daddy?"

"They did, and I said I was found under a cabbage patch," I explain. "Because that's what Mama always says."

Mac groans. "You're lucky *you* didn't end up in the mad-house, saying that," he says. "Look, kiddo, everybody has a father, okay? You, your mom, even the baby Jesus had a father. That's just the way it is. Even I have a father, the sonofabitch."

I do not know what that means, *sunnufabish*, but it doesn't sound good.

"Does Theo have a father?" I ask.

Mac frowns. "Who's talking about Theo? I'm talking about *you*, Aoife."

But I'm talking about *Theo*.

"Listen, Aoife, I didn't bring you here to explain the facts of life," says Mac. "I came to talk to you about something, uh, really serious."

That sounds just like what Mama said before she started talking to Theo. *Aoife, I want to talk to you about something important.* But she never told me what it was.

"Okay?"

Mac starts up the truck again and pulls out onto the road. "Now I have made . . . I've made a lot of mistakes, I know that. To be honest, Alf, lots of times your mom hasn't been able to count on me when it really mattered. I know I've been kind of in and out of your life. That's what I'm trying to talk to you about."

It's true that there were long times where we never saw Uncle Mac at all. Mama had other special friends, like Uncle Alex and Uncle Tim, who I don't remember so good except that he smelled like popcorn butter. But they weren't full-time real uncles like Uncle Donny, and they went away. And then Mac would come back and be Mama's special friend again.

"I know she blames me for bailing on you guys when you were born, and—plenty of other things, too," says Mac. "But I want to do better this time. Okay, kiddo?"

He's looking at me like he's saying something really important. But I don't understand what it is. I still want to know where we're going and what the surprise is.

"Aoife, I'm trying to explain to you . . . crap, I'm no good at this." Mac puts out his cigarette in the ashtray in the middle of the car. He rubs his eyes. "This is harder than I thought. Your mom didn't want to tell you this because she didn't want to confuse you. And, ah, because I obviously haven't been, uh, what you deserve. But you weren't found in a cabbage patch, okay, Alf? You got an old man looking out for you."

Teddy has fallen asleep and is snoring away in the back seat. "Do you mean God?" I ask. Because I knew that already. God is an old man, just like Santa Claus. And he watches out for us.

"Wha—no, Aoife, I'm talking about me, Mac. I'm saying *I'm* your father."

That doesn't really make any sense. "Like . . . like Father Paul is?"

"No! Not like Father Paul. Like your *mom*, only a dad."

I don't really know what to say. Theo and I never had a father before, and we've had Mac pretty much all along, so I'm not sure what this means.

"Oh. Okay," I say, nodding.

"Just—okay? That's all you've got to say?"

I don't have anything else to say. I'm just hoping that *Ben, 1998* will turn into what Hannah would call our *top suspect.* Because I don't want my father to be the murderer.

"We're here," says Mac, gruffly.

I look up and realize we're at the zoo. "I love the zoo!" I say, wiggling in my seat. I love surprises! "I wanna see the tigers, and the giraffes, and the *bears!*"

"C'mon, then," he says, opening the car door. "We'd better hurry, if we're going to see all of that."

"The polar bears *and* the grizzled bears!" I say. "Mac, Teddy wants to see *all the bears.*"

111

"Yeah, yeah, we won't miss a single bear," says Mac, taking my hand as we walk across the parking lot. "Just don't wander off in there, okay? I don't want to find out you got eaten by an African wild dog."

"I don't wander off," I say, wrinkling my nose—doesn't Mac know that I'm a big girl now and I always behave?

"That's right. You're a good girl, aren't you, Alfie. That's why your uncle Mac—that's why your . . . ol' buddy Mac—is going to take you to the zoo, as a reward for being so good."

We wait in line with the rest of the kids, a lot of whom are from the city and don't know how to act. Mac and I *comport ourselves with dignity*, as Mama would say, and wait patiently until we get up to the man in the box. Mac buys us tickets and complains about how expensive they are. He's on a budget, just like Mama and I are, not like Uncle Donny. Then we go in through what Mac calls the turnstile and we're in the *zoo!* Teddy is dancing around and around because he loves, loves, loves the zoo, too.

"Look, they got seal lions!" I say, forgetting for a second to comport myself with dignity and yelling. "Can we see the seal lions, Mac? And then the bears?"

"Sure, we paid good money enough. We oughta see every flea-ridden animal in the joint," says Mac. But he doesn't sound mad for real, and he takes my hand as we go over to the animal house.

I know I can't remember my whole life, but I'm pretty sure this afternoon is the happiest I've ever been in forever. We go see *all* the animals, and Mac buys us Dippin' Dots, and then we get a hot dog each with just ketchup, no relish, no mustard. And we eat it the same way, with extra ketchup, because we both like ketchup.

Teddy has the best time ever, too, because he gets to see all his family of bears in the zoo. They look kind of fiercer than Teddy does, and they don't wave back when I wave to them, not even when Teddy says hi, but sometimes bears are like that.

And Mac buys us snow cones, because it's soo hot. And we both get cherry, which is my favorite. Murderers don't take people to the zoo and buy them snow cones, do they?

"All right, all right, sit down before you pass out," says Mac. We get a spot at one of the metal tables, and the seat is hot on my legs. "For goodness' sakes, take it easy, Aoife."

I tip my head, because he never calls me Aoife. He says it just about right, as good as Sister Mary Celeste at least.

We sit quietly and suck on our snow cones through straws.

"Hey Mac?" I say.

"What?"

"What did you and Uncle Donny have a fight about? Are you mad at him now?" Because if Mac isn't the murderer, then I want him and Uncle Donny to like each other and then we can all have fun together.

"We weren't fighting," says Mac, and I laugh when he sticks out his tongue at me and it's extra red. "Sometimes adults just have a disagreement, that's all."

"Hannah says that Uncle Donny is going to marry her mom and then we'll be sisters," I blurt out, all at once. I didn't even know I was going to say it until I already had.

Mac chuckles, but I don't see what's so funny.

"Do you think he will?" I ask.

"Uh, no, Alf. I don't think your uncle is going to marry the cougar next door."

I wouldn't say that Hannah's mom reminds me of a cougar. I would say that she reminds me of a groundhog. But it's fun that Mac knows how to play the game, too. "He *might* marry her," I say, seriously.

"Well, kiddo, I guess you're old enough now to understand that your uncle is, uh, of the homosexual persuasion. You know? So I don't think you have to worry about any woman making off with him."

But I don't get what he means. I look at Mac, waiting.

He sighs. "He's a fruit," he says.

But I don't know why he says that. Uncle Donny doesn't seem anything like an apple or an orange to me. He really seems more like a penguin.

"Look, a lot of people in this world end up paired up to somebody, right? Not everybody, sure, but most people, they meet someone, they get married, right?"

"Okay," I say. This doesn't really seem to be true—Mama isn't married, and neither is Mac, or Hannah's mom, or Father Paul, or Stephanie—but I guess it's true on TV.

"So most of the time, a lady marries, you know, a gentleman. Right? But sometimes, uh, a guy like your uncle Donny, you know, and he ends up marrying, ah, another man instead. Uh, instead of a lady."

"That's not true," I say. "Uncle Donny isn't married to *anyone*."

"Okay, yeah, but if he *was*, it wouldn't be to a lady. All right?"

I try to understand what Mac is saying, but it doesn't really make any sense. "So, Uncle Donny would marry you?" I say. "Or Father Paul?"

"Uh, no, those are two people he would definitely *not* marry," says Mac. "He'd marry, you know, another guy like himself, who also likes the gentlemen."

Oh.

Mac looks at me, but he doesn't say anything. After a minute, he lights up another cigarette.

"Sir, you can't smoke that here," says the snow cone man.

"Jesus Christ," says Mac. "I'm outside, ain't I? What do you want from me? C'mon, Alfie, we're done here anyway, right?"

I guess we are, because Teddy's feet have started to hurt and he's already seen all the animals. But I drag the toes of my shoes on the ground all the way back to the gate because I don't ever want today to end. I want to stay here at the zoo, forever, and turn into a monkey and live with my monkey friends.

We walk all the way back to the truck, and Mac unlocks the door and I climb in, feeling like my feet weigh a hundred pounds.

That's when I remember that, if I want Mama to come home, I need to solve more clues. I promised the saints I would.

I try to think of a good question. "Did you ever take Theo to the zoo when he was my age?" I ask.

"Ah, I hadn't met Theo yet when he was your age," says Mac, lighting another cigarette as he gets in. He starts the car, and at first it makes a big noise but then it starts.

I laugh. "That doesn't make sense," I point out. "You said you were our father. You must have met him at least a few times."

"I said I was *your* father," says Mac.

But—but Theo is my brother. I thought that meant we have the same parents. I'm pretty sure that is what that means. Right?

Mac's cell phone rings. He looks at the number and mutters under his breath before answering it. "Yello, Don. No, she's with me . . . Because I picked her up from the church, that's why. Well maybe she shouldn't have been walking by herself with nobody but a teenager looking out for her, then! . . . No. No, I'm bringing her home right now. Keep your pants on Donny, Jesus." He hangs up and reaches for the AC dial, turning it higher because it's warm in the car with the sun beating down.

"But—how can you be my father and not Theo's? Was Theo found in the cabbage patch? You said *everyone* has a father."

It's quiet except for the rattling of the truck. "Theo's father is dead, a long time ago," says Mac.

"Oh." It's sad that Theo's father died, even though it's exciting to be solving parts of the mystery. "He's still my brother though, right?" I ask.

"Yeppo. He's still your brother." Mac doesn't look like he wants to keep talking about this.

"Do you miss Theo? Is that why you don't like to talk about him? Mama really misses him and that's why it's not good to bring him up too much."

"Uh, you know, there's things about me and Theo that are—are hard to explain," says Mac at last. He uses the same voice that everybody uses when they talk about Theo. It doesn't sound right on him because he's usually pretty loud. "He wasn't too happy with me, back in those days."

I want to ask Mac to help me investigate so that Mama comes home. I want to tell him about the saints and the mantle over the fireplace. But before I can say that, I have a different problem.

"I think I ate too much snow cone," I say. "I don't feel so good. Do you have a bucket?"

"Christ," says Mac, reaching back and rummaging around in the back seat. "All right, hold it, Alfie, *hold it!*"

* * *

When we get home, Mac pulls up right in front of the house in his beat-up truck. I've been resting against the window, watching the telephone poles bob past.

I didn't get sick. Mac stopped the car on the side of the road and we let some fresh air in. "Well, kid. End of the line," says Mac. "Guess we better go inside and face the music."

I don't understand what he means. "Are we in trouble?" I ask. I hope we're not in trouble because of skipping Bible study. It won't be fair if we are, because Uncle Donny said I didn't even have to go.

"Eh, some people don't think a man has the right to take his own kid out for the day without police supervision," says Mac. "I tell you, Alfie, back in the day we didn't have someone looking over our shoulder all the time, and we came out okay."

Mac walks me up the front steps and inside, where Uncle Donny is waiting.

"You're going to prison, Mac," he says, his voice tight and pinchy like new shoes. But he has a smile on his face as he takes my shoulder and guides me into the living room. His smile is funny. His eyes aren't scrunched at the corners at all.

"Here she is!" he says.

There are three ladies I've never seen before, sitting on the sofa with clipboards. "Aoife, these nice people are here to see you, okay? They're from Child Protective Services, and they just want to have a little chat with us."

Chapter Eight

Hannah said that big scary men would drag you off to Children's Prison, but these are definitely old women—older than Mama but not as old as Sister Mary Celeste. Hopefully that means I haven't been too bad yet.

"Well, hello ladies. Ah, Don, sorry I dropped her off a little later than we agreed," calls Mac. His voice seems cheerful, but something about it sounds fake. "I guess I'll head back now, but you folks have a good night, okay?" He nods in their direction, but he's already turned around and is heading out the door.

Uncle Donny does not walk him to the door to see him out. He keeps his back turned to Mac until he hears the door closed. Mama would say that is not good manners.

"Sorry about that," says Uncle Donny, keeping his hands tight around my shoulders. "Little caregiver timing mix-up there. As you can see, Aoife's fine, aren't you kiddo?"

"I went to the zoo!" I tell him. "It was a surprise!"

"It sure was," says Uncle Donny. "Aoife, these are some of my friends. This is Miz Carrie, and this is Miz Lori. Can you say hi to them?"

I peek over at Miz Carrie and Miz Lori. Miz Carrie has short dark hair speckled gray, and Miz Lori has blonde hair cut around her shoulders. They are both a little fat. If they were animals, they'd be hedgehogs. Both of them.

"Hi," I say.

Teddy goes to hide behind the sofa, because sometimes when he meets new people he's shy. But he doesn't know that his fuzzy bear backside is sticking out from behind the couch because he's too big to fit behind it. I want to giggle, but I don't, because I just remembered that Uncle Donny told me not to talk about Teddy in front of the *sea-pee-ess* ladies. I close my eyes and ask Teddy inside my head to please, please not get me in trouble.

"Well hello, Eva," says the dark-haired one, Miz Lori. Or maybe it's Miz Carrie. Oh no, I already forgot which one is which! "We were just noticing how unusual your name is."

New grown-ups always want to talk about my name. I don't know why they never have anything more interesting to ask me.

"It's my gramma's name," I say, because that's what I always say.

"That's right, your gramma Aoife," says Donny. "Boy, she was a cantankerous lady. I once saw her yell at a store clerk for forty-five minutes in a Macy's!"

I stare at him. Mama never tells that story. Every time I say I'm named for my gramma, Mama always says, "Your gramma Aoife, God rest her soul." Uncle Donny just smiles at me, big, but I can't tell if he's joking.

"So, ladies, as you can see, we're doing all right here," says Uncle Donny. "Just muddling along, you know how it is, one day at a time."

Both the Miz Carrie/Loris nod, but neither of them really smile.

"Well, as I was saying, Mr. Scott, in the state of Michigan, police and hospital workers are mandatory reporters," says the light-haired one. Her voice is very calm, like she's reading a bedtime story. It almost makes me feel sleepy again. "This means that if they have any reason to suspect any child is being abused or neglected, they *must* file a report with Child Protective Services."

"All right, well, there's no abuse or neglect going on here," says Uncle Donny. "Look at this child—she's not hungry, she's wearing clean clothes, she's just fine!"

Although my shorts are actually dirty from last week, but I don't mention that.

One of the Miz Ladies writes something down in her notebook.

Uncle Donny clears his throat. "You've seen the fridge, you've seen the bedrooms, everything aboveboard."

If the Miz Ladies looked at the fridge, I'm glad they looked after Uncle Donny came and cleaned it up.

"Ongoing lack of supervision *is* a form of neglect, and we're also required to evaluate the risk of potential future neglect," says one of the Miz Ladies. "Now, I'm not saying abuse has occurred, but we need to ensure that the child is not at risk. Ms. Scott is clearly struggling. We need to make sure there's a support network in place."

"You know, we're two miles from the boundary of Detroit. I'm pretty sure there are a hell of a lot of children that could use more assistance than Aoife," says Uncle Donny.

"This is a county agency, sir."

The other Miz Lady leans forward. "You do understand that *Eee-fah* here was left unattended in the parking lot of the mall during the incident we were discussing." She is trying to say it right, but it sounds funny anyway. She says the first part, *Ee*, with the exact same amount of attention as the second part, *Fah*.

"Siobhan is usually doing better than that," says Uncle Donny, but he doesn't sound very sure.

"Do you mind if we ask you some questions, sweetheart?" asks the lighter-haired one.

"Okay," I say. Is that a good answer?

Miz Whoever smiles, but in a sad way. Like Sister Mary Celeste when she announced it was the last day of kindergarten at Sacred Heart. Some of the boys cheered, but at least one of the girls cried.

"Okay, *Ee-fah*," says one of the ladies, "Well, what can you tell us about your day today?"

"I went to the zoo with Mac, and he told me he's my dad," I say.

There's silence, and I look up. Everyone is looking at me.

"What?" says Uncle Donny. His voice is strange.

"Yeah, I thought I was going to go to Family Bible Study, but we went to the zoo instead. It was a *surprise*! And I like surprises, especially if there's bears involved."

"Aoife," Uncle Donny cuts in, "what did you mean, Mac told you he's your father?"

"Yeah, he said he was. He said, 'Your old man will watch out for you,' and he didn't mean God, he meant himself. I checked. But Mama always says she found me in a cabbage patch. Mama *always* says that. Did Mac put me in the cabbage patch?"

"Is this . . . Mac her father?" the blonde Miz Lady asks Uncle Donny. "The file doesn't have an entry."

"That's a question for Siobhan, when she gets home," says Uncle Donny.

"He's not Theo's father, though," I say, remembering the important part of the conversation. "I asked him, and he said he wasn't."

I am watching the dark-haired one's face. When I say Theo's name, her eyes look away from me, towards the light-haired one, but nobody says anything. "Well, Eva," says the dark-haired one, "that must have been a very exciting day for you. How do you feel about Mac saying he's your father?"

She's back to saying my name flat wrong instead of kind of wrong. I don't try to tell her the right way. I just push my hair out of my eyes, because it's coming out of the ponytail I made. "Okay, I guess," I say, because it's true.

"Baby, this is probably something you should talk about with your mother, maybe when you're older," says Uncle Donny. To the ladies, he adds, "I'm sorry, Mac should have talked to Siobhan before just . . . springing it on the kid like that."

"I liked that he springed it," I say. "I like the zoo."

"Uh-huh. Well, as you can see, ladies, Aoife is fine. She's being supervised by a surplus of substitute parents. I think we can all agree there's no problem here."

"Mac says you're a *fruit*," I tell Uncle Donny. Both the ladies freeze. "Is that true?"

"Aoife, that's not a very nice thing to say," says the dark-haired lady. And for once, she says my name just about right.

I look around. Nobody wants to look at me, but I don't know why. "That's what Mac said," I explain. "What does it mean? Does it mean you're not going to marry Hannah's mom?"

"Okay, well, as you can see, we've got a lot going on here," says Uncle Donny. "I'd like to talk to Aoife about this in private, if you don't mind, so perhaps we can wrap it up, hmm, ladies?"

"Is it not true?" I ask. I don't know why everyone's getting so mad. I'm just asking a question. Sister Mary Celeste says there are no stupid questions.

"I think we can all agree that this 'Mac,' who has no legal claim to be Aoife's father at the moment, does not seem to be an ideal caretaker," says the dark-haired lady. "Hmm?"

"Uh, yes," says Uncle Donny. "I'll, uh, keep him away from her until Siobhan's back."

"But I like Mac! He took me to the zoo!" Also, I really hope he didn't kill my brother.

"Take it up with your mother," says Uncle Donny, rubbing his face with both hands.

"If you don't mind, Mr. Scott, I'd like to ask Eva some questions that she should answer on her own," says either Miz Lori or Miz Carrie.

"Sure, how can this go any worse? You just go ahead."

"Would you mind coming with me into the kitchen?" the light-haired one asks him.

Uncle Donny looks at me and starts to say something, but then he closes his mouth and doesn't. "Sure," he says.

So he gets up and follows her, and I stay with the dark-haired one. I think about asking if she's Miz Carrie or Miz Lori, but I don't.

"Well, sweetheart," says Miz Lady. "I'd like to get to know you a little bit. Would that be okay?"

"Okay," I say. Although I think maybe I do mind, because I'm pretty sure if I don't answer right they will call in the men to drag me away.

Teddy comes to climb into my lap, even though he's supposed to stay out of the way. I don't tell him to get down.

"I was wondering, do you like having your uncle Donny stay with you?"

I think about saying that it's hard to sleep with him coming into my room at night. I'm extra tired from being woken up all the time. But I just nod instead, because it's bad to complain.

"Okay." She makes a note on her clipboard.

I wish I wasn't here. I need to tell Hannah all the clues I've found.

"Now tell me, Eva, do you feel safe in your home?"

I don't really know what she means by that. How could you not feel safe in your home? That is what your home is, the place that feels safe. But Teddy nods his head real big, so I nod my head, too.

"Okay. Do you have any bruises or marks you would like to show me?"

"I skinned my knee," I say, trying to help. I was trying to make cartwheels, but I fell. That was last week. I lift up my leg so she can see, although there's not really much of a mark left anymore.

"Thank you, sweetheart," she says. "Anything else?"

Say no, says Teddy.

"No," I say. I wiggle my loose tooth back and forth with my tongue. "I don't think so."

"Thank you for answering my questions so well," says Miz Lady. "You're doing a great job. Last one. Now, honey, in the last few months, has anyone touched you in a way that you didn't like?"

N–O, Teddy spells out.

I think about Hannah, who pushed my hand away the other day when I was trying to take Totally Rad Barbie and she only wanted me to have Chemical Engineer Barbie, who's not as good.

No! says Teddy, a lot louder.

So I say *no*, too. I don't want to go to Children's Prison.

"All right, Mr. Scott, you can come back in now," calls Miz Lady. "Eva did a great job answering all my questions, didn't you, Eva?"

I guess I did. I don't know. I look over at Uncle Donny to see if he knows, but he looks like he doesn't know either. Nobody has called in the scary men yet.

"Okay," I say. "Can I go play now?"

"Aoife, be polite," says Uncle Donny. I don't see what was so rude about that. I don't like Miz Lori or Miz Carrie. I want them to leave.

The dark-haired one looks at me. "We're almost done here, sweetheart," she says. She takes out her clipboard and turns to Uncle Donny. "Now, as you know, our last visit with the Scott family was just under three years ago."

I don't know what she's talking about. I've never seen her before.

"At that time, there was no evidence of sufficient abuse or neglect to proceed with a safety plan for Aoife."

"You said this was an independent investigation," says Uncle Donny. "We're not reopening all that stuff. This is specific to the present."

"Of course, Mr. Scott."

"I have to apologize," says Uncle Donny. "You see, I'm an attorney, so I understand how . . . difficult the law can be to navigate, for the average citizen, given the inherent bureaucracies of county agencies."

"Of course, Mr. Scott. Our purpose is to strengthen Michigan families by providing access to services, that's all. We're not trying to make things more difficult."

"I'm sure."

Teddy has crawled off my lap and is lying in the big sunbeam from the front window like a kitty cat. I wish I could lie down there and take a nap with him.

"Now, this is a second investigation, independent of the first. I've had a phone call with Aoife's teacher, and her report was positive, but she did note some concerning signs."

"You talked to Sister Mary Celeste?" I say. I looove Sister Mary Celeste. She is the nicest of all the sisters and is my favorite.

"Chill out for a minute, Aoife," says Uncle Donny, taking me onto his lap and bouncing me up and down. "Let us finish this conversation so the nice ladies can leave, huh?"

I would like that. I try to chill out.

"Now, at the moment we're most concerned about Ms. Scott's ability to provide sufficient supervision."

"Siobhan barely lets the kid out of her sight," says Uncle Donny. "She's a great mom."

"Yeah!" I say. Mama is the greatest.

"Nobody is saying she isn't doing her best, Mr. Scott. But in cases in which a preponderance of evidence of child abuse or neglect is not found, the department must still assist the child's family in voluntarily participating in community-based services commensurate with risk level determined by the risk assessment."

I don't know what any of that means. "I miss Mama," I say quietly. That's what I know.

"I bet you do, sweetheart," she says. "Hopefully you'll be able to talk to her soon."

But Mama said "soon" before, and that was *ages* ago.

"I think that's enough," says Uncle Donny. "Are we done here, ladies? Because I for one am feeling pretty done."

The ladies all stand, too. "Remember, Mr. Scott, nobody here is trying to get anyone in trouble," says the light-haired one, in a voice like Mama uses to call the next-door cat. *It's okay, kitty kitty, don't be scared.*

"I understand perfectly," he says.

"Aoife, thank you very much for talking to us," says the dark-haired one, putting away her notes.

"You're welcome," I say. *Please don't take me to Children's Prison.*

Uncle Donny takes my hand, and we show the Carrie/Loris back to the door. They shake Uncle Donny's hand goodbye and then they shake my hand, too. I try to shake it real nice, like a grown-up. But I hold on real tight to Uncle Donny with the other hand. The Carrie/Loris drive away, and then it's just us again. I say a special thank-you to all the saints.

"Well, that went just great," says Uncle Donny, rubbing his forehead. I think he does not feel like it went great.

"Can I go play outside?" I ask. I still need to tell Hannah about what Mac said, and how I hope he's not Theo's murderer because he's my father now. Hannah will explain it to me. She can explain things much better than I can.

"I guess you're not hungry for dinner yet," says Uncle Donny, looking at his watch.

"Nuh-uh. We had Dippin' Dots and hot dogs and a snow cone."

"Great," says Uncle Donny, but not in the way that really means *great*. He clears his throat. I don't think he's going to let me go play just yet.

Uncle Donny kneels down in front of me. "Listen, Aoife, it's really important that you never, ever get into a car with someone unless your ma or I say it's okay," he says. "Even if you know the person, okay? You should still have called me to ask."

That doesn't really make sense. I get in cars with people all the time—the church van, the bus to the YMCA, Hannah's mom's car when she wants to take us out for ice cream. Uncle Donny is silly. Plus, if I hadn't gotten in the truck with Mac, I wouldn't have learned about Theo's father. So I'm not quite as sorry as Uncle Donny wants me to be. But I nod anyway.

"Did Mac really tell you he's your father?" he asks.

"Uh-huh." Everyone else is so impressed, I'm beginning to realize this is a really big deal. But I've got too much to think about already. I still need to solve a whole mystery to bring Mama home. "That's what he said."

"Well, I don't want you to put too much stock in what Mac says, okay? Anybody can say anything; it doesn't make it true. And Mac is—well, I don't think you should be listening to him, okay?"

"You don't like Mac," I say.

"Not especially, no. I know he can be . . . He can seem like he's fun sometimes, but he is not a good person for you to be around."

"Is it because of how he broke Mama's plate from the Old Country?"

Uncle Donny frowns. "That's the kind of thing I don't like about him. There are things about Mac that—well, it's hard to explain."

"You mean when he yells," I say.

"Does he yell at you?" Uncle Donny drops down to look into my face. We have the exact same eyes. It makes me want to tell him one of my secrets.

"He yells at Mama late at night sometimes," I whisper.

"But he's never hurt you? Never raised his voice at you?"

I look at Uncle Donny's face. He's got a good, kind face. His skin is so soft you could pet it. I put my hand on his scratchy cheek to see. You have to get away from the stubble, but then it's smooth and clean.

"I love you, Uncle Donny," I say.

"I love you too, kiddo. So much. That's why I don't ever want to see you get hurt. Nobody should ever yell at you or hurt you." Uncle Donny puts his arms around my shoulders and pulls me into his neck, which smells good. I close my eyes.

"Mama yelled at me. She told me to get away from her."

I feel Uncle Donny's breath blow out hard. "Oh, Aoife," he says. "I know she did. And I bet she is really, really sorry for yelling at you. I know she didn't mean it."

So maybe Mac didn't mean it either.

If I close my eyes and try to remember, I can just barely picture . . . I remember us hiding because someone scary was downstairs. The two of us, me and Theo. And Theo put his arm over my shoulder, just like Uncle Donny is doing now. And I never remembered that before, but all of a sudden it came into my head because I was trying to remember being shouted at.

And I remember how the plate from the Old Country broke into a million pieces when it hit the wall.

"Aoife, what is it?" asks Uncle Donny.

"What's what?" I say.

"You zoned out on me, kiddo. Couldn't you hear me calling you?"

"No," I say. "But I hear you now. Can I go play?"

"Uh, okay," says Uncle Donny. "Sure, go play. I've got a phone call to make. But stay within sight. I don't need another heart attack."

So I say I won't give him another one on purpose.

As I cross the lawn, I can hear Uncle Donny yelling on the phone inside. Mama told me that sometimes lawyers yell at people. I don't know who he's talking to, but he sure sounds mad. I'm glad he is not yelling at me.

I can't wait to tell Hannah all the things I've figured out in our case. She's going to be really impressed. I wonder if she's solved *anything* while I've solved so many things!

I knock on her door, but her mom says she's out at a birthday party and isn't back yet. So Teddy and I play in the sprinkler out on the front lawn. We keep close to the house because I don't want to make Uncle Donny sad.

I can't wait to ask Hannah to do the name-searching thing on her dad's computer, and look up JOHN MACMILLIAN COREY. Hopefully we can prove that Mac didn't kill Theo. I can't do the name-searching thing myself. You have to be a big girl to use the computer. Plus you have to be able to read words even when they are little or there's lots of them or they're boring.

Teddy and I are running through the water when Hannah comes home from her party.

"Hi Hannah!" I say, waving as she gets out of a minivan I've never seen before. But there are people in the car that I don't know, so I stop waving.

Two moms come out, too, with two girls about Hannah's age. I've never seen any of them before, so I don't go over. They're older than me, and have smooth hair, tied up in ponytails with ribbon. Hannah's mom was working in the front yard, and she comes down the driveway to chat with the strangers.

I'm still wearing my play clothes, but I'm sprinkled wet all over. Hannah's wearing a real dress like I would only wear to church.

Teddy thinks the girls all look stupid in their dresses. He doesn't like shiny shoes because he likes to bite shiny things. He doesn't even like it when I get dressed up for church, because he knows we're not going to the park to play. He makes faces at all the girls and Hannah as they stand around on the sidewalk waiting for their moms to finish talking.

They're looking at me, but I don't say hi again, because Hannah didn't answer me the first time and I guess she doesn't want to play in the sprinkler in her party dress.

"Who's that?" asks one of the girls. The feeling of their eyes on me makes me hot all over.

"That's my neighbor, but she's only six," says Hannah. She waves at me, but not with a lot of enthusiasm. I know better than to do more than wave back. Instead I turn off the sprinkler, because I don't want to jump in the water while all the bigger girls are watching.

"M-o-o-o-m, come on!" says one of the girls loudly. She stamps her foot, but the moms are talking and not paying attention.

"Why don't you tell your mom to hurry up?" asks one of the girls, to Hannah.

I know why she doesn't ask—it's because Hannah's mom is a sharp lady who says we need to act respectful when we talk to grown-ups. Mama says we are lucky to have such good neighbors, but we're all a little afraid of Hannah's mom anyway.

"I'm sure she'll be quick," says Hannah.

"She's slow," says the other little girl. "Like *you*, Hannah." The other girls both laugh. When I look up, Hannah is all red in the face, looking at her shoes.

It doesn't even make sense, because Hannah runs much faster than me. Whenever we race anywhere, she always wins.

"Is that why your daddy left?" asks the other girl. "Because you and your mom are so slow?"

"Because they're fat," says the other girl.

"My dad didn't leave, they just got divorced," says Hannah loudly. "I still see him every month." Even I can tell that this answer is not going to impress the other girls, who are still laughing together.

"You probably don't even *have* a dad," says one of them. "Where is he right now?"

"I'm going to get my mom," says Hannah. She walks up the driveway, and when she gets closer to me, she frowns in my direction. "Why are you listening in on me and my friends?" she says angrily.

"I'm not listening," I say, which isn't true. I was listening.

"Well, nobody likes nosy little girls, so go home," says Hannah. She hurries up the steps to the house and shuts the door. She didn't even go get her mom like she said. All the moms are still talking, not paying any attention.

Hannah's friends are right—Hannah's mom is bigger than the other mothers are. I guess she does walk more slowly, too.

I picture Mama standing here talking to these other moms. She doesn't look like any of them. The other moms, even Hannah's, all have short hair and bangs. Mama has long hair all the way down her back. And the other moms wear regular clothes, but Mama only wears dresses and long cardigans.

Even though they're both wearing nice jewelry, my mama is thinner than *both* of these new moms. She's the best mama.

I look back at the other girls, who are still standing on the sidewalk laughing together. They are both thinner than Hannah, and they look better in their party dresses. I guess they make fun of Hannah because there's two of them and only one of her.

When I'm in the third grade, I hope I look like them instead of round like Hannah. Then maybe they won't make fun of me, since my father's not around, either.

"I'd better go see what's gotten into that girl," says Hannah's mom, looking towards the closed front door. "She's always so sensitive."

"All right, well, you girls have a good afternoon," says one of the new moms. They both smile big, their mouths painted with lipstick. I don't like how it looks.

"Bye now."

The girls all get in the car and their moms pile in with them. Teddy blows raspberries at them while they drive away.

I don't go knock on the door right away because I know Hannah is going to change out of her fancy dress and her shiny shoes, and then we can talk about the mystery. Instead, I turn the water back on, and Teddy makes me laugh by chasing after the drops from the sprinkler and trying to catch them on his tongue like raindrops.

Finally Hannah comes out of the side yard. Her face is puffy and red, and her voice sounds stuffed up. I turn the hose off at the wall. She looks up the road where the van drove away, but it's gone.

"Don't talk to my friends when they come to my house," says Hannah.

"I won't," I promise.

She sniffs.

"Do you want to talk about the mystery?" I ask. Because I have a lot to tell her.

But Hannah says, "No, not now."

That makes me confused. How else are we going to look up the name-searching thing?

"Do you want to do cartwheels?" she asks. I don't really want to, but it seems like Hannah does. So the two of us practice cartwheels for a while. Hannah's still wearing a skirt, just not a party dress, so it's funny when her pale legs stick up. But neither of us goes all the way over. Teddy can turn cartwheels all day long—he rolls over and over, like a brown furry ball—but neither of us has the trick to it.

Mama knew the trick. I try to picture the way she looked, turning one on the sidewalk when we were practicing last week. *Push with your arms*, Mama said. *Kick your feet up.*

So instead of putting my hands forward, I keep them up above my head. For a while my feet stay on the ground and I bend sideways. Then all of a sudden, everything turns over on itself. I'm only on my hands for a second, but it's easy to balance that way, and then my feet come back on the other side and I fall over. But I could have stood up.

"I did it!" I say.

"That doesn't count," says Hannah.

I stand up and do it again, thinking *sideways, sideways* instead of *forward, forward*. This time my feet know to stay

133

planted for just the right amount of time and then they're up in the air, and my hands are as strong and as steady as legs. It's still fast, but this time I'm ready, and my feet keep going forwards until they're right-side-down again, and now suddenly I'm standing again. I feel a little dizzy, my brain all weighed down from flipping in circles, but it feels good, and I laugh and laugh.

But Mama isn't here to see it. It doesn't really matter, if nobody but Hannah knows.

Hannah still can't do it. She gets the start right, but she's not moving fast enough to get her feet off the ground.

"Keep trying," I say. "Go sideways, not forwards."

"This is stupid," she says, pushing her hair out of her face. "Cartwheels are for babies, anyway."

"They're not for babies! My mama does cartwheels."

But Hannah is already brushing off her hands and turning away. "They're dumb," she says. "I don't want to do this anymore."

I shake my head. "You're just mad because you can't do it and me and Teddy can."

"Teddy isn't *real*," says Hannah. "He can't do a cartwheel anyway because you made him up."

Teddy is going to untie the bows on Hannah's sneakers. "He is real! He's right there!"

"You're crazy," says Hannah. "That's what everybody thinks, but they're too scared to tell you the truth. You're crazy, just like your mom."

That's not true. Nobody thinks that about me and nobody thinks that about Mama. Hannah is a liar.

"You better just be quiet," I warn her.

"It's *true*," says Hannah. Her face has gotten all red, her bangs sticking to her face. "Your mama is locked up in a mental ward because she's *insane*, and you're just like her. In fact, your whole family is crazy, so there!"

I don't even know what happens, but suddenly my hands are on Hannah's shoulders and I push her down on the grass just like the bigger boy cousin pushes the littler one. For a minute I think Teddy must have done it, not me. I've never pushed Hannah or anyone else before, and she's bigger than me, so you'd think it wouldn't work. But I'm moving faster, and just like a cartwheel, it's over before I know it and she's on her butt.

"You're a liar and a sneak!" I yell at her. I don't even know anything bad enough to say.

"You're a little *slut!*" Hannah screams back, just as loud. I don't know what that means, but I think it must be the worst thing ever. Nobody has ever, ever said something like that to me before, and it feels like being kicked in the stomach, which Sasha Rajanhor did to me once on accident.

Teddy has all his teeth showing and he wants to bite, bite.

"Hannah!" It's Hannah's mom, standing in their doorway. "I think it's time to come inside now, if you and Aoife can't play nicely."

"It's her fault," says Hannah, getting up from the grass. She has dirt on her palms from falling. "She's the one who's always talking to her stupid imaginary friend like a crazy person, and then when I told her so, she pushed me down."

That isn't even true. But I know I'm not going to be able to explain it properly. Hannah is older, and she's better at talking to adults. They'll never understand.

"I don't want to play with you *ever again*," I say. That'll teach her. She'll have to hang out with those girls from school who don't even like her. "And you're going to go to *hell*." I've never even told her that before, but it's true.

Then I turn around and run back to my own house. I didn't even get to tell her about what Mac said, but I'm glad now that I have a secret, especially one she would want to know about so much.

"Hell isn't even real," she calls after me. "It's just made-up, and only stupid, crazy people like you believe it."

I let the door swing hard against the doorway with a crash, Teddy right at my feet.

Chapter Nine

I go straight upstairs and get ready for bed even though it's too early.

I miss Mama so bad. If she was here, I wouldn't care what stupid thing Hannah said. And the *sea-pee-ess* ladies wouldn't be bothering us anymore. And she could explain how come she said she found me in a cabbage patch when Mac says he's my dad. Mama would make everything okay. But she won't come home until I find Theo's killer.

I walk out of the bathroom with my toothbrush hanging out of my mouth. Theo's last picture is looking at me from the end of the hall. Nobody has kissed him goodnight since Mama left.

The last picture is not my favorite photo of Theo. In his scrapbook there's one where I'm just a tiny baby and he's eight years old. He's sitting and smiling with me on his lap. That's my favorite. It's weird to think that even though Theo is dead, I'll always be the second child. I'll always be his younger sister.

Mama doesn't have my scrapbook made. She says it's harder for the second child. But if she did, that picture would be in both of them.

I go back to the bathroom and spit.

Theo's eyes, just like Mama's, are watching me walk past. If I don't solve this mystery, I'll be letting both of them down.

Maybe I don't need Hannah to look for clues. Maybe I don't need anyone. I can try to solve the mystery all by myself. Then everyone will thank me, and Hannah will be so jealous.

I tiptoe down the hall because I don't want Uncle Donny to hear me and come see what I'm doing. I get to Theo's door and I wait to make sure *the coasts are clear*, which means nobody's coming. They are clear.

I know I'm not allowed to play in here. Stupid Hannah is usually the one who wants to, not me. But this time I'm not playing—I'm *investigating*—so it's okay. Teddy pushes past my legs as I inch the door open and creep inside.

"Hi Theo," I whisper, just in case. "I'm very sorry I ran away last time. I didn't mean to. But this time I'll be brave."

Teddy isn't worried that Ghost Theo will be mad at us, of course. He's only interested in playing with Theo's action figures. He thinks it's funny to set them up in silly poses.

I tell myself I do not hear any tapping, so I don't. I walk around the room with my hands behind my back, looking for clues. We already checked Theo's drawers and bookshelves once. The clues must be somewhere else.

Teddy knocks over one of the Star Wars action figures, the little guy with the sword. I hear Uncle Donny moving downstairs, and I hold my breath.

"Stop messing around, Teddy," I whisper. I walk to the desk and set Little Sword Guy on his feet again. I can see in the dust exactly where he was standing.

But I've never noticed this box before. The action figures are hiding it, the big ones in front of it and the little ones on top. It's a pretty wooden box, with a glass front. I move all the action figures carefully to one side to see better.

There's a bunch of pieces of ribbon inside and some pins. Those are called medals. Each one is different. There's even a patch like Hannah got from Girl Scouts (which I'm not allowed to join, because we're on a budget, but I'm going to be an altar girl some-day, which is way better). I don't know why Theo had these medals and patches. I don't think he was a Boy Scout, or even an altar boy. I know he was really good at lots of things, but these don't look like the plastic trophies on his shelves—I think these are for grown-ups.

I pick up the box—it's heavier than I thought—and tucked underneath there's a folded piece of yellow paper. It crackles when I unfold it.

It's a page cut out of the newspaper. There's a picture of a man and a lot of text. I recognize him—a man in a tan uniform with thick plastic glasses. It's BEN, 1998.

The newspaper is full of words. I can read, but I can't always read every tiny little word. The headline is big, though:

LO-CAL space MAR-INE space KILL-ED. IN. TRAIN-ING space EX-ER-CISE. I know those words. *Marine* means *ocean*, like Marine Biologist Barbie.

This paper is saying that BEN, 1998 was killed while exercising.

I look into his handsome, smiling face, and I am sad. Mama says we shouldn't be sad when people are in heaven, but she breaks that rule all the time.

I wonder why Theo kept this box and this newspaper here in his room, guarded by his action figures. "Teddy, what do you think it means?" I ask him. I don't know if it's a clue or not. Usually Hannah tells me.

Teddy doesn't care. But it must have meant something special.

Well, I am too smart now to believe that Theo was found in a cabbage patch. Mac said Theo's father is dead. And now I know BEN, 1998 is dead.

I am a great detective.

Teddy shrugs.

I wonder what would have happened if Mama had married BEN, 1998. Maybe I would never have been born. But also, maybe Theo would never have died.

Carefully I fold the newspaper back up and put it back where it was, with the box of medals sitting on it. Then I set the action figures back on top of the box just how I found them.

"Maybe we should just go to bed, Teddy," I say. "We'll have to find more clues in the morning."

I'm almost starting to get sleepy for real. Teddy is wide awake, though. He's bouncing along beside me like one of the characters on Hannah's video games as we go back down the hall.

"It's time to sleep now, Teddy," I complain. But he never listens to me.

"Are you just up here talking to yourself?" asks Uncle Donny, coming up the stairs. I'm glad he doesn't know where I was coming from. "Wow. Are you really getting ready for bed? Don't you even want a story first?"

"I'm too tired for a story," I say, walking to my room.

"Listen, Aoife, I hope I didn't make you feel bad when we were talking to the CPS ladies," says Uncle Donny, sitting on the mattress. I crawl in the other side. "I didn't mean to make it sound like you were in trouble. I just don't want them to think we've got any problems we can't handle. We're doing okay, aren't we, Aoife? You and your uncle Donny?"

I don't want to talk about the *sea-pee-ess* ladies. I don't want to talk about how we're doing, either. I don't want to talk about anything, I want to go to sleep.

"Yeah, we're okay," I say, fake yawning.

Uncle Donny turns out the lamp. "Good. Okay. Well, nighty-night, early bird. See you in the morning."

"See you when you come in here later," I say, but it's slurred into the pillow. He pulls the door shut softly, and then I hear his familiar steps on the carpet, moving away.

Teddy sits on the side of the bed where Uncle Donny just was. His weight tugs at the blankets. "Quit it," I say, trying to push him off.

I try to go to sleep, but Uncle Donny's right—it's really early. It's still light outside, and the light is coming in a different way than usual, right in my face. Plus, everyone outside is awake. I can hear Hannah's cousins playing in the yard next door, shouting and screaming. I know they're shooting each other with squirt guns, because Hannah's bigger boy cousin Liam said he was going to bring his new one over.

There are cars on the street, too. We live pretty close to the highway, so you can always hear that in the background, but now I can hear wheels *shush, shush*ing past the house outside. People are coming home. Parents are coming home to their kids. But not at my house.

I'm falling asleep. "Goodnight, Teddy," I say.

Sweet dreams.

The last thing I think about is Hannah's surprised face when I pushed her. She looked scared. Nobody's ever been scared of me before. Her mouth was open, and her eyes were wide, and then she was *flying*.

* * *

We're in the water, going up and down on the waves, me and Teddy. I have an awful feeling like there's something right beneath our feet, like at any second my toes are going to brush against it, or maybe it will reach up and grab me. And I'm feeling sick, being pushed around by the waves, up and down, side to side, and up and down.

I open my eyes. Teddy is bouncing on the bed.

"Stop it, Teddy," I say. "You woke me up." He's never done that before.

He's a bear the same size as me today.

I know a secret, says Teddy. I sit up in the bed. It's so late at night now that even the highway is quiet.

"What secret?"

It's in your pocket, says Teddy.

I don't want to get out of bed to find my shorts. Even though it's summer, it still feels chilly because I was sleeping. But Teddy told me to do it, so I get up in my bare feet and walk to the dresser. The shorts I was wearing are slung over the desk. Usually Mama comes to pick up my laundry and put it in the hamper, but Uncle Donny hasn't. I put my hand in one pocket—nothing. I put my hand in the other side.

It's Mac's cigarette lighter. Silver, with a picture of a bird on it, and USMC.

"Teddy, why did you take this?" I ask him. I don't understand. Teddy has never moved anything in real life before.

We need it, he says.

"Oh, Teddy." Taking the lighter from Mac's car is stealing, which is a *mortal sin*. "We're going to get in so much trouble."

But Teddy never cares about that.

"What do we even need it for?"

It's a secret, says Teddy.

"I can keep secrets," I say.

Watch, Teddy says. *I'll show you another one.*

He tilts his head towards the door and listens. I climb back into bed and listen, too. I don't hear anything special at first, but then I hear the *creak, creak, creak* of Uncle Donny's feet on the stairs. Then he comes down the hallway.

"It's just Uncle Donny," I tell Teddy. "So what?"

Wait.

Uncle Donny opens the door, just like he always does. I think for sure he will see me sitting in the bed and say something. But he just stands in the doorway, looking at the bed. He doesn't seem to notice me at all.

"Uncle Donny?" I ask.

But he doesn't answer.

Wait for it, says Teddy. *We're just getting to the good part.*

After a few minutes, Uncle Donny turns around and walks back out into the hallway, just like he always does. He doesn't pull the door shut, though.

Come on, says Teddy. He picks up the lighter off the dresser. *Let's go.*

"Go where, Teddy?" Teddy is already out the door, walking heavily on all fours. He's following Uncle Donny down the stairs. I hear Uncle Donny's two feet, and then Teddy's four.

I don't know what to do. I wish Mama was here. She always knows what to do.

I climb out of bed and go after them.

The hallway is stuffy. It looks different late at night, with long shadows from the bars on the staircase. I don't like to walk through them, because my legs look striped, like they're covered in bruises. I hurry to catch up with Teddy.

Uncle Donny goes all the way downstairs. I never knew where he went after he left my room, but he walks straight to the front door without pausing.

Come on, says Teddy. *Don't you want to see? I'm doing this for you, Aoife.*

"Where are we *going*?" I ask. I wish I was back in bed, under the covers, where it's warm and dark.

Uncle Donny doesn't seem to hear my voice. He unlocks the front door and pulls it open.

See? He wants you to go, says Teddy. *He wants you to go find the murderer. Come on, Aoife, this is your big chance.*

Uncle Donny just stands there, holding the door open. I can't see the yard or the bushes, just the white street. It's silent out there, like it's holding its breath. Waiting to see what I will do.

"Are you sure?" I say. There could be a huge dog, right there in the shadows, just waiting to bite me as soon as I set a foot outside.

Don't you want to be brave? asks Teddy. *Don't you want to be like Joan of Arc?*

"Well, ye-e-esss . . ."

Uncle Donny is still just standing there, holding the door open, letting the cold air out, as Mama would say.

"Uncle Donny, are you sure I should go?" I ask.

He's not going to answer, says Teddy. And sure enough, Uncle Donny doesn't. He doesn't even blink.

"I don't know," I say.

If you solve the murder tonight, your mama can come home tomorrow, says Teddy. *Remember? Isn't that the deal you made?*

I did say I would take up the mantle of the Lord, didn't I? Maybe this is it. I bet Joan was afraid, but she listened to the voices of the saints. They probably sounded something like Teddy.

"Maybe you're right," I say. If even Uncle Donny wants me to go solve the mystery, it must be the right thing to do. Right?

Right, says Teddy.

So I walk past Uncle Donny, out into the blue darkness. Behind me, I hear him slowly close the door and lock it shut again.

*   *   *

For a while I just stand in the driveway and wait until I can see in the dark. It doesn't take long. Even in the middle of the night there's orange glow over the trees, which Mama says is the city of Detroit. Between that and the moon, which hangs in the sky like a big capital D, there's not a single star overhead.

I'm not cold in my pajamas. The air-conditioning machines buzz like bees, so loud I want to clap my hands over my ears. From somewhere far away I can hear a horn honking, or maybe it's a truck backing up.

There are no dogs waiting to bite me, at least not that I see yet. I don't look real hard, just in case. Mama says that sometimes bad people from the city wander around the neighborhood at night, and they don't have any homes so they sleep in corners or under bridges or in alleys. I don't look for them either.

It's time to get going, says Teddy.

The neighbor's house—not Hannah's, the other side—has lights over their driveway, which light up as Teddy and I walk through their grass. In front of the lights there's insects swirling everywhere, and they make shadows on the wall, like bats, or the flying monkeys from *The Wizard of Oz*. I don't like how it looks, but Teddy tells me not to be a baby.

We make it across the grass. We walk down their driveway and into the road. I'm not wearing any shoes. The tar is still a little warm under my toes.

C'mon, says Teddy. *Don't drag your feet.*

"Where are we going, anyway?" I ask.

It's a surprise, he says.

Even though we're in a fight, I kind of wish Hannah was here. She likes investigating a lot more than I do.

You're brave, Aoife, remember?

Teddy's right, I'm brave. Just like Joan of Arc.

We walk past the quiet houses, and all the windows are eyes, watching me. There are no cars rolling by on the street. It's easier to walk right in the middle of the road, where there are fewer stones or sharp bits of glass, but every once in a while something pokes into my foot.

We keep walking.

When we finally make it to the corner, I see the cat from next door, sitting under the streetlight. She turns to watch me, her tail flicking, and even though I think she's going to run away when we get close, she doesn't. Teddy takes us right past her.

When we get to the end of the road, Teddy cuts across someone's lawn instead of walking all the way around the circle, so I follow him even though somebody has planted flowers and they might be mad. Maybe it's okay in the dark, when nobody can see our footprints in the dirt.

As I look back, the cat uncurls itself and follows us. I want to stop and try to pet her, but Teddy says we have to hurry.

The three of us cut between the houses. It feels like the whole neighborhood moved out at the same time except for me and Teddy and the cat, and now we live here all alone. But then there's the sound of a car on the road and Teddy tugs my shirt sleeve.

Get down, says Teddy.

So I get on my hands and knees in the grass, hoping I will look like just another one of the bushes in the side yard. The grass smells good this close, and it's cool against my palms and my toes. Teddy and I crouch low as the car goes past. The cat stands there like a regular cat, but she's small, so that's okay.

C'mon, says Teddy, standing back up again when the car is gone. He makes a bear-shadow against the brick wall of the house, from the streetlamp. *Let's go.*

He leads us through a gap in the fence, and I realize we're taking a shortcut to the park.

"Teddy, I can't walk through the brambles," I say. "I'm not wearing any shoes."

But he doesn't stop, so I have to keep up. I tell myself I have to be brave, like Saint Joan. I keep walking.

The kitty is still following us. She doesn't make any noise at all as she walks, just like Teddy. All I can hear is the sound of my own feet in the grass.

This way.

I hear the squeaking of the swing set first, before we even get to the playground. There's someone there, I think, hiding in the dark.

Get back, Aoife, says Teddy.

We creep around the fence, keeping low, Teddy and I. There's a streetlamp on the corner, so if I look kind of out of the corner of my eyes, I can see shapes. There's someone standing in the playground smoking a cigarette, a man, in a dark jacket with a black hat. I can smell a nasty, burned-rubber kind of smell, and I don't like it. It takes a second before I can see that there's another man standing in the corner, all in gray. They're talking in low voices and laughing, and there's a woman with them, too. I can't see her at first, but I can hear her voice. I hear the sound of the swings again, and I realize the woman, whoever she is, must be sitting in the seat kicking herself off the ground, just like I do.

I wonder if these are homeless people like Mama warned me about. But they're not asleep, so maybe not. Maybe they have nice homes and also are nice to little girls. Or maybe they're thugs from the city.

It makes me feel funny to see these grown-ups hanging out in our place. The playground is for Hannah and me, and for kids, not for strangers to laugh in and smoke nasty-smelling cigarettes.

Aoife, keep away from them, says Teddy. *Let's go.*

"But Teddy, they shouldn't be there!" I whisper. "They're ruining it!"

Let's go, Aoife! I feel a cold wind pick up, and I don't want to make Teddy mad. So we creep low, away from the playground. Teddy is ahead of me, getting farther away, and I have to hurry to keep up. The kitty follows behind us, not trying to keep up. We make a big circle around the edge of the trees where the strangers can't see us.

This way, says Teddy, slipping into the bushes.

Now I can hear the sound of the water trickling from the creek. Teddy is making straight for it, and I'm not sure I want to go, but the strangers will see me if I go back.

The kitty stops following us when we get to the edge of the grass. She sits at the edge of the tree line and watches us, like she's trying to figure out what we're doing. I don't know either.

Down the hill, says Teddy. He disappears into the branches, and I bite my lip. "Bye-bye, kitty," I whisper, and then I follow Teddy towards the trees.

Even though my feet are tough on the bottoms from playing outside, it still hurts to walk on the branches in the dark. I try to keep up anyway. I only cut myself a little.

Now that we're under the trees, the moon doesn't reach us anymore. There are old, dried-up leaves from last year under my feet, and as the hill gets steeper, they slide out from under me. But it feels good on my toes where it's slimy and cool underneath.

"Teddy, I'm getting slugs under my toenails," I say.

Almost there, says Teddy. *Keep walking.*

I know where we're going, of course. We're going to the Secret Place. I just don't know why.

Hannah and I climb down here all the time, but it's a lot harder in the dark. I can't see where I'm going, and the hillside is slippery even in bare feet. There's fallen branches and I stub my toe a couple times before remembering how to slide-walk. I put my hands out so I don't bump into any trees.

Look, says Teddy. *We're almost there.*

He's right—I can see the rock because it sticks out over the river and there's no trees blocking it from the moon. When I look down, I can see a little shine of silver from the capital-D moon reflecting on the water. And with the extra light, it's not hard to scramble over the last little bit and onto the smooth, cool stone.

"Teddy, we made it!" I say. The water is louder here. Earlier in the year the whole river was full, but there's not that much in it now, just enough to run between the rocks. Soon it will be totally dry and we can walk down there in the mud and look for toads.

Light the candle, says Teddy. *I want to show you now.*

"What candle?"

In your hand, says Teddy.

I look down, and he's right. I'm holding the apple candle from Hannah's house. Teddy must have taken it out from under Theo's bed and brought it along.

"Teddy, this is Hannah's," I say. "We shouldn't have it out here without permission."

We need it, says Teddy. *Now, it's time to light the candle.*

"Are we having a séance?" I ask, because that's what Hannah did with the candle. Teddy doesn't answer me, because he's busy leaning over the edge of the rock to watch the water.

So I sit down on the rock, far from the edge that I can't really see very well. From low down, everything beyond the rock is just dark-purple dark.

Here, says Teddy, and he hands me Mac's silver lighter. *Hurry up*, he says. *Do it.*

I'm a little afraid of the lighter, because I know the fire is going to burst out of it. But I hold it in one hand and try to push down the little lever, just like Hannah showed me. Nothing happens. The lever is stiff.

Faster, says Teddy. *Harder.*

I'm afraid to push it faster or harder, because I know fire is going to come out, and I'm afraid of fire. But Teddy says to do it, and I want to be brave like Joan of Arc, so I do. The little *snick* sound happens, and then the fire pops out the end of the lighter.

"Teddy, I did it!" I say.

The flame goes out because I let go of the lever. But it still counts.

Again, says Teddy. *Hold it over the wick first.*

It's hard to do so many things at once. I put the lighter right up against the wick of the apple candle and try to hold it still while I push the lever down again, fast enough to make the *snick*. It takes me a couple times, but I'm not afraid anymore.

The flame comes on, and I hold it over the wick like Hannah did. The lighter gets hot in my hands.

Good enough, says Teddy. And when I let go of the lever, the candle stays lit. My fingers are pinchy and hot feeling, so I shake them out, and that feels a little better.

The Secret Place looks scary with just the candle. I forgot how the fire makes things look creepy. The apple candle burns kind of red, and it makes everything flickery and pink.

"What was the point of that?" I ask Teddy.

Because, says Teddy, *You can see me now.*

I look over, and there's a boy sitting on the rock with me. I don't think I've ever seen him before. He's got dark hair, and tan skin, and thick eyebrows.

This is my secret place, says Teddy. *You can see me, right? For real?*

"I thought the séance was supposed to summon my brother," I say. "You're not Theo." I know what Theo looks like because his picture is in our hallway, and this is definitely not him. "Are you a saint?" He doesn't look like a saint.

Of course not, he says. *Aoife, don't you remember me? I'm Teddy. Who else would I be?*

"Oh." But I don't understand, because Teddy is a bear. A big, friendly bear who likes honey and pinecones. I don't understand who this boy is.

I've been trying to explain to you, says Teddy. *What happened to your brother, why your mom is crazy.*

"Mama's not crazy," I say, mad. "She's just a little confused right now."

Your mom is crazy because of Theo, because of what he did, says Teddy.

"But—what did he do?"

He killed me, says Teddy.

Dear Donny,

I've had another slip. They say it may be a while still, and it kills me to think of Aoife waiting for me. She doesn't remember things that happened a few years ago, but she'll remember every day now that we are separated. I told her we'd watch the fireworks together, and for the last month she asked me each morning, Is it today? Is it today? Soon, *I told her.* Soon, baby.

I don't want her to realize that grown-ups don't keep their promises, that she'll have to look out for herself. I remember learning the same lessons myself, and how much it changed me.

I just wanted a few more years for her.

One of the nurses told me that one-quarter of a patient's first-order relatives will end up being diagnosed themselves. "Yeah," *I told her,* "well, Aoife is my magical three-quarters." *The doctor tells me not to worry.* "It's normal for little children to have imaginary friends."

Donny, I know there are things that we are both aware of and do not discuss. I can't believe that it's right, but I can't cast any stones myself. I have had two children outside of marriage. I lost one of them to the demons and not long ago I almost killed the other in my delirium.

Just—

Just watch out for my baby, Donny. She's our last best chance.

Siobhan

Chapter Ten

～

Teddy's not a saint—he's a *ghost*. I scream. I'm trying to back up, against the wall of the creek bed, but I accidentally kick the candle away with my foot. It goes flying over the edge of the rock. When I look down, I see it falling, still lit—then it hits the rocks in the creek bed with a dull *thunk*.

The fire goes out and Teddy is gone.

"Teddy?" I call.

He doesn't answer.

"Teddy, come back! I'm sorry!"

There's nothing.

I don't know what to do next. Why did Teddy go away? Why did he say that, about Theo and Mama? Why did he bring me out here if it wasn't to help me figure out who killed Theo? Maybe he was teasing me, like Hannah in the séance. And I got scared and now he's run away.

I get up from the rock, sniffing. I want to go home. I want my bed and I want Gramma Aoife's rosary and *The Illustrated Volume of the Saints*. I broke the apple candle and now I'm going to be in big trouble. And I already made Hannah so mad she won't play with me anymore, and now I did the same thing to Teddy. I pick up the lighter very carefully—it's still pretty warm—because I know Mac will be sad if I don't give it back. Maybe I can hide it in his car and he'll never know it was gone. I can't tell him Teddy took it, because people always blame me for what Teddy does.

It's hard to see in the dark again, after the candle. I know I need to go up the steep slope to get back to the park, but it's dark and I'm afraid I'll slip. I squish up against the side of the hill so I won't fall off the edge and put my head down on my knees. Even though it's warm outside, it's chilly here by the creek, so I curl up in a little ball. My head is heavy and my nose is stuffed up from crying. I want to cry more, but I'm too tired even to start. I'm so tired it's hard to keep my eyes open.

One minute I'm in the Secret Place and the next I'm in a shining white hallway, a little bit like the hall in the hospital where they took Mama. Everything is very clean and bright, and it smells like lemons, like it was just washed. And there's music, people singing, so beautiful that I feel my eyes fill up with tears until they spill out, like the line in Mama's favorite psalm, *my cup runneth over*, which means *overflowed*.

At first I can't even hear what the voices are singing because all I can think about is how pretty it is. Like one time in church, the choir was singing in Latin, *mi-ser-i-cor-des si-cut Pa-ter*, and usually Mama says the choir is not that good, but that day they were beautiful, and the light came in through the big window and Mama put her head down in her hands and started to cry, real quiet. I didn't even know what to do, but later Mama said she was moved by the Spirit. Because the singing was so good, that's why. And this is like that.

The singing breaks up into different voices, high ones and low ones, and then I can hear one in particular, singing *Eeee-fah, Eee-fah*, and then I know for sure it's the Blessed Saints come to visit me again, just like they did in church.

"Hello!" I shout, "I hear you!" I hope they know I've been trying real hard to solve Theo's murder, just like I promised . . . I've found clues, and I've interviewed Stephanie and Mac, and I followed Teddy and wasn't afraid because I thought he was going to lead me to the answer, even though I knew I might get in big trouble, and maybe even would have to go away to Children's Prison. But after all that I still haven't figured it out yet.

The saints probably already know the answer, because saints sit at the feet of the Lord and He knows everything. He can even see into the heart of the wicked, so He already knows who killed Theo. But the saints don't tell me, they just keep singing, and the hallway is blinding white as I walk down it, following the music. The room gets lighter until I can't see anything at all, except for the beautiful capital-D moon that is hanging in front of me lighting up the whole sky.

Aoife, says a voice that sounds like bells ringing. *Listen.*

"I'm listening!"

If the voice tells me to raise an army against the wicked King of France, I guess I'll travel all the way to the president tonight and tell him to send me right away. But instead, the saints show me a giant hand, finger pointed at the moon. And all at once I understand that the moon is just like the spotlight at the car dealerships on Woodward Avenue, not just lighting up the night sky but also pointing to the place I'm supposed to go, just like the star that led people to the baby Jesus. I just need to *follow it*. And the saints will lead me to the answers so that I can bring my mama home.

"I understand," I promise, as the voices start to fade. "I'll go exactly where you say!"

I open my eyes in the gray dark, and I'm lying on the flat rock at the Secret Place.

I sit up, pushing my hair out of my face. I can see the silver light of the moon reflecting off the water, but I need to get to the top of the hill to see where it is. I bite my lip hard, but I'm not a baby, and I know how to get back up to the park. I have to climb.

It's difficult to climb while I've got the silver lighter in my hand. And it's much harder going up than coming down was. My feet are all scratched up, and it hurts worse to walk back over the sticks and things. Plus, before I had Teddy telling me what to do, and now I'm all alone.

I don't think I've ever been alone before. Usually Mama or Hannah or Sister Mary Celeste or Stephanie or *someone* is around, and anyway, there's always Teddy. And now there's nobody but me. If I grab the wrong branch, I'll probably slide all the way down the hill and right over the edge.

But I don't grab the wrong branch. I make it all the way to the top of the hill, and push through the brambles into the park.

The first thing I do as soon as I'm clear of the trees is look up at the sky, trying to find the moon. The last time I saw it, it was hanging over the city of Detroit, and I hope I don't have to go all the way there—but if the saints tell me to, then I will, and I'll be brave like Joan of Arc.

It's not over Detroit now. Sometime while I was in the Secret Place, the moon moved across the sky. I can see it coming out from behind the clouds off to the side of the park, low on the horizon.

It's a *sign*.

I start to run across the grass, and my bare feet don't even hurt anymore. It's not hard to run fast when I know the saints are watching out for me. I feel like I could do anything, like I could fly.

"Hey!" yells someone. I realize it's the men smoking on the playground—they've seen me in the light of the streetlamp. "Hey! Hey, little girl!"

I hear the gate around the playground crash as someone lets it slam shut behind them, and they might be chasing after me, but I don't know because I don't even turn around to see. I keep running, fast as lightning, following the moon. Someone is still yelling behind me, but I'm already across the grass and into the road, straight across it, quick like a bunny and into the bushes on the other side. You should always cross a road slowly and carefully, but I know the saints wouldn't let a car hit me. Outside the circle from the lamp, the voices will never, ever find me, and I lean over with my hands on my knees, panting.

The moon is still floating over the street, and when I've caught my breath for just a minute, I creep out of the bushes and start walking again. It takes me to the corner, where the neighbor's cat is waiting, flicking its tail in S curves while it watches me getting closer.

"Hi, kitty!" I whisper. I'm glad to see her, because it's lonely going on an adventure without Teddy. "Do you want to help me solve the mystery of my brother's murder?"

The kitty doesn't answer, but when I keep walking, she gets to her feet and follows a few steps behind me. I think she might want tuna, but I don't have any.

"We have to keep moving, kitty," I say. "Do you see where the moon is sinking? We have to follow it!"

So the two of us follow the sign that the saints made for us, running barefoot through the gray light. And it's only after we cut down three different streets and over the roundabout that I realize the saints are taking us straight to Mr. Rutledge's house.

But this time I'm not afraid. Knowing that the saints are beside me, I only run faster. I'll face anything to bring back Mama, even a mean old man like Mr. Rutledge.

It's further to Mr. Rutledge's house than I thought, and I can't run the whole way, but I keep walking even when I get a stitch in my side. From where I'm standing at the end of the street, Mr. Rutledge's house looks almost exactly like ours, just like most of the houses in the neighborhood: square, brick, and low to the ground. The yard is all long grass and dandelions, just like ours before Hannah's mom paid one of the boy cousins (not one of the younger ones, the older one) to mow it for us.

I look up at the big heavy moon hanging over the house, so close that it might land on the roof. Mr. Rutledge could be inside the house right now, and Mama always tells me to stay away from him. But I know the saints have led me here to do something important, and they wouldn't have given me a sign to follow if it wasn't going to lead to the right place.

So what are you waiting for?

Teddy!

When I turn around, he's right behind me, and he's back to being my Teddy, a bear again, which makes me very happy.

"Teddy, you scared me!" I say. "Why did you look like a little boy before? Were you playing a trick? Why did you go away?"

I promise I'll explain everything later, Teddy says. *We need to go inside now.*

Teddy is right. The moon is already sinking into the house, and we might not have a lot of time to learn whatever it is the saints want to tell me. But I'm still upset at Teddy for being so mysterious, and for disappearing and leaving me all alone.

Aoife, don't be mad. I'm sorry.

"But why can't you tell me what's going on?"

I'm trying to tell you. But you have to trust me. You want to solve the mystery, don't you?

"Of course I do!"

Well, come on, then, says Teddy.

So Teddy leads the way, and I follow him, down the street to the front walk. The kitty waits until we sink into the shadows, and then she walks away down the street without us, without looking back. Kitties aren't as loyal as bears.

This is it, says Teddy, looking at Mr. Rutledge's house. *We're home.*

"You're silly, Teddy. This is Mr. Rutledge's house, not ours."

But of course Teddy doesn't listen to me—he never does. He creeps down the sidewalk to the front door, but then instead of knocking, he follows the line of bushes around the side of the house. I think about saying we shouldn't go in, but I don't say it, just follow Teddy into the shadows.

He's kneeling down in some spiky plants, trying to open a low window. I wouldn't have even known that it was there—we don't have windows there in our house—but somehow Teddy knew. It's just a little window, too small for anyone bigger than me to fit through, but there's no way to see what's inside. It looks like it's stuck shut, or maybe locked.

It takes both of us together to lift the window, and now I can see that the metal piece that should be holding it closed is rusted straight through, so the window opens slowly when we pull at just the right angle. It makes a low screech like an animal, and we both freeze—but nobody comes to see what it is, so after a minute we relax again.

I look up again. The moon is setting over the house. It looks like an angel has landed up there on the roof, just like on top of a Christmas tree. "Let's go," I say.

Teddy should be too big to squeeze through the window, but luckily he can be any size, so he says it won't be hard for him to fit. Both of us slip feetfirst through the window and into a dark basement—Teddy first, and then me, taking a deep breath and sliding in behind him. For a minute I hang from the window frame, my legs kicking out into nothing.

Let go, Aoife, says Teddy.

And once I've got my breath, I do, and drop.

The window must be higher up than I thought, because for a second I'm falling in the blackness, and I almost make a noise, but I bite down hard and keep in everything except a loud breath. Then my feet hit what feels like carpet and my knees go out, so I fall forward hard, catching myself on my hands. My palms are stinging, but I shake them off and don't let myself think about that.

Here in the basement it's another kind of dark, way worse than outside on the street. I'm afraid to take even one step forward, in case I run straight into something or step off a cliff. I don't know why there would be a cliff in the basement, but it feels like that's what could happen. It's damp down here, and smells bad—an old, moldy smell, like the fridge before Uncle Donny cleared it out.

There's a quiet *click*, and then Teddy holds up Mac's lighter. I thought I was holding it, but it's not in my hand anymore. The light from one lighter isn't much to go on, but at least it's enough to see that I'm just standing in a square of empty carpet. The basement is full up with stuff, and Teddy and I are in a far corner next to a big shelf of boxes. I don't know why this house has a basement when ours doesn't, but it must be nice to have somewhere to keep all the extra boxes.

Teddy walks back to the window and gives it a really hard tug, and it slides shut with another rusty creak.

"Teddy, how are we going to get out?" I ask, but he doesn't answer. He just holds up the lighter so we can see better.

Mr. Rutledge has a dog, I remember suddenly—Roo, the pink-eyed poodle that walks past us without knowing we're there. Even a blind dog will bark if people come into his house, right? But there's no barking. Mama always says that Roo *looks ready to drop*, and I wonder if maybe he died, which would be good for me, but I'd feel bad, too.

"Do you see the door?" I ask Teddy. Because if nobody's barking, then we might as well keep going.

He points across the room, and I start walking in that direction even though I don't see much—bears can probably see better in the low light than I can. I try to be real quiet and so does Teddy, and we squeeze around the shelves in the dark. I don't know why the saints brought us here, but it seems like we should try to keep from being loud until we figure it out.

Just like Teddy said, there's a metal door in the wall right where he pointed, half hidden in the dark. I move boxes out of the way as Teddy cracks it open slowly, afraid it will creak. Then he holds the lighter up so we can see what's behind it. If it were me, I'd have burned my fingers by now, but Teddy's fingers don't ever get hurt.

We're looking at a flight of wooden stairs and, at the top, another door. This time I go first, trying to keep on the outside of each step because the middle part of the stair is the loudest. I don't want to go *creak, creak* like Uncle Donny in the middle of the night.

At the top of the stairs, I put my hand on the knob and turn it. But the door doesn't open. All of a sudden I can imagine us trapped in the dark like this, with both the door ahead of us and the door behind us locked. Teddy and I would starve to death.

Push harder, says Teddy. I take a deep breath and do as he says, and Teddy comes next to me and puts his bear weight against the door and pushes, too, and very slowly the door starts to move. There's something pushed in front of it, but Teddy and I together are strong enough to move it.

The moonlight pours in the windows on the other side of the door—just like our house, all the windows face the street and the light comes in from outside—and Teddy lets the lighter go out. We're in a hallway just like the one that leads to our living room from the front door. It smells a little like dog. There's a big box pushed into the middle of the hallway, and that's what was blocking the door. I can see the black writing on the outside.

Except for all the noise I'm making, the house is silent, and I'm pretty sure there's nobody home—anyway, the saints wouldn't have led me here if Mr. Rutledge was waiting to catch me.

"Teddy, where do you think we should go?" I whisper.

Upstairs, says Teddy.

Upstairs is probably where the bedrooms are, or at least that's how it is in our house. It's also closer to the moon, so I guess that makes sense. The two of us creep down the hallway, making a little-girl-and-a-big-bear-shaped shadow against the wall. It's weird that Mr. Rutledge's house is kind of like ours and kind of not. We have carpet on the main floor and Mr. Rutledge has wood, which feels smooth and cold under my sore feet. Our walls are painted white, but his are covered in wallpaper that might be dark red, but looks gray in this light. It's like stepping inside a mirror world, like the house we could have lived in.

Hurry, says Teddy.

"I don't know what you're in such a hurry for," I say. It's not like we even know what we're looking for yet, so how can we get there any faster?

But Teddy pushes ahead of me and puts his front paws on the first step of the stairs. *This way.*

More stairs. At least these have a wide piece of carpet that runs up the middle. Although the little strings brushing against the underside of my feet just make them hurt worse.

Don't make a sound, says Teddy, although I'm not. Teddy just likes to tell me what to do.

Mr. Rutledge has photographs over the stairs just like we do. Most of ours are pictures of Theo. I can't see who these are of until we get high enough to get light through the window from the streetlight across the street. Then I see an old brown-colored picture of two people getting married, even if I can't see their faces exactly in the dark.

"These are cool," I tell Teddy. "They must be from a long time ago. Do you think this is Mr. Rutledge?"

Keep up, says Teddy. *It's this way.*

I climb the next stair and look at the next picture. It's of a smiling woman with a fat baby (or maybe a puppy?) in her arms. Her husband—it must be her husband—is standing behind her with his arm around her. They look like a real nice family, and for just a second, I miss Mama so bad that it makes me feel like I'm going to be sick.

Aoife, come on!

Teddy has gotten to the top of the stairs now, and he's waiting for me, standing up on his back legs the way he does when he gets excited. I climb up the next two stairs and look at a big picture in a round frame at the very top of the staircase, right where Theo's last picture is hanging in our house. Just then a car comes around the corner and the headlights come in through all the windows, and suddenly I'm looking straight into the face of a little boy just about Theo's age. He's got curly hair and thick, beetle-y eyebrows, and a very round brown face.

"But—Teddy," I say, forgetting to be quiet. "Teddy, this picture . . . it's of *you*."

When I turn back around to look at Teddy again—bear-Teddy, my Teddy—he's not standing where he was.

"Teddy?" I call, remembering to be quiet again, although it's sort of too late for that now. He doesn't answer. But I hear a sound down the hall that could be bear-feet, walking over the wood floors, so I think he must have gone on up ahead. He's probably looking for clues.

I climb the rest of the way up the stairs. "Teddy?"

If Mr. Rutledge's house is just like ours, the first room after the stairs will be my bedroom. I open the door and turn on the light, almost expecting to see my own pink walls and butterfly pillows. But this room is boring looking, pale-tan wallpaper and a dark-blue carpet and a big desk with a desktop computer. That makes sense, I guess, because Mr. Rutledge is old, so he uses the kind of giant monitor they have at school, not a cool thin screen like Hannah's family has.

There's not going to be anything about Theo's murder in this room. It doesn't even look like anybody's been in here for a long time, because there's dust on the computer monitor and all the papers. I turn the light off and pull the door closed.

The next room along the hall is the bathroom, and I have to use it by now, so I do real quick and make sure to wash my hands extra good even though there's no soap. No toilet paper, either, so I have to drip dry like we do at our house when Mama hasn't felt up to going to the store. You just do a little shimmy over the bowl before you pull up your underwear, and it's not that bad.

But this bathroom smells funny, not like ours, which smells like pine trees, or Hannah's mom's, which smells like apples because of the apple candle (at least, it used to, before Teddy took the candle and I broke it. Maybe it won't smell that way anymore?). Mr. Rutledge's bathroom smells like moss.

The next door down the hall is what would be our guest room, except that we don't have a basement, so actually it's full of stuff—the computer, wrapped up in a box and taped shut so that the demons can't get out, and the old sofa bed that Mama moved up there when Hannah's mom gave us a new one with springs that don't stick out. So I'm not all that excited to look inside here, but right away I know that this room is what the saints brought me here to see, because the moonlight is filling up the window.

It's a little boy's room, with dark-blue painted walls and framed pictures of race cars. There's a bed shaped like a rocket ship—way better than my bed, which is little and square and not shaped like anything—and the sheets and the pillows are all decorated with moons and stars.

I walk all the way into the room, closing the door behind me. It smells dusty and I wish I could open the window. What it reminds me of really is Theo's room, back in our house, even though it's in the wrong place, because Theo's room is the next one down. But it smells like that, dried up and sad.

I've never seen Mr. Rutledge with a little boy. Mr. Rutledge is always alone except for Roo. I don't know why he would have a room like this in his house, but he does have that picture of the boy who looks like Teddy at the top of the stairs.

I walk to the desk in the corner, which is full of books. I wish I had some nice books like this. All of ours are chewed up before we even get them because Mama picks them up from the church book sale. I open the front cover of one that is about crayons in a crayon box—I love crayons—and inside, someone has written in blue marker, NED SLATER. Lots of my books have names written in the front of them, too—names that aren't mine, I mean, from the other kids that had them first. But I open another book (it's called *Free to a Good Home*, and it looks like someone finds a box of puppies by the side of the road), and the inside says NED SLATER, too. The same person wrote it both times in block letters. I put the books back, but I know it's a clue.

There's a teddy bear on the bed. A big tan-colored one that's bigger than the pillow, with a chewed-up ear. I like teddy bears, too. Part of me wants to climb into that rocket-ship bed and go to sleep like Goldilocks, except she also got to eat a lot of porridge. I do understand that story a little better now, because it makes a lot more sense why she would get into the little bear's bed and fall asleep after a whole night walking around.

There are two pairs of sneakers in the closet—one blue, one yellow—each with white stripes around the edge, and white laces. I don't like to look at those shoes. I close my eyes.

I shouldn't have thought about porridge, because it reminds me I'm hungry, too. But eating any of Mr. Rutledge's food would be stealing—not just *borrowing* his bed, which might be okay with Jesus. So I try not to think about being hungry and I just keep looking at the little-boy things in the room.

I'm not sure why the saints brought me here to learn about Theo when all I keep finding is more about Ned Slater. There must be a part of the mystery that I'm missing. The saints are trying to tell me something, but I don't know what it is.

I sit on the bed. That's okay. I lean against the wall and I'm not lying down, I'm not under the covers, I'm just sitting. My eyes hurt, though. And I feel kind of dizzy, and kind of sick to my stomach, I guess because I'm hungry maybe. And even though the bed is full of dust, it's very soft. I wish Teddy would stop playing around and come back to tell me what to do.

Those shoes are watching me.

*   *   *

Then I'm back at the Secret Place. It's raining and the raindrops are like glass beads, they shine in the light, falling real slow. There's two boys on the rock, a little one and a bigger one. I can't hear what they're saying, and their faces are blurry, like ghosts. I can see right through them to the big trunks of trees behind them. I feel like I've seen them before, though, both of them. They're older than me by a lot, and they don't like it when I follow them around, but Mama says they have to let me come if I want and they have to keep an eye on me. And if I can't keep up, they have to wait for me, because I'm little and they're big.

But now they both have angry voices, and I'm scared, even though they're ignoring me. I scoot up the rock on my bottom, away from the edge.

*   *   *

Aoife, wake up!

I open my eyes and I'm still in the rocket-ship bed. But there are lights swinging across the wall, coming through the curtains on the window, and I realize it's a truck, pulling into the driveway. Mr. Rutledge is home!

I get up off the bed, my heart thumping *bum, bum, bum*. My hands are shaking as I pull the blanket straight where I crumpled it. I don't know when I fell asleep, but it can't have been long, because it's still not even morning yet. I don't know what Mr. Rutledge does all night, when he should be home in bed asleep like everybody else, but he's home now. And I have to go, *right now*.

I keep well away from the window and run back to the door. I can hear a car door slamming and a little dog barking. Dogs always know when people are in the house, I think, and I couldn't hide under the bed or behind the curtains from Roo even if I could hide from Mr. Rutledge. So I have to try and get out of the house without him seeing me.

"Teddy, come on," I whisper as quiet as I can. "We have to go!" I'm going to be in big, *big* trouble if Mr. Rutledge finds me in his house.

But Teddy doesn't answer.

All I can think is that the saints—even though I haven't solved the whole mystery yet—probably brought me here because *Mr. Rutledge killed Theo*. Maybe he was driving around in his black truck just like he is now, and he found Theo and killed him. That's why Mama says not to play in front of his house. And now I'm all alone in Mr. Rutledge's house late at night and he's going to kill me, too.

I have to get out.

I creep out the door and back down the hallway, still trying to keep to the edges and not make noise. I hear the key in the front door, so loud in the quiet, and then I hear the door opening. The dog runs in first, barking, and then I hear the heavy feet of Mr. Rutledge. "Can it, Roo," he grumbles. His voice makes the hair on my arms stand up.

I duck down low in the hallway, leaning against the railing and trying to hold my breath so he won't hear me. I hear him putting stuff down and slamming the door. If he comes up the stairs, I'll never get away.

Blessed Mary, and all the saints, especially Joan, I pray, under my breath. *Please don't let Mr. Rutledge come up the stairs and catch me.*

Roo is still barking, barking, and I think he must know I'm here. But he doesn't come any closer. I can hear his toenails scraping on the wood floor like he's being pulled away backwards. Is he on a leash?

"Quit it!" says Mr. Rutledge, sharply. Roo whines and whines, but he stops barking. I guess that's the problem with a dog that barks a lot—you can't tell when he's trying to tell you something special. Lucky for me.

Mr. Rutledge goes down the hallway, and I hear him muttering and groaning to himself. In our house that hallway leads to the living room and the kitchen, although I'm not sure it's the same here. I can't get back down into the basement without him seeing me, even if I could open that window again. Which I probably can't, since it was above my head. Maybe I can creep right down the stairs and out the front door before he even knows I'm here? But how can I be sure he won't come back and catch me? It's hard to think straight. I just want to run straight home to Uncle Donny.

If I wait longer, he might let Roo off the leash and then he'll come for me and I'll be caught. I can hear Mr. Rutledge rummaging around and the sound of couch springs squeaking. Maybe he sleeps downstairs like Mama does when she has bad dreams. He might be tired, since he was out in the middle of the night.

I put my bare feet right up against the edge of the wall and creep, creep, down the hallway, holding my breath. *Hail Mary, full of grace, the Lord is with thee—*

Roo starts barking again when I get to the top of the stairs.

"Shut up!" yells Mr. Rutledge, but I hear the couch squeak like somebody's getting up out of it.

Blessed art thou among women, and blessed is the fruit of thy womb—

I tiptoe down the stairs, sure at any moment that he's going to catch me. The hardest step is the one halfway down, where I won't be hidden by the railings anymore. I'll be right out in the open where anybody can see me. I don't want to put my foot down. I'm frozen. I'm going to be sick.

I pretend that Saints Joan and Catherine are with me, a shining line of beautiful women, cheering me on. I close my eyes. I step down.

The dog comes running down the hallway, making a racket. I run down the last six steps like a shot rubber band, and Roo comes right up to my heels, barking that high-pitched bark. I think for sure that he's going to bite me, right through my pajama pants, but maybe because he kind of knows me, or because the saints are protecting me, or just because he can't see that well, being old and blind, he just jumps around my legs, barking.

"What the fuck?" I hear Mr. Rutledge say, and that's a *bad word*. I think that he shouldn't say such a bad word, but I just run clear across the hallway and pull open the first door I come to. My hands won't work properly to open the lock. I know Mr. Rutledge can hear me, and I can hear him coming down the hallway, but I can't get it—until finally I manage to throw open the door and half fall out down the steps.

It turns out that the door leads out into the garage—our house doesn't have a garage so Mama has to park the van in the driveway—but it's too late now, and I keep on, straight down the steps, hoping the door closed behind me.

"Hey! Who's out there? I know you're there!" yells Mr. Rutledge.

I can't open the big garage door. I don't have the button. There must be a regular door to the outside somewhere, but I can't see it in the dark.

I'm *trapped*.

I squish down between the wall and the rusted old car that's taking up most of the space, trying to crawl underneath, even though the bottom of the door is digging into my arms and cutting me. There's sharp stuff—broken glass?—here among the old leaves on the cement, but I couldn't move even if I wanted to.

"I know you're out there!"

I close my eyes and cover my face. This is probably just what it was like when Mr. Rutledge murdered Theo. I try to stay still, still.

I hear a *chuck-chuck* sound, and then there is a noise so loud I clap my hands over my ears and duck because there are little shavings of wood falling all around me. I turn around and there's little holes blown clear through the garage door behind me and over my head, and there is a cloud of dust in the air that makes me cough.

He shot off a firework right here in the garage.

But with the streetlights shining in, I can see the door to the outside. I see it.

"I'm calling the police, you hear me!" yells Mr. Rutledge, and I duck lower and don't move. *I'm not here. I'm at home, safe and sound.*

I hear Roo barking, and then I hear the clicking of his little nails on the cement floor, getting closer, and then he is barking and snapping at my face, and I fall backwards onto my butt and skin my palms. I hear the inside door slam and I know this is my chance. I'm already climbing up to my feet and pulling hard on the doorknob that leads out of the garage. But it's locked, and I can't get out. Mr. Rutledge is going to be right back any second, and I can't get out.

Except there's a doggy door down by my feet. It's locked on the inside with a latch, but I can open it. I'm already through before I can think about it, crawling on my hands and knees. Roo comes with me, pushing past me, but he doesn't try to bite me, just barks and barks. I fall forward and hit my palms and my knees. I smack my chin, and I feel my loose tooth fall right out *and I swallow it.* I don't make a sound. I bite my lip and think *don't cry, don't cry.*

"I have the police on the phone, do you hear me! They're on their way here now, you piece of shit!"

I'm already on my feet, Roo jumping up with me, and then I run through the shadows. Across the street and into the grass. All the way down the sidewalk in the dark. I run and run even though I'm tired and my feet are hurting from the cracks in the pavement, which have sharp little stones in them, and I scuff my toes on the cement.

Roo runs part of the way with me, but at some point he breaks off, still barking, and gets left behind. I hope the cat from next door was smart enough to go home and not get attacked. I don't stop for anything. I just run straight into the shapes of bushes and trees. I let the darkness swallow me up.

Chapter Eleven

I can hear sirens coming closer, and I remember Mr. Rutledge said he was calling the police. I can't believe there are police looking for me. They'll take me to Children's Prison when they find out that Teddy and I stole Mac's cigarette lighter and broke into Mr. Rutledge's basement.

And I swallowed my tooth! I'm not even going to get a quarter for it. It's going to sit in my stomach like a watermelon seed, growing out of my ears like Hannah said.

It's only when I remember the lighter that I realize for the first time that Teddy isn't with me. He must have stayed back inside the house, but I don't know why he'd do that—he never used to appear and disappear like this. He used to always, always be there, wherever I was. I hope he's okay back in Mr. Rutledge's house. He does like dogs, so maybe he wanted to stay and play with Roo? I wish he had come with me, because I'm scared, and I don't care what I did, I don't want the police people to catch me. I have to hide.

I run in the direction of the dark for as long as I can. When I can't go anymore, I stop and lean over, trying not to throw up. It takes me a while to catch my breath and realize that I'm lost.

It's starting to get just a little lighter, and it probably won't be too much longer before there are cars on the road and people walking around, and they're going to ask why I'm in my pajamas, and maybe they could point me back to my house or call Uncle Donny.

But Uncle Donny is the one who held the door open. He wanted me to go solve the mystery. I'm not sure he'll even let me back in, since I only found one clue and I don't even know what it means.

I can't go to Hannah's house because she's mad at me.

And even though Mac says he's my dad, that doesn't mean anything—he's been my dad all along, and mostly he wasn't around. I don't even know where he lives. I only learned his whole name yesterday.

So I just keep walking, keeping the sound of the sirens behind me. I'm really tired and I'm so hungry my stomach is eating itself. I got a little bit of sleep on and off—some on the rock, maybe, and some in Ned Slater's rocket-ship bed, but I don't think it was nearly enough, because I'm about to fall asleep standing up. And I really miss Teddy.

I wish I'd worn shoes to bed tonight, because the bottoms of my feet *really* hurt. And my knees hurt from crawling on the cement, and my palms are scuffed up from the garage floor, and I have bits of wood in my hair from the firework Mr. Rutledge shot off in the garage.

I'm just starting to think that maybe the best thing to do would be to find a dark space under some bushes and go to sleep like someone from the city, when I hear a low chime— *dong, dong, dong, dong, dong*—five times, for five o'clock in the morning.

It's the church bell ringing.

It's almost exciting to hear the five-o'clock bells, which I don't think I've ever heard before in my whole life. Best of all, church means *sanctuary*—that's what Mama always says—and *sanctuary* means Mr. Rutledge can't get me. Even if I wasn't on a mission from the saints, Jesus would protect me in the church, which is his Father's house. So instead of looking for my house or anything on the street that I recognize, I look up above the buildings to try and find the church steeple. And there it is, over the trees, looking down on me just like God does.

It's a lot easier to find a street to get there, and I only take one that dead-ends without taking me to the church. The whole time I'm half waiting for Mr. Rutledge to come out of the bushes and grab me. I don't even know what I would do if he did, except maybe pray. Praying worked last time, at least, because the saints did take me to the garage and then the doggy door instead of letting Mr. Rutledge catch me.

I'm too tired to run anymore, but I walk slowly on my sore feet until I get to the Sacred Heart of Mary. I already know exactly where to go. I don't even need the saints to tell me, because the chapel off on the far end of the church is never, ever locked.

I cross the grass where we play red rover when we have a substitute counselor at church camp. It feels so good under my feet, way better than the gravel around the road or the twigs I've been walking on all night.

Still looking out for Mr. Rutledge, I sneak around the back to the door of the chapel. Just like I knew it would be, it's unlocked. Inside, the windows are purple and pink stained glass, and there's wooden benches, and a cross, and the box that looks like a tiny coffin for a baby doll, but which Mama says is part of the altar and that I shouldn't say that.

I hear a car driving by real slow on the road, and I can see a big flashlight lighting up all the windows, but I don't duck down even though I think about it, because I know the saints will protect me here. They'll turn the glass windows black so Mr. Rutledge and the people from Children's Prison can't see me inside.

The windows look the same to me, but it must work, because the sound of the engine doesn't stop, it just creeps down the road, shining the flashlight into the bushes as it goes.

I say an extra-special *thank you* to all the saints, particularly Saint Catherine and Blessed Saint Joan, and of course to Holy Mary, Mother of God. I don't mention Jesus because he is probably too busy to come down here and intercede with Mr. Rutledge for me (but of course I am always grateful to him anyway, all the time). I know I ought to say a Hail Mary and an Our Father or something, but I'm so, so tired now that I can't hardly remember the words—that is, I mean, of course I remember them, but I keep forgetting where I am in the prayer after just a couple lines, and have to start over.

I've still got so much to do, and I'm running out of time. But what am I supposed to do next? Why would the saints lead me all this way but not show me the answer? I'm still missing part of the jigsaw. I almost wish Hannah and I were still friends in case she could explain it. I know I need to figure it out, but it doesn't make any sense.

I'm sitting up on the pew, but then my head gets heavy, so I let it slide down, down, to the wooden seat, and then I pull my knees up in my torn pajama pants and curl into a ball, which makes me think of Teddy, who likes to sleep in a furry blob. That makes me sad, but I'm too tired to even really be sad, so I just close my eyes and send a last thank-you prayer especially to Saint Joan for helping me to be brave, and then between one blink and the next I fall asleep.

* * *

In my dream, the first thing I see is the bird. Mama said it was a starling. We found it dead in the grass when we went outside in the morning on our way to church.

What happened to it? I asked.

It fell, she said.

It looks like an angel, I said.

It was almost grown, but maybe not quite all the way. It looked perfect, except for being dead. Its feet were spread pointing two different directions, and its wings were spread, and its feathers looked soft and fluffy. But it was dead. Its eyes were open. And Mama said that God's eye is on the fall of a starling. But she also said that the bugs would eat it, or the next-door kitty, and she moved it under the bushes so I wouldn't see.

I used to picture the little bird falling from the nest. Maybe it got too close to the edge by accident.

Or maybe the other birds pushed it out.

In my dream, the bird's wings twitch, and Mama and I step back. It gets up and shakes itself off, and its eyes, which were dried up like raisins, are little black beads again. The starling hop-hops down onto the grass, and then in the next breath it takes off and flies away.

* * *

The next time I open my eyes, everything is pink. I'm cold. I don't want to move, but then I realize that the reason I woke up is because someone is outside the door, turning the knob.

Has Mr. Rutledge found me? I sit up although everything hurts and my head feels swimmy like I'm still half asleep. Teddy isn't back yet. I wish he was here. Would Mr. Rutledge break down the door of a church to get in? He might because I don't think he's even Catholic. He never comes to service. The door opens and I want to scream, but I bite down hard on my lip to keep the sound in.

But it's not Mr. Rutledge. It's Father Paul. When I see him, in his weekday clothes, his bald head, and his big wire glasses, I'm so relieved that I start to cry.

"Aoife? What on earth are you doing here this early?"

"I'm sleeping," I say, sobbing. At least, I was trying to, before he woke me up.

Father Paul kneels down in front of me so he can look at me square. "Aoife, what happened?"

I'm not sure what to say. No one thing happened, but everything. I didn't solve the mystery even though I tried to be very brave. I had a really weird dream.

I try to push my hair out of my face, but my fingers get stuck in the tangles. My feet hurt, and I need to brush my teeth. I'm still tired. I sort of wish he would go away and come back later. "I was following the saints," I say. "But then—they almost got me in big trouble. Why would they do that? And Teddy *left!*"

I put my head down in my hands and I'm still sobbing.

"Aoife." Father Paul puts his hand on my shoulder. "Aoife, this is important. How did you get here? Does your mother know you're here?"

"My mama's at the hospital because she's *crazy*," I say, starting to cry harder. "And Uncle Donny opened the door last night and Teddy told me to go! And I was just following the saints, but then I got l-l-lost." It's hard to talk at all, because every time I breathe it all just goes into pushing out more tears.

"Lost? But why are you in your pajamas? Where are your shoes?"

"My house!" I say. Where I wish I was now.

Father Paul looks confused, but he doesn't look mad. "I think you'd better come on back to the office with me," he says, standing up and holding out his hand, "and maybe we can give your mother a call, hmm?"

That just makes me cry harder and harder, until I think I'm going to throw up. "She's not *there*," I say, trying to talk through my tears and not doing a good job. "She *left* and I *can't get her back*."

"Come along and we'll get this all sorted out," says Father Paul. "Who is at your house right now? We can go find your home phone number in the church directory."

"Uncle Donny," I say, still sniffing. By now all the snot is running down my face and my nose hurts and my eyes hurt from crying, and my head hurts, too. "My uncle Donny is at home."

"Would it be okay if I called your uncle Donny?"

I take a few breaths and try to stop crying. You can stop crying if you really, really have to. It's a secret that Teddy showed me once, a long time ago. "He might be mad at me," I say.

"How about I'll talk to him first, and I'll make sure he's not angry with you?"

I don't answer, but I reach out to take Father Paul's hand when he offers it again.

"You know, Aoife, if you don't feel safe with your uncle, I can call someone else. I won't call him if you don't want me to."

That sounds a lot like when the Carrie/Loris asked me if I *feel safe in my home*. I don't know why grown-ups keep asking me that. Of course I feel safe with Uncle Donny, and it's not like I know how to reach Mama at the hospital even if they let her talk on the phone, which I don't think they want to do again.

"Can we call him for you?"

"Okay," I say. And then I follow Father Paul to the office, where the nice secretary is waiting with the phone.

* * *

"Jesus God, Aoife," says Uncle Donny. He picks me up and squeezes me tight, tight.

I would tell him not to take the Lord's name in vain, but I don't think he is. He sounds like he really means it.

"Hi Uncle Donny," I whisper.

"Aoife, I thought you were asleep upstairs. What the hell?"

"She says she got lost," says Father Paul. He doesn't seem very warm towards Uncle Donny. I don't know why.

"Lost? Aoife, why were you even out of the house? You do know we're going to get a report from CPS literally any minute, right? And you decide to run away *now*?"

I guess he didn't want me to solve the mystery after all. I don't understand. "I was following the moon and then the kitty was there and then Teddy *went away*. And I'm tired. I wanna go to sleep." I like being high up in Uncle Donny's arms. He smells good. I lean against his shoulder. My head still hurts.

"Look at your *feet*," says Uncle Donny.

"I wanna go home. Can we go back to bed now?"

"Kiddo, I'm about two seconds away from calling the police. Tell me why you left the house."

"Teddy made me go out, but then he disappeared," I say.

"What?"

"I was walking, and Teddy had a candle, but then the candle broke, and Teddy disappeared."

"Does any of this make sense to you?" asks Father Paul.

Uncle Donny puts his hand over my head and sways side to side. "I think she was sleepwalking," he says. "It's a family tendency. I used to do it myself, as a child."

Nobody was walking in their sleep. Teddy was doing it all. He made Uncle Donny open the door and he told me to follow him.

"I've never heard of Aoife having the same problem, but I guess I shouldn't be surprised. She must have gotten up in the night and gone out, eh munchkin?" He jiggles me on his shoulder. "It's amazing that she didn't hurt anything more than her feet."

I was awake, and I only walked because Teddy told me to. But I don't bother trying to argue with him, partly because I'm so tired and partly because I already know he's not going to understand.

"Thank God you're all right, Aoife," says Uncle Donny, still rocking me back and forth. "Do you know how sad I would be if anything happened to you?"

"I'm sorry," I say, sniffing. "I didn't mean to make you sad."

"I think maybe it would be best to take Aoife home and let her get some rest," says Father Paul.

"Yeah, I'll take her straight back. I'm sorry, we've had a lot of—ah—changes at home lately, and I think perhaps it's got her stirred up. But I've got the number for a professional, and believe me I'll be making an appointment right away. Just—thank you very much, uh, sir. Really." Uncle Donny juggles me around to shake Father Paul's hand with the hand that's not under my knees.

"Aoife, I hope you're feeling better soon," says Father Paul.

I don't know about that, so I don't say anything, because it would be wrong to tell a holy priest that I'd feel better soon if I didn't think I would.

"Night-night, Father Paul," I say instead.

Uncle Donny takes me out to the parking lot, and I fall asleep in his shiny car.

Chapter Twelve

❧

I don't dream a thing, and when I finally wake up I'm back in my own bed.

Uncle Donny is sitting at the end of the bed, looking at my feet. "Boy, it looks like you really scuffed these up," he says.

I sit up. It's bright and sunny outside. "I'm still tired," I say. "I want to go back to sleep."

"Sorry, kiddo, but it's already noon. If I let you sleep all day, you'll never get back on schedule," says Uncle Donny. "You don't want to end up turning into a night owl, do you?"

I don't want to be an owl. I want to be a bear, like Teddy.

Then I remember Teddy is gone. Usually when you wake up in the morning, whatever was wrong last night is a lot better— Mama always tells me that—but now I've woken up and I remember everything and it just makes me want to cry again.

"Anyway," says Uncle Donny, "if you sleep all day, you'll miss the fireworks!"

But . . . but that means today is the Fourth of July. And Mama isn't home. And it's all my fault because I didn't solve the mystery in time, even though I did my absolute best last night.

"Come on, lazybones. Up and at 'em." Uncle Donny jiggles my arm.

I don't know what else to do, so I get up. Uncle Donny watches me brush my teeth and then he runs me a bath. It hurts to put my feet in the water, but I don't cry. Uncle Donny asks if I want bubbles, but I say no.

He makes me oatmeal, but I'm not hungry. I feel funny and floaty after not getting much sleep last night, and missing Mama feels like I swallowed a rock and now its sitting in my stomach.

I thought if I followed the signs and was brave, the saints would help me solve the mystery. But I didn't learn who killed my brother at all.

Uncle Donny brings in the mail, but he won't let me look at it. He says there's nothing in it for me.

"Uncle Donny, Mama isn't going to be home in time to watch the fireworks, is she?"

Uncle Donny bites his lip. "No, kiddo, she's not going to be able to," he says. "I know it's real important to you, and you don't know how much I wish I could make it happen. But your ma . . . well, she's pretty sick, and even though the doctors are trying really hard to help her, and I know she's trying too . . . she's not better yet. So she needs to stay at the hospital."

I look at my feet. Lots of people told me that Mama wasn't coming home, but on TV it always seems like at the last second something comes up and everything turns out fine. The soldier makes it home in time for Christmas, and the superhero catches the piece of burning building right before it hits the girl.

But I guess Joan of Arc only became a saint after she died . . . God didn't send the angels to rescue her before she was murdered by the wicked English soldiers. Maybe it's like that.

The afternoon goes slow. Uncle Donny sets up his computer so I can watch *Mr. Wonderbean*, and for a while I do. Later he asks if I want to watch the fireworks downtown with Hannah's family, but I say no. I draw on the front sidewalk in chalk and watch Hannah's mom loading up boxes and a cooler and a glow-in-the-dark Hula-Hoop. Then they all pile into the minivan—all the boy cousins, and Hannah, her mom and grandma, and her aunt and the new baby, which is crying loudly. They back down the driveway and make a slow turn and then pull away.

I draw bears on the sidewalk. I hope it will make Teddy come back, but it doesn't. After a while, the cat from next door comes over and sits next to me. This time I know not to grab for her, and she doesn't run away. After a while, I start drawing cats instead of bears. When I put my hand out, she rubs her head against it and purrs.

It's still light outside. Today is always going to be the day Mama didn't come back in time for the fireworks, forever and ever.

Uncle Donny comes out when it's almost time for dinner. "Aoife, do you want to go to the lake with your favorite uncle?" he asks me. "We could probably see some great fireworks from there."

He is my favorite uncle, but I shake my head no. I don't want to go anywhere.

"Nice cats," he says, looking at my pictures. He puts out a can of tuna for the next-door kitty, just like Mama always does, and we sit on the step and watch her eat it.

Then Uncle Donny puts *Toy Story* on the laptop, and we watch it while we eat dinner—frozen pizza, which is Teddy's favorite. It feels weird to eat it without him. Uncle Donny doesn't watch the whole movie with me—I can hear him walking around upstairs—but he does come back down to watch the last part. He makes me laugh by doing the Woody voice.

When it starts to get dark, we can hear popping noises far away. I turn up the ending music louder because I don't want to hear.

"You know, when your ma and I were little, we used to have a family tradition," says Uncle Donny.

I don't look away from the screen. "Yeah?"

"Yeah. How about we put this on pause for a minute and you come upstairs with me?"

"I don't know," I say.

Uncle Donny holds his hand out. "C'mon." So I get up and go with him.

We go up the stairs and into Mama's room, and I see that the window is open. Uncle Donny has taken off the screen, too. "Careful," he says. He puts his head out the window, with his hands on the frame, and then he lifts one foot over the edge, and then the other. "Go slow," he says.

I creep towards the window, and even though it makes my heart beat hard in my chest, I climb up just like him, and he waits on the other side to help me out. Then we're standing on the gritty hot surface of the roof. Right outside Mama's window, it's not so slanted, and we can walk as long as we're careful. Uncle Donny tells me to keep one hand on the wall of the house. Together, we creep around the corner and over by where the chimney comes out of the roof.

"When we were growing up, we used to live in Chicago, and we didn't have a lot of money," says Uncle Donny as he inches along, with his hand tight around mine. "This was back when your ma was close to the age you are now."

I can't imagine Mama ever being the same age as me. I wonder if we would have played together and been friends or if we would have fought like me and Hannah.

"Every Fourth of July, we'd go out on the roof, and if you looked in just the right spot, you could see the fireworks over Lake Michigan. In fact, that's just about the only thing I can remember from back that long ago. Of course you wouldn't be able to do it anymore—things have gotten a lot more built up than when I was a kid. But—look! There they are!"

I look where he's pointing. He's right. The fireworks start off like a little pinprick on the horizon. Then they bloom into a shower of light—red, and blue, and golden yellow.

"Wow," I say quietly.

"Here, come sit." Uncle Donny shows me how we can sit against the chimney with our feet hanging over the edge of the roof. It's a little scary, but the fireworks are so pretty that I forget to be afraid. They're far away and kind of small, but with the two of us out here together, I think we might have the best view in the whole city.

"It's pretty," I say. Teddy would love this.

I can hear the music playing from far away, echo-y and quiet. It sounds like a marching band, like when Mama and I went to the Flag Day parade. They're playing a song that Mama taught me silly words to:

Be kind to your web-footed friends, for a duck may be somebody's mother . . .

The fireworks are timed to go off at exciting points in the song. Uncle Donny hums along. Maybe he knows the same made-up words as Mama. "I'm sorry your ma couldn't take you to the lake," he says. "I know you really wanted to go, and I know she really wanted to take you."

The fireworks are making the shapes of stars, getting bigger and bigger until they just blur away.

"It's okay," I say, which isn't true at all. I just don't want Uncle Donny to know that it's all my fault anyway.

"I bet when your ma is less confused, she'll take us all to the lake together."

"Can Mac come, too?"

Uncle Donny snorts. "Ah, probably not Mac, baby. But the three of us."

"Is it because Mac called you a fruit?"

"Uh, yes, among other things. But the point is, when your ma is feeling better, we'll go out there, and we'll bring sparklers. Have you ever seen a sparkler, Aoife? It's like a little mini firework you can hold right in your hand."

I know Uncle Donny is just saying this to make me feel better. I try not to let it work. The fireworks get faster, and the music, which is now playing *The Star-Spangled Banner*, is drowned out by the *pop-pop-pop* of them all going off so fast, one after another. There's more smoke than light, after a while, but each new firework is bright again for a little while.

"Uncle Donny, do you think prayers really work?" I ask.

Uncle Donny sucks in a breath. "Ooh, kiddo, I am so not the man to ask this stuff," he says.

I think about this. "Is Mama really going to get better?" I ask.

"Of course she is! Don't be silly! And it'll be just like it was before. Okay? It's just going to take a while, that's all."

"But . . . Mama was confused before, too, sometimes," I say. "Right?"

The fireworks are all gone now.

Uncle Donny sighs. "All right, well, maybe I shoulda started by saying that there's different kinds of better. There's the kind like when you catch a cold, and after a few days it goes away completely. And then there's the kind that . . . maybe it doesn't get worse, and that's as good as we can do. And we may always be trying to manage it, but it's never really gone. And that's the kind your ma has."

Somehow I knew he was going to say something like that. I nod and look back out at the horizon, where the fireworks aren't anymore. Quietly, I can still hear the band playing something I don't recognize. In the end we are both looking at the black sky.

"End of the show," says Uncle Donny. He takes my hand again and we go back inside together, careful, careful, because the fireworks are over.

"What about miracles?" I ask, as I brush my teeth and Uncle Donny watches. "Do you think miracles are real?" I spit.

"To tell you the truth, Aoife, your uncle Donny is a skeptic. Let's just say . . . let's just say there's a whole lot of things about my life that the pope and I wouldn't quite see eye to eye on, okay?" Uncle Donny takes a pair of clean pajamas out of the drawer and puts them on the bed.

"But the saints are real."

"Well, they were real *people*. I mean, some of them. Right? But they're also stories, like, a way to talk about certain ideas or teach us certain lessons. So they're real in that sense. Okay?"

But either things are real, or they're not. If the saints are just a story, then they're not *real*. But I saw them. They were as real as I am, as real as Teddy. They sent me a vision and a sign, and they led me to the chapel and turned the windows black. Didn't they?

"But Father Paul thinks they're *really* real, right?" I ask, pulling back the blankets. "And Sister Mary Celeste does, too."

"Well, yes, they probably do. But you know, honey, nobody really knows the truth about this, uh, stuff. Like your mother, for example. She would say that one hundred percent of the things you hear in church are one hundred percent real life. So that's all of it, uh . . . the life of Christ, the saints, God, heaven, communion—all of it. And that's a perfectly fine thing to believe, okay? You can decide to believe that if you want to, just like your ma."

"But Mama believes in angels and ghosts, too."

Uncle Donny makes a face. "Ghosts? Really?"

I think about Mama setting out a cupcake for Theo on his birthday every year. I nod my head yes.

"Ah—okay. Well, some people believe in ghosts. Now I personally do not think that ghosts are real life. But some people do."

"What about demons?"

"No," says Uncle Donny, and his voice is tight. "No, I don't believe that demons are real."

"But Mama saw them," I say. "When they came out of the TV and the computer."

Uncle Donny rubs his forehead. He does that a lot, I've noticed.

"Well, this is something we could talk about with your ma when she gets home, but, uh, well, sometimes it's hard to know where the lines are, because she—you know, like you said, she gets confused sometimes. I know that your ma *believes* that the things she sees are real, so she's . . . telling the truth about . . . that. Ah Christ, Aoife, I don't know what's real or not, okay? Nobody *really* knows. Not me, not Father Paul, nobody. So for me, if you're asking me what I believe—none of it is real. I don't think there's a . . . a giant old white guy in the sky who watches and judges us, and tells us that some things are right and some things are arbitrarily wrong. And I don't believe in spirits or saints or demons or ghosts. But that's just me, okay?"

"But what about prayers?" I say, because he didn't say before. "You mean you can pray as hard as you want for something, and it still won't come true?"

"Well, honey, I think—I think that when you pray, it's a good thing to do, okay? Like, I think that it can make you feel better, and that's good, and I think . . . I think asking the, uh, universe for what you want is . . . uh, it's worthwhile to do, even if you're sort of only praying to . . . yourself, I guess. Okay?"

I don't say okay, because I don't want to go to hell, but I let him kiss my head and tuck me in and say goodnight.

"In the morning, we're going to go talk to Dr. Pearlman again," says Uncle Donny. "These are the kinds of things I want you to talk to her about, okay?"

I'm not so sure that sounds okay.

"I've put a special lock on the door, so don't worry about walking anywhere tonight," says Uncle Donny, before he heads out into the hallway. He still doesn't know he's the one who unlocked the door last time.

The moon is right outside my window, which is wide open. It looks *huge*, like it's about to come into my bedroom and land on the floor. I remember the sign of the saints. But Uncle Donny says the saints aren't real.

So I climb out of bed to close the curtains.

Dear Aoife,

When you and Theo were born, I told myself that I was going to give you a better life than your uncle and I had growing up. You were never going to be hungry or frightened. You were never going to huddle together in a corner and listen to the sounds of bones breaking. That wasn't going to happen to my children, no. They were going to grow up strong and healthy and secure, like kids on television.

But the truth is, I couldn't give that to you even though I tried. There have been lots of times when we have been hungry, you and me both, and you stopped asking for a snack because you knew there wasn't going to be any. And in that car on the way to the mall I made you fear for your life, which my father did to me and I swore I would never do. I made a lot of mistakes. And I'm more sorry than you'll ever know.

Last night I sat on a hillside with ten crazy people and watched something as beautiful and terrifying as any of us could have imagined. We were too far away to hear any music, and the attendants were definitely not sure this was a good idea. But we were laughing and screaming, and some people clapped, and some cried, and it looked like the end of the world, the city burning under a riot of color and sound, like a war zone, like the End of Days. And we all sang together, "The Stars and Stripes Forever," those silly words Ma used to sing. Until we couldn't see a thing except the reflections behind our eyeballs.

My whole life I guess I've struggled, and sometimes it seems easier to go out like a firework, all in a pop. There are times I'm sure you would be better off without me, times when it seems like I'm only going to hold you back. There are a million ways that I could make an exit before I screw up both our lives even more. I think I must have considered every one of them, more this week than any other.

But today we cheered and blessed America and drummed along on our knees to imaginary music. And my heart was a Saint Catherine's wheel after all, but not the way I used to think, not torturing my poor body on the rack, but spinning and shouting in glory.

Hold on, baby.

If you can keep trying, I swear I will too.

Chapter Thirteen

Uncle Donny is trying to get us out the door. He wants us to go see Dr. Pearlman *first thing*.

I did not sleep so good, and now I'm tired. "Do we have to go?" I ask. I'd much rather never leave the house again.

"I think it's important," says Uncle Donny. "Come on, I'll make you breakfast and you can eat in the car."

It's oatmeal again. Uncle Donny tells me to finish my milk and brushes my hair. He does a good job this time, and uses fewer clips.

"All right, are you ready to jet?" asks Uncle Donny. He sounds like he's trying to sound happy even though he doesn't really mean it. Mama does that sometimes, too, but I'm not fooled anymore.

"I want to stay here," I say.

"Ah, no, Aoife, we need to go." Uncle Donny doesn't even give me the chance to disagree.

As we pull away, I see Hannah come out of her house and stand on the front porch, but I don't wave and she doesn't either. She called Mama crazy and she said I was crazy, too, and we're not friends anymore.

"Are you ready to see Dr. Pearlman again?" asks Uncle Donny. "You remember her from the hospital, right? You liked her."

I'm not sure that's true—I mostly just liked the play dough— but I don't bother to say that.

"Now I want you to feel comfortable talking about anything, okay? This is your chance to really get stuff off your chest."

I don't have anything on my chest. I put my head on my arms and look out the window.

"Tough crowd," says Uncle Donny.

I remember Mama and me in the car singing Princess Jasmine and how Mama always sings the harmony parts because she knows they don't stick in my head. Uncle Donny does not play any music.

We pull into a parking lot. I thought we were going to go back to the hospital where Dr. Pearlman works, but instead we are in front of a brick building that looks like someone's house. But outside there's a sign, so I know it's a store.

"Whelp, end of the line," says Uncle Donny. I don't say anything, because I don't feel like talking. Maybe I'll never talk again, and my throat will close up. That sounds okay.

We get out. Uncle Donny puts his big hand on my shoulder as we walk in. Inside there's a big wooden desk with a pretty red-haired lady sitting behind it.

"Hi," says Uncle Donny. "Uh, Scott? The first name is— well, it's spelled A-O-I-F-E."

"*EE-fah*," I say.

"Oh, yes! You have an appointment for ten o'clock. Dr. Pearlman is just running a few minutes behind, if you don't mind taking a seat. There's coffee in the corner and juice for your daughter."

"He's not my dad," I say.

The girl looks at us. "Ah, sorry, I wasn't thinking," she says
to Uncle Donny, not to me.

"Of course, no problem. C'mon, kiddo," says Uncle Donny,
putting his hand back on my shoulder and pushing me towards
the juice.

"Look, there's lots of books for you," he says, pointing to a
low table that's just for kids. There are lots of books in bright
colors, but they just remind me of the books in Mr. Rutledge's
house, with Ned Slater's name in them. That's as far as I've gotten solving the mystery, and I don't even know what it means.
So I don't want to read any books today.

"Can I have juice?" I say instead, but I don't say *please* like
you're supposed to.

Uncle Donny squeezes my shoulder and then lets go. "Sure
thing," he says, and he goes over to pour some for me.

I pick up a book with a bear on the front and open it to the
middle, where the baby bear has gotten lost and is trying to find
his den in the woods. If Uncle Donny is right, and the saints
aren't real, then Ned Slater doesn't matter to bringing Mama
home anyway. It doesn't matter why Mr. Rutledge has all his
things in the room with the rocket-ship bed.

"Uh, Miss Scott?" calls the pretty lady. "Dr. Pearlman is
ready for you. Right through there."

Uncle Donny brings the juice and leads the way down a
hallway with ugly carpeting. I put the book under my arm
and bring it with us. Nobody tells me I can't. Dr. Pearlman
comes to the door and waves to me. She's still wearing big
round earrings, just like the last time I saw her, but no necklace this time. She still looks like a bird. Maybe those earrings
are her eggs.

"Dr. Pearlman, hi, good to see you again," says Uncle Donny,
holding the cup out to me so he can shake her hand. But I don't

take it, and he frowns at me and carries it into the office and puts in on the desk.

"Hello, sweetheart," says Dr. Pearlman. "Do you remember me from the hospital?"

I don't like to think about the hospital, because it reminds me that Mama is still gone. "Uh-huh."

"I've heard you had an exciting couple of days since then," says Dr. Pearlman.

"I guess."

"And you had a pretty big adventure all by yourself?"

I nod yes.

"I'd like to talk to you about that for a little bit, if that would be okay with you. Would you like your uncle Donny to stay? Or it can be just us girls if you'd rather."

"Yeah, I don't mind either way, Aoife," says Uncle Donny.

"Uncle Donny can stay," I say. "I don't care."

The back of the bear book does not have any names in it. It is not like the books in Mr. Rutledge's house.

"Okay." Dr. Pearlman takes a notepad out of her drawer and sets it on the desk in front of her. "So, Eva, your uncle Donny says you've been having some trouble lately. I'd like to ask you a few questions to see if we can help you feel better."

My trouble is that I still need to figure out how to bring Mama home, and I don't know how. Especially if Uncle Donny is right about the saints.

"Eva, how do you feel when you think about the day when your mommy went to the hospital?"

"I don't like to think about it," I say, which is true.

"Okay. That makes sense. I bet it was pretty scary, huh? Maybe it makes you feel sad?"

I guess. I don't want to remember. If you don't think about things, sometimes they go away.

"Sometimes when things are scary or sad, people can feel like it's hard to concentrate afterwards, or they keep feeling sad or scared after it's over. They can even have trouble sleeping. That's okay that's a normal way to feel."

I don't know what to say, so I just keep nodding. I want to go home. "Okay," I say. I miss Teddy. He would be doing something fun to make me laugh.

"You know, nobody here would be mad at you if you said you were still feeling sad or scared."

"I'm not," I say. "I just want Mama to come back."

Dr. Pearlman makes a sad face. "I know you do, sweetheart. You know, I hear you've had some other big changes lately, too. You had a conversation with a friend of your mom's, Mac?"

Does she mean the trip to the zoo? That feels like a long time ago, but I nod anyway. Who cares about that?

"And I understand Mac told you something important?"

I wonder if Dr. Pearlman is talking about the dad part of it, which is not really very important compared to trying to figure out if he might have killed Theo. But I don't think she knows about me investigating the case, and I don't want to tell her. "He told me he's my father," I guess.

Dr. Pearlman is nodding, so I know I guessed right. "Wow!" she says, even though she must have already known what he said. I think her and Uncle Donny have been talking. "That is big news. And how did you feel when he said that?"

I can't actually remember. "No special way, I guess," I say.

"No? How do you feel about it now?"

I don't want to say *I don't care*, because that sounds mean. "Happy?" I ask. "Although . . ." I shouldn't keep talking. I don't want to talk about any of this.

"Although what?" asks Dr. Pearlman.

I look at her kind eyes. "I don't really understand why Mama lied," I say. "Mama said she found me in a cabbage patch. Mama *always* says that."

"Aoife, maybe that's something you should talk about with your ma when she gets home, because I know she would want to discuss that with you herself," says Uncle Donny.

"It's all right," Dr. Pearlman tells him. "Eva, sometimes grown-ups say things, and they don't mean they're literally true. Do you know what *literally* means?"

I shake my head no.

"For example, when someone says, 'I'm so hungry, I could eat an elephant.' Now, they don't mean they would actually *eat* an *elephant*, do they? They just mean they feel as if they could, in their imagination. So sometimes when adults say things, they may be explaining how something feels, but not how it really truly happened."

"That's stupid," I say.

"Aoife, be polite," says Uncle Donny.

"Sorry." I'm not really sorry.

"It's okay to be upset, Eva," says Dr. Pearlman.

"It's *EE-fah*," I say. "*Fah, fah*, with an *f*."

"I'm sorry," says Uncle Donny. "It's been a really long week."

"That's okay, that's fine. Thank you for telling me, Aoife. Am I saying it right now?"

She is, pretty much. But I'm still mad. I nod, but I don't look at Dr. Pearlman. I look at the book in my lap. The pages are curling.

"She was asking—in the car on the way home—if her ma was, you know, gone away *like Theo*," Uncle Donny butted in.

That was *private*, I think. If I had wanted to ask Dr. Pearlman about Theo, I would have asked her! "No I didn't," I say.

"She did," says Uncle Donny.

Dr. Pearlman sighs. "Sweetheart, I know it's scary that your mommy had to go away. But just like I told you at the hospital, my friends there are going to do everything they can to help her so she can be less confused. I know it's hard to understand, but what you really need to remember is that your mommy loves you very, very much and she wants to get better so she can come home and be with you. Okay?"

But I'm pretty sure Mama won't come home until *I'm* not confused anymore.

Dr. Pearlman seems sad. The corners of her eyes are turned down. "Do you remember your brother well?" she asks.

"No."

"But you remember that one day he went away," she says.

"I think she would have been too young to remember," says Uncle Donny, but I am already nodding. I remember Mama crying, and explaining that Theo was gone away to a place where he couldn't come back.

It was a sad day.

"I do remember," I say. I remember that night we went to church and said a special prayer for Theo's soul. Mama lit two candles because one wasn't enough.

"She was only four," Uncle Donny says.

"Actually, studies suggest that children Aoife's age can retain very early memories, even though most adults don't clearly remember much before eight years of age."

And I do remember some things.

I run my thumb along the edge of the bear book,

"And by the way, how's Teddy doing?" asks Dr. Pearlman, smiling.

But I don't want to talk about Teddy, ever again. Teddy went away when I needed him, and he still hasn't come back. "Teddy's just made-up," I say.

If grown-ups can lie, then I can, too.

I can feel Dr. Pearlman and Uncle Donny looking at each other, and I hate it.

"I'm really sorry if I made you feel like it's not okay to talk about Teddy, kiddo," says Uncle Donny finally. "You can talk about him if you want to."

"I don't want to talk about him. He's just pretend. I made him up because I wanted a special friend," I say.

"Sweetheart, however you're feeling right now is okay," says Dr. Pearlman. "Nobody is going to get angry with you or try to tell you that you're wrong. I promise."

But Dr. Pearlman already said that sometimes when adults say things, they don't really mean them. That's why Mama said I was born in a cabbage patch, and why she said she would be home *soon*, even though neither of those things were true. So maybe Dr. Pearlman isn't telling the truth either—maybe she's just saying how she *feels*.

"I guess that brings us to two nights ago. Can you tell me what happened that night?" asks Dr. Pearlman.

I have to think fast.

"I was having a dream about . . . cats," I say. "I was following a cat, and we walked around the neighborhood. But then I woke up by the church and I was scared."

"Sleepwalking runs in the family," says Uncle Donny, rubbing his forehead.

"Sometimes a change of routine can be a trigger, particularly if a child isn't getting enough sleep. Are you having trouble sleeping?"

"Sometimes," I say. Mostly because Uncle Donny wakes me up.

"I know it can be scary to wake up and not know where you are. But there are techniques your family can use to make sure you don't accidentally leave the house again, okay? I'm going to work with you all to make sure you stay safe. I don't want you to worry about that happening a second time."

I'm not really all that worried, but I say okay anyway.

Dr. Pearlman is talking to Uncle Donny, but I'm not listening anymore. I am thinking about what she said, that sometimes grown-ups only say what they feel like. That is not real. What you feel like is only a lie.

The only things that are real are what you can see and hear. I am real. Uncle Donny is real. Teddy is real.

Maybe when Uncle Donny said the saints aren't real, he meant they're not *literally* real life. They are just explaining how something feels. But I remember standing at the base of Mr. Rutledge's stairs, afraid to run. I remember the saints cheering me on, and then I could be brave. And they told me how to bring Mama home. If I don't believe in them, then how am I supposed to see her again?

I saw them myself. And I heard them in the church and I saw them at the Secret Place. And they took me to Mr. Rutledge's house, but I still don't understand why.

"Aoife, honey, do you understand?" says Dr. Pearlman.

"Yes," I say.

And Ned Slater was real, too. I saw a picture of him. I held his book. I slept in his bed.

Dr. Pearlman talks more, and I look down at my hands. I have a splinter under my thumb because of Mr. Rutledge's firework that he threw at me. And the bottom of my feet still hurt in my shoes.

There is only one person I could ask about Ned Slater, but I am afraid.

"So Aoife, do you think you can be patient a little longer?" asks Uncle Donny.

No, I can't be patient. Mama is counting on me. And that is not just how I feel, but it is literally true.

But I still say "Yes," because I can lie, too.

* * *

So that evening after dinner, when Uncle Donny is inside doing math problems and I'm supposed to be drawing on the steps with chalk, I walk out to the end of the street.

The kitty from next door is sitting in the lawn, watching me. The sight of her makes me think about Teddy. I don't know if I'm ever going to watch him catch fireflies again.

It's quiet out here.

Kitty and I walk together to the corner where I'm not supposed to go to.

"Do you think he'll come?" I ask the kitty. She flicks her tail at me. I don't know if that means yes or no.

I'm waiting long enough that I think Uncle Donny is going to realize I left the steps. But then I can hear the jingling of a small dog on a long leash. It makes me shudder, because the last time I heard that sound I almost got caught in the garage. But I know how to be brave now. I don't run away. I wait.

Mr. Rutledge comes around the corner with Roo. When he sees me, he crosses to the other side of the street. He doesn't look over again, just keeps walking.

I remember how angry he sounded when he was yelling, *You piece of shit*. I remember how he threw that firework in the garage, and it knocked splinters out of the door.

But I have to do it. For Mama.

I cross the street to catch up to him and take a deep breath. "Excuse me," I say. My voice comes out soft, and he doesn't hear me. I clear my throat. "Excuse me, Mr. Rutledge."

Mr. Rutledge ignores me. He keeps walking, and Roo pulls on the end of his leash to come and sniff at my shoes. I can't feel a thing below my knees.

"Hello, Mr. Rutledge, I'm Aoife Scott, and I'm sorry but I really need to talk to you." I can't even believe I got that out all the way.

He sniffs but keeps walking, so I walk next to him.

"I need to ask you—"

"What you need to do, little girl, is go home and not bother me."

He must still be mad about the other day. "I'm really sorry I broke into your house," I say, because it's good to apologize if somebody is mad at you, especially if you need to ask them something.

"What?" Mr. Rutledge stops walking. "What the hell are you talking about?"

"The other day," I say. "When I broke into your house. I'm very sorry. So can I ask you a question now?" Because I need to ask about Ned Slater.

"I don't know why you think this is a funny game, but it's not, and you shouldn't talk about things you don't understand."

"It's true," I say. And then I think of a way I can prove it. "I bet you found a silver cigarette lighter on the basement stairs. With letters on it."

He snorts.

"But . . . doesn't that prove it?"

"Someone has been telling you stories. Believe me, between me and the police, we searched every room. There was no lighter in that house. And I know for damn sure that it wasn't a kindergartner I was shooting at—it was a bunch of thugs that broke in. Now, don't you know it's very rude to bother a grown-up who doesn't want to deal with you?" He pulls on Roo's leash, not looking at me.

But . . . I know Teddy left that lighter there, because I don't have it now. I don't know why he didn't find it.

I need Mr. Rutledge to help even if he doesn't believe me. "Please, I just need to ask you one thing, because I'm trying to find out what happened to my brother."

"Your brother?" says Mr. Rutledge. I don't like how he sounds, so tight and hard.

"Yes, see, my brother Theo was murdered, a long, long time ago, and if I figure out who killed him, my mama can stop being so confused and come home from the hospital."

When he speaks, Mr. Rutledge's voice is ice cold like a snow cone, pointy like a stick, ready to stab me. "What the hell is the matter with you? Are you stupid?"

"I don't . . . think so?"

He pulls the leash, hard. "Then you're crazy," he says. "Your brother ain't dead."

"Wha—what?" I don't know why he's saying such a stupid thing, but I hate it. I want to hit the words out of his mouth.

"Maybe you just better go ask him," he says, turning his back on me and walking away. "You go ask him why your mother is confused." Then he jerks Roo back so that his front feet come off the ground, and they walk away fast.

But I'm too stunned to follow him.

He could just be lying. Grown-ups lie all the time, and I don't have to believe them anymore.

He must be lying.

Right?

* * *

I walk home by myself. Uncle Donny is just finishing the dishes. He never even noticed that I left the sidewalk.

Ask your brother, said Mr. Rutledge. Maybe he meant like— like in a prayer. A séance.

I creep up the stairs with my feet on the outside of each step, right next to the railing, where it won't make a creak, which is better than how Uncle Donny does it. I stop when I'm at the top step, right next to the last picture of Theo.

He's looking right at the camera, just like Ned Slater was in the picture hanging in Mr. Rutledge's house.

"Hey, Aoife," says Uncle Donny. "Whatcha lookin' at?" He came upstairs when I wasn't looking. It's funny that he's a lot louder at night than he is during the day.

"This picture of Theo," I say, which is true.

"I can see that," says Uncle Donny. "What are you thinking about?"

If Mr. Rutledge *were* telling the truth, then somewhere out in the world, Theo would have kept getting older. This wasn't the last picture ever taken, just the last one we have hanging up. I look into my brother's face and try to imagine him as a real person.

I take a deep breath. "Uncle Donny . . . Theo is . . . Theo's dead, right?"

Somehow the question comes out sounding normal. It's like I didn't even say it, like I'm listening to someone else talk with my voice.

"What?"

"He's dead. He died. Didn't he?"

Uncle Donny kneels down in front of me and puts his hand on my shoulders. It's funny, because I'm on the top step and he's on the landing, so he has to kneel really low to reach.

"Aoife," he says. "Did someone tell you that Theo is dead?"

I think back, I really do, because I'm sure someone said it at one time. "Mama said that Theo . . . had to go away," I say, and I'm afraid that I might start to cry now, but I don't want to stop talking. "And everyone says that I shouldn't ask questions because it will upset Mama, but Mama said Theo was gone to a faraway place, and I thought—I thought it was like Gramma Aoife?"

"Oh, baby," says Uncle Donny, and he pulls me into a tight hug. He puts his chin on top of my head, and it feels heavy but also good.

"Nobody ever talks about Theo," I say, blinking back my tears, "except Mama, but . . . Mama gets confused sometimes. But then Mr.—somebody told me that—that Theo isn't dead. Is Theo not dead?"

"I'm so sorry, honey," says Uncle Donny. He keeps rock-rocking me, and I think he's not going to tell me anything, just like nobody ever tells me anything. But then he starts talking again. "What happened with Theo is—well, it's something that's very hard for even grown-ups to understand, and I think that nobody knew exactly how to explain it to you. But that was our fault, even though it was really confusing; we should have tried to find a way that would have made sense to you."

"Is he . . . not dead?"

"No, baby. He's not dead."

Mr. Rutledge wasn't lying. It doesn't make any sense—it's like saying that Sleeping Beauty is real, and I could poke her with my finger and see her asleep in the bed. I know that some things are real and some are just made-up. But I can't believe Theo is alive.

"Listen, I know this must all feel really strange right now, but as soon as your ma comes home, we're all going to talk about it together, okay? And it will make a lot more sense."

But Mr. Rutledge said to ask my brother why Mama is confused. "I want to talk about it now," I say.

"Ah. Well, you see, your ma is the best one to explain this to you, and I really shouldn't—I mean, I'm just an uncle, you know? I don't want Siobhan to come home and find that I've, ah, said all the wrong things, and, uh, made things worse."

I don't see how anything can be worse than me thinking my brother is dead. "Please?" I say. "It's really important."

"Uh, well, you see, your—he—Theo has some special problems; he has an illness that makes him—it makes it hard for him to think right sometimes. And he's living somewhere where they can help him with those problems, okay? A special place just for people like him."

But if Theo isn't dead . . . when Mama said she was *visiting* Theo, I always thought she meant like the time we visited Gramma Aoife in the grassy field. But I guess she really was *visiting* Theo. She meant she was literally going to go see him, in real live person. And that means . . . that means I could do that too. Just like Mr. Rutledge said, I could go see him for real, and talk to him and get answers. I could find out the truth, and then if Mama is confused, I can explain it to her.

"I want to go visit Theo," I say.

"Oooh. Yeah, see, that's going to be a little bit of a problem," says Uncle Donny, pulling back. He sits on the landing with his legs crossed, and I climb up the last step to sit next to him, looking up.

"But I want to," I say. "I want to go see if Theo is real and talk to him."

Uncle Donny lets out his breath in a burst.

"Why haven't I been able to see him all this time? Hasn't he asked about me?"

"Listen, Aoife. These are good questions you're asking about Theo. I'm glad you're asking them. But sometimes there are just—things you can't really understand until you're older, and this is one of these things. I promise, someday you're going to get all the answers about your brother. But right now you may need to be a little patient, okay?"

But this is the final piece of the mystery, and this is my chance to solve it.

"Aoife, we've talked about a lot of things," says Uncle Donny. "And I'm sorry that we didn't understand what you were thinking about Theo or how you were feeling. I think we should just have a nice quiet day and we can talk about this again later, all right?"

"I want to go visit Theo," I say.

Uncle Donny sighs. "Remember what I said about your ma? I don't want us to do anything too hasty while your ma isn't home, so we should wait."

"I have to go now," I say. "Today. I want to talk to him right away."

"We couldn't do that even if we wanted to, baby. Theo's doctors have to give us permission before we can talk to Theo," says Uncle Donny.

"Can we ask them, please?"

"Honey." Uncle Donny kneels down again and looks into my eyes. "I know you want to see your brother after all this time. But we're just going to have to wait, okay? I know it's hard. Why don't we go watch a movie downstairs, okay? Just the two of us."

I know Uncle Donny isn't going to change his mind. He's just like Mama, and once he makes a decision, that's it. So I don't try to argue with him. But I can be like Mama too, and I've made a decision as well. I'm going to talk to Theo no matter what anybody says, because that's the only way to bring Mama home. This is the secret that Teddy was trying to tell me. I just know it.

"I don't feel like watching a movie," I say. "Can I play outside?"

"You want to go next door and play with Hannah?"

"No. Hannah is mean," I say. "We're not friends anymore."

"Aha. Well, I don't want you to leave the yard if you play outside. I'm going to be watching you from the kitchen, okay? I have eyes in the back of my head."

Now that Dr. Pearlman pointed it out, grown-ups really do lie all the time.

Chapter Fourteen

≈

I don't have good Barbies like Hannah does, but I have two of them at least. Uncle Donny watches me from the hallway as I go into my room and pull the box out from under my bed. The Barbies aren't wearing any clothes and their hair is tangled, and most of their accessories are missing. Father Paul gave me one of them from the box at church for behaving well in day school. She came dressed as a schoolteacher, but I lost her shoes.

Uncle Donny goes downstairs, and the minute I hear him leave I tiptoe into Mama's room. Just like before, I get the feeling that the room is waiting for Mama to come back, just like I am. But this time, I'm not looking for the rosary or *The Illustrated Volume of the Saints*. Instead I go to the side table where Mama's phone is plugged in and charging. I take it, tiptoe back to the Barbies, and hide it underneath all the clothes. Then I carry the whole bin downstairs.

Uncle Donny has cut up an apple and put out a jar of peanut butter for a snack, but I'm not hungry.

"You didn't eat any dinner," says Uncle Donny. "Please eat at least a few slices."

So I do, but they don't taste like anything. I swallow them anyway and then ask again if I can go outside.

Uncle Donny seems sad, but he says okay. "Just until it gets dark. And remember, you have to stay in the yard," he says.

"I will," I say.

I take the box of Barbies and I sit on the back porch. Uncle Donny will be able to see me from the kitchen window but only if he's standing at the sink, and I know he won't stand at the sink the whole time.

I take out both Barbies and put them on the sidewalk. Hannah likes to pretend that Barbies are real people and give them names and make up stories about them. But to me Barbies were never as much fun as Teddy.

I don't really play with them, I just lay out their clothes on the step with a space for each of the missing pieces, and then I brush Teacher Barbie's hair.

I hear a little *mrow*, and the cat from next door is rolling around on the hot cement in front of me. "Hello, kitty," I say.

The cat looks like it's trying to scratch an itch between its shoulders with the crack in the pavement. Then it rolls over onto its front and comes to rub its face on the side of the Barbie bin until I pet its head. I'm glad we're friends now.

"Kitty, I have to do something naughty," I tell it. She starts to purr and flops down so I can stroke the fur along her back.

I look up and make sure Uncle Donny isn't watching anymore. I can hear him whistling and I know he's probably cleaning the kitchen, which is what he does when he's upset. I know he would be angry with me if he knew what I was doing, but the most important thing is that I keep trying. That's what I promised I would do.

I turn my back to the window and take the phone out of the box. I know how to open Mama's phone: *1113*. Me plus Mama plus Theo equals three. The phone comes to life and I open the contacts, scrolling through the list. I already know who to call. There's only one person left.

The phone rings. Then it cuts off, and a gruff voice says, "Hello?"

I don't say anything at first because I'm scared.

"Siobhan? That you, baby?"

"It's me. Aoife."

"Alfie? What are you calling me for on your mom's phone?"

"I need your help, Mac," I whisper. If I'm loud, Uncle Donny will wonder who I'm talking to, and I don't want him to come out and stop me.

"What the hell are you talking about, kid? Is everything okay?"

"I need to go see Theo, and Uncle Donny won't let me."

"Ah, jeez."

Mac must have put the phone down or something, because I hear it clunk and clatter on the other end, and for a minute I think he's going to hang up on me. But then I hear him breathing and I know he's still there.

"You said you were my dad," I say, feeling brave just saying those words out loud. "If you're really my dad, then you'll help me, right? That's what dads do. Isn't it?"

"I've been your father for less than a week; can't you give me a freaking break?" Mac grumbles.

I don't think that's how it works, but I don't say anything.

"Does your uncle say why he won't take you?" he asks at last.

"He says we should wait until Mama comes home and we can talk about it then. But I need to talk to Theo *now*, right away. Today."

"Your uncle's right," says Mac. "It makes more sense to wait until Siobhan gets back."

"But that isn't going to be today or tomorrow or soon," I say. Not unless I figure out the last secret. That's what I can't tell

Mac, because he won't understand. I forgot to keep my voice down for a second, and I look over my shoulder in case Uncle Donny heard me, but I don't see him at the window, so it doesn't seem like he did.

Mac sighs. "Yeah, probably not."

"But if you're my father and Uncle Donny's just my uncle, then you get to decide what I can do, not him, right? That's how it works, right?"

"When did you get so smart?" says Mac.

"Isn't it?"

"Well—yeah. Yeah, kiddo, that's how it works."

"So you'll help me?"

Mac sighs. "I guess if this is the first favor you've ever asked me for, I can't really say no, can I? It's not like I've got a college fund for you or I'll buy you a car or anything."

Lucky for me, I don't want a car or a college fund. I just want to talk to Theo.

"All right, tell you what. I'll give your uncle a call and see what I can do. And if I don't like what I hear, well, I've got a few cards up my sleeve that I could probably play. No promises though, okay? And it won't be today, so get that idea out of your head."

"Thank you, Mac!" I say. Right after I say it, I wonder if I should have called him *Dad*, but the word sounds too funny in my mind. He's just Mac, that's all. I hope he doesn't mind.

"Yeah, yeah, now get off the phone. I've got stuff to do today, you know."

"Goodbye," I say. As soon as Mac calls him, Uncle Donny is going to know that I went behind his back, but I don't care.

"See ya, Alfie."

The phone beeps and goes silent. I hide it back under the Barbie clothes and stand up, brushing off my shorts to go inside.

I hear the pop of a screen door closing, and I turn around to see Hannah coming out of her house. Hannah and I are mad at each other, so I don't say anything. I just look down at the doll box and pick it up without watching her walk across the yard, but I know that's what she's doing because I can hear her shoes on the grass. Plus, the neighbor kitty gets up and slinks away when she gets close.

"Hey, Aoife," she says, just as I'm turning around to go back inside.

"Hey," I say, still looking down.

"Everybody's talking about you. I heard that you ran away in the middle of the night."

Mama always says that Father Paul's secretary does not know how to keep a secret. I guess she's right.

I know Hannah would want to hear all about Theo and Ned Slater, and what Uncle Donny told me. In fact, I'm pretty sure Hannah would enjoy the whole mystery way more than I do. But right now, it feels like it should be just for our family. I think I understand now why nobody wanted to talk about Theo—nobody knows what to say.

So I don't tell Hannah anything, at least, not for now. I keep it a secret, buried like a Saint Benedict medal.

"I have to go inside," I say.

"I'm glad you're all right," Hannah says.

That makes me feel good. It's not really making me happy to stay mad at her anyway. I walk back over. "Hannah, I broke the apple candle," I say. "Teddy stole it, and it got broken. Do you think your mom is going to be mad at me?"

"Nobody cares about the apple candle, Aoife," she says, seriously. "You could have gotten hit by a car, or an evil serial killer could have found you and murdered you! And the last thing I would have done was call your family crazy! You don't know how freaked out everybody has been, just thinking about it."

"It's all right," I say, looking down. The truth is, I think my family actually is crazy. Even Uncle Donny walks in his sleep, and is a *fruit* according to Mac. Mama is locked in a hospital, and so's Theo. And my best friend might have been a ghost.

I hear the phone ring inside my house. I know I'm going to get into big trouble soon.

"I'm glad you're all right," says Hannah. She puts her arms around me and gives me a hug. Usually we don't hug, but right now it feels okay.

"Are you still mad at me?" she asks.

"No. You're my best friend," I tell her. And now that Teddy's gone, it's true. "I could never be mad at you."

I can hear Uncle Donny raising his voice. The sound of shouting is my least-favorite sound.

"You're my best friend, too," says Hannah. "Forever and ever. Okay? Pinkie swear."

She puts her pinkie in mine, and we squeeze them together and swear.

"Aoife!" yells Uncle Donny from the kitchen. "Can you come in here, please? I need to talk to you. Right now."

I pick up the box of Barbies and wave goodbye to Hannah. I'm glad she's my friend again, even though I'll probably never be allowed to play with her after Uncle Donny finds out what I've done.

Uncle Donny is still on the phone when I come inside. He's holding it against his shoulder and frowning at me. "Aoife, did you call Mac?" he says.

"Yes," I say.

"I wish you hadn't done that. I told you that you need to be patient and wait until your ma is home before we talk more about Theo."

"I know," I say. I'm not sorry, so I don't say that I am. "But Mac says he's my father, so he can say different if he wants to, right?"

I can hear a grumbly voice that must be Mac answering back, but I can't hear what he's saying. Uncle Donny frowns harder. "I'm going to put the phone on speaker," he says, "so stop swearing." He pushes a button on the handset and holds the phone up.

"Mac?" I say.

"Yeah, kiddo. I hear you."

"Did you ask him? Did you tell him I get to go see Theo now?"

"Aoife, this isn't up to Mac, it's up to your mother," says Uncle Donny, cutting off whatever Mac was going to say. "And since your mother is unavailable right now, that means it's up to me. And I'm saying no."

"Maybe it ain't up to you," says Mac.

"Look, she's too young to understand this," says Uncle Donny. "She's only six years old, for Chrissake. We should wait a little longer."

"I can understand!" I say. "I want to know."

"It will be fine," says Mac. "I told Siobhan from the start, children are tough. You're tough, right, Alfie?"

"Yeah!" I say, nodding.

"But how are you supposed to *explain* something like this?" Uncle Donny says. He sounds like he's getting upset again. "No, this is a terrible idea. We need to wait."

"Well, we could ask Siobhan," says Mac calmly. "Maybe she'll have a different answer."

"Yeah!" I say. "Uncle Donny, let's talk to Mama! And we can ask her together!"

"Thanks, Mac. Thanks a lot. Aoife, your ma has a lot on her plate right now, and I'm not going to add any stress to her life. This doesn't need to be dealt with right now, and we can wait."

"We should call her," I say. "We should call her right now."

"Aw, Don, don't be such a wet blanket," says Mac. "Siobhan can handle a little controversy. Take off the kid gloves, for Chrissake, and just ask her. That's what she would want you to do. What's the alternative? She gets out of the clinic and this all lands in her lap at once? We take care of it now and by the time she's home, things will be running smooth again."

Uncle Donny doesn't look convinced, but I know this is my best chance. "Please, please, please," I beg, pulling on his jacket. "Just ask her. I know she'll say yes if you tell her that—tell her that it's *very important* that I talk to Theo *right away*. Okay? Tell her that it's what I want for my next birthday present and all my Christmas presents, okay?"

"Maybe it's better to have her understand instead of guessing," says Mac. "It's only because we've done a shit job explaining so far that's she's confused."

"*Please, please, please, please!*"

"Ah, jeez," says Uncle Donny, rolling his eyes. "All right, I'm going on the record here saying that I think this is a bad idea. Aoife, we're going to be talking later about how you went about this. I'm disappointed in your behavior today."

That makes me feel a little bad, but I still want him to ask Mama. "Now, I'll talk to her. But you're not listening in this time, and if she says no, then she says no and that's it, no more arguing. You wait patiently and you *don't* bother her about this when she does come home. Okay?"

"Okay!" I say, with a big thumbs-up.

"I want to be in on this phone call, Don," says Mac.

"What? You?"

"Yeah, me. You know I'm pretty—intimately involved here, Donny."

I don't know what that word *in-tim-ate-ly* means or why Mac says he's involved. But I know he'll do a better job of convincing Mama than Uncle Donny, so I nod my head *yes, yes, yes*.

"Well, I guess this is all one big family affair," says Uncle Donny.

He doesn't sound happy at all, and I bite my lip but I'm still not sorry. I love Uncle Donny and Mac, but I love Mama more than anyone in the whole wide world. Maybe we missed the fireworks, but I still want to sit on her lap and listen to her stories, and I want to show her my cartwheels, and I want her to sing Princess Jasmine to me again.

"Goodbye, Mac, thanks so much for all your help," says Uncle Donny. I can tell he doesn't mean it.

"Goodbye, Mac, thank you!" I yell into the phone. "I'm glad you're my father after all!" Uncle Donny covers his ears and makes a face before he hangs up.

"Not even a week in and she's already playing the parents against each other. It must be instinct."

Sometimes Uncle Donny is only talking to himself, particularly when he grumbles.

"Aoife, go upstairs to your room," he says. "And I'll be checking both phones, so don't even think about getting on the other line, because I'll know."

I nod my head and pick up the box of Barbies again, and as I climb the stairs, I say a special prayer to Blessed Joan and Catherine and Michael and anybody else who might be listening. *Please, please help Mama understand.* I know sometimes the saints visit Mama, too, so maybe they can explain it to her better than I can.

I can hear Uncle Donny talking downstairs. He's probably calling the hospital right now. I sit on the floor of my room with a box of Legos, but I'm not trying to build anything. I'm just snapping a blue block to a bigger yellow block and then unsnapping it again. Then I put it back together. *Snick, snap. Snick, snap.*

Uncle Donny's voice sounds frustrated. I wonder how Mama sounds and if she's still confused, or if she's feeling better.

It's weird to think that Mama knew Theo was alive the whole time. That I'm the only one who thought he was dead.

I hear Uncle Donny walking across the floor in the living room. It sounds like he's standing at the base of the stairs when he says, "Okay. Okay, all right. Thanks, Siobhan. Feel better. We love you." Then I hear him press the button—*beep!*—and the phone hangs up.

I wait for him to come up the stairs, but he doesn't come up right away. I hold my breath, and for some reason I think he might be holding his breath, too.

I can't stand it anymore. "Uncle Donny?" I call. "What did Mama say?"

Finally I hear his footsteps on the stairs, the usual *creak, creak, creak.* I turn around when he gets to the doorframe and he's standing there watching me.

"Well, kiddo—" he says.

"She agreed, didn't she?"

"Your ma said if you want to go talk to your brother, I can take you there," says Uncle Donny. "I still think it would be better for us to wait until your ma comes home, and then we could all go together. Doesn't that sound good?"

"I want to talk to him *now*," I say.

"Are you sure you wouldn't rather talk on the phone first? We could call your brother if you want, if his doctors say that's okay."

But I don't want to talk on the phone. If my brother is really real, I want to see him so that I can know. A phone call isn't good enough. I shake my head without saying anything.

Uncle Donny rubs his face. "Are you sure? Because it might be scary. Your brother is still working on getting better, and he might still be . . . confused."

That does sound a little scary. "Can you and Mac come with me?" I ask.

"Mac isn't Theo's father, so he doesn't have permission to visit. But if you're sure you want to go, I'll be right there with you."

"Then I want to go."

"If you aren't sure, we don't have to go," says Uncle Donny.

"I want to go, even if it's scary," I say.

Uncle Donny sighs. "Brave girl," he says, but he doesn't sound happy about it.

"Can we go today?"

"Not today, but we can go tomorrow afternoon."

So that's it. One day, and I'll see my brother.

Chapter Fifteen

The next day, Uncle Donny and I get into his shiny car and we drive away. We go on the same highway that Mac took us on when we went to the zoo, but I know we're not going to the zoo this time. We drive on the freeway that cuts right through the city of Detroit, with high, light-gray cement walls on either side and tall buildings made of glass. We go past the brick downtown churches with their pointy tops. All the way past the factories, and still we keep driving even after that, out the other side and back into the kind of place our house is again.

"The suburbs just go on and on out here," says Uncle Donny, looking out the window. "How many strip malls does one state need? And how many fast-food joints? No wonder we have an obesity crisis."

Uncle Donny always complains when he's nervous. I'm nervous, too. I wish we could have brought the next-door cat, but she's not like Teddy so she can't come with us everywhere we go. That's why bears are better than cats. I miss Teddy, but I don't think he's coming back anymore. Maybe he lives with Mr. Rutledge now.

Finally the traffic thins out. We're in the country. *The boondocks*, Uncle Donny calls it. There are real cows in the fields, like in the picture books at school. It's sunny outside and looks friendly.

"Theo lives in a nice place," I say, looking out the window. We're passing a red barn with horsies in the field, which are rolling around in the dirt like the cat from next door.

"Sure, you could say that," says Uncle Donny. He doesn't really sound like he means it, but I think it looks nice. I like how the plants are all growing in straight lines, like the stripes on Uncle Donny's work suit. It looks a lot more tidy than Mama's garden, even back when she was weeding it.

I can't believe Mama has to drive all this way every other weekend. No wonder she's gone all day. It's funny to think how many times Stephanie and Hannah and I played in the park for hours and hours and I didn't even know that she was with my brother. She never said anything when she came back, except that usually she wanted to lie down afterwards and sometimes her eyes were red from crying.

That's the other reason I thought it was like when we visited Gramma Aoife, because it made Mama sad to stand in that field, and she cried, even though Gramma Aoife has gone to heaven to be with the angels. Now that Mama has been away, though, I understand why she was so sad not to be with her ma. I'm glad my mother is only in the hospital and not in heaven, even though it might be a sin to think that.

You know what is funny? She never, ever talked about how Theo was doing or delivered a message or anything. For years and years. I don't know why she did that. I don't like it.

We keep on driving. Uncle Donny doesn't put on the radio or anything. I look out the window and imagine music. It's funny to be in a place where there's no houses, and almost no cars on the road. There's no sidewalks and no people walking their dogs or their babies in strollers like at home. There's no shops and no fast-food restaurants. Nothing but fields until a truck rolls past us.

"Okay, getting close," says Uncle Donny. "There, off to your right—there it is."

I look where he's pointing, because I don't know left from right. At first I can't see it behind the trees, but then we get closer. There's a bunch of brown buildings, squatting low on the hillside behind a long fence.

"Is this where Theo lives?" I ask.

"This is where Theo is trying to get better, remember? Like a hospital."

It does look a little like that. The buildings are all the same, built out of the same kind of bricks. There's a big parking lot and lots of signs. We turn into the driveway. I'm too excited to be nervous.

"That says VISITORS' PARKING," I say, pointing to the sign we just passed.

"That's right," says Uncle Donny. "Because we're here visiting Theo." He pulls into a parking spot and stops the car.

"How are you feeling?" he asks.

"Okay," I say.

"You might not recognize Theo," he tells me. "That's okay. You haven't seen him since you were four years old, so that's normal. Whatever you feel is okay, all right? There's not really a right way to feel sometimes."

"Okay," I say. "Did Theo . . . did he do something bad?"

"What makes you ask that?"

I look out the window and shrug.

Uncle Donny rubs his face with his hand. It pulls his scratchy cheeks down and he looks old.

"Is he a bad guy?" I ask. It's going to be extra weird seeing my brother for the first time if he's also a bad guy. I hadn't really thought about that.

"No, he's not—he's not a bad guy," says Uncle Donny. "He's just a boy."

"I thought he was almost grown up," I say. "You said he was almost sixteen."

"That's still just a child," says Uncle Donny quietly. "But he—he had a lot of trouble, growing up. He lost his father very young, and things were tough sometimes at home. Theo was always a very—a very sensitive boy, and he has an illness, remember I told you? It makes it so that he . . . isn't always in control of his choices. Does that make sense?"

I don't know if it does or not.

"Listen, I understand that this is scary, sweetheart. I don't even know if Theo is going to want to talk today. I don't know if he's going to understand who we are. But I don't want you to be scared, okay? We're just here so you two can get to know each other a little. It's going to be a short visit, and I'm going to be right here with you the whole time."

"Okay," I say. So we get out of the car.

Uncle Donny locks the doors behind us, and he takes my hand. But neither of us starts walking towards the entrance. It's a regular-looking place, and it does look kind of like the hospital where I met Dr. Pearlman. But for some reason I don't want to go inside, and it doesn't seem like Uncle Donny does either.

"It's okay to be scared, baby," says Uncle Donny. "It's normal."

I'm not sure if I'm scared or not. It's more like, I know I'm about to learn something and then I'll never be able to not-know it again. When my brother Theo was dead, even though I didn't know what happened to him, I thought I knew what was going to happen next: he was going to keep on being dead. But now that I know he's alive, I'm not sure what's going to happen anymore.

"Uncle Donny, are you Theo's uncle, too?" I ask.

"Yep."

"But Mac is only my dad, and not Theo's dad, because Theo's dad is dead." I think I know who Theo's dad is.

"That's right."

And I'm his sister, the only one he has. And he's my only brother in the whole world.

Uncle Donny shakes himself off first and says, "Are you ready, Queen La-T-Aoife?" I nod my head even though I'm not sure. Maybe I wish we could get back in the car and drive home. But now that we're here, this is happening one way or another.

We hold hands and walk inside together.

It's not as bright inside as a hospital. There are signs posted on the door, with lots of writing, too much and too small for me to read. Uncle Donny doesn't let us stop to look at them. He has my hand in his and is pulling me along to the front desk, where a woman in a brown hat is sitting behind the table.

Uncle Donny gets us checked in at the desk. "You all here for Theodore?" says the brown-hat lady. "We've been missing Miz Scott."

"Ah, yes, something . . . came up unexpectedly," says Uncle Donny, combing through his hair with his hand.

"Happens to the best of us," says the woman. She looks over at me and Uncle Donny. "Brought the whole family this time, huh?"

Uncle Donny smiles tightly. "Sure did. Uh, we have permission, if you check the file . . ."

"Sure, no problem," says the brown-hat lady, looking down at me. "I'm going to call down and have them bring him into the visitors' room, so you-all can have the chance to talk. If you could just take a seat right there, I'll let you know when they're ready for you."

"Great," says Uncle Donny. He takes my hand and leads me to a corner where there are orange plastic chairs against the wall under the window. It looks sunny outside, and a big part of me wants to be out there and not in here.

There's a woman sitting in the far corner with her head down in her hands. I don't know if she's crying or asleep. She doesn't move. Uncle Donny pulls me towards chairs across the room, and both of us pretend not to notice her.

Even if Uncle Donny hadn't told me this place was a kind of hospital, I would have known. It smells like it's been cleaned extra hard, but it's still grubby.

I'm watching the brown-hat lady at the front desk. Sometimes she gets a call that takes her through the door behind her. There's a red light over the door, but when she presses a button on her desk, the light goes from red to green. When she walks through the door and closes it behind her, the light goes red again.

"Can Theo leave whenever he wants?" I ask.

Uncle Donny doesn't answer right away. I wait.

"Theo has to listen to his doctors," he says at last, "because they're trying to make him better. So if they say it's okay, then he could leave, but they haven't said it's okay yet. And they might not say it for a long time."

I think that means *no*. I realize where we are now. We're in Children's Prison. Just like Hannah said.

My whole life I've imagined Children's Prison, and now I'm right in the middle of it. I thought I would be afraid, but I can be brave. I am here with an army from France.

"Mr. Scott?" says the brown-hat lady. "I think they're ready for you."

As we stand up, everything turns gold—the hallway, the lady, me and Uncle Donny. I look down at my hands and they're shining, with light coming out from the ends of every fingertip.

"Mr. Scott, I have to be honest with you, I'm not sure it's such a good idea for her to come in," says the brown-hat lady.

"Ah. Is he having a—a bad day?" asks Uncle Donny.

She sucks her teeth and shakes her head. "Well, you know how he can get," she says. "But then, it'd be a shame for her to come all this way and not see her brother."

The whole room is gold, shining gold. "I want to go," I say, walking through the golden room.

"Aoife . . ." Uncle Donny says.

"I want to go," I say again. There are people singing very softly, I think. It's beautiful.

"All right. C'mere, squirt," says Uncle Donny. He picks me up and walks down the hallway behind the lady. She presses the button and the light turns color, and I know it must be green, but it looks gold because everything is gold.

Uncle Donny is saying something, but I can't hear him because of the music. It sounds a little like the organ at church and a little like standing right next to Mac's speakers when they're turned all the way up.

Behind the desk, the lady has three televisions. Uncle Donny carries me past before I can get a good look, but they're not showing anything good, just fuzzy pictures of people. We go through the door and I feel the ground shiver when it closes behind us, even though I can't hear it. In the room behind us, I know the light must be turning from green to red.

On the other side of the door, there's a hallway with tiles just like at the hospital. They're probably white, but all I can see is *gold, gold, gold*. The smell is stronger here. Another person in brown, a man this time, is sitting in a chair. As we walk I hear what sounds like trumpets, so loud that it makes me want to clap my hands over my ears, although I don't because I know it would make everybody ask questions. I can tell from their faces that nobody else hears the trumpets but me. They sound happy, like the school bell at the end of the day. They get louder and faster, and then with the last note the trumpets all stop at once, and I can hear Uncle Donny breathing again, and the whirring of what is probably the air conditioning, and the sound of a door closing far away. Only the beautiful soft singing carries on, quietly in the background. But everything is still bright gold, and me, Uncle Donny, and all the worker people are all glowing.

The man behind the counter has a bin in front of him. Uncle Donny takes his wallet and keys out of his pocket and puts them in.

"Step through," says the man. He's got a bunch of TVs in front of him, too.

Uncle Donny boosts me higher to walk through what looks like a turnstile at the zoo.

"Don't give Theodore anything," says the man. "Understand?"

"Got it," says Uncle Donny. He doesn't put me down, even though I'm a big girl and I can walk.

"Straight down this hallway, then go through the glass doors on your left."

We couldn't get lost because there's a gold stripe right down the hallway, getting lighter and lighter until it almost hurts my eyes to look at it.

"All right, Aoife," says Uncle Donny.

"Uncle Donny, can you put me down?" I ask.

"Sure, kiddo." Uncle Donny bends down low enough that my feet touch the ground, and when I'm standing again he holds his hand out for me to take. The floor is still glowing gold, like I'm standing on top of a cloud full of sunshine, but it feels normal under my feet.

He puts his hand on a door, and although he can't see it, the door lights up like Christmas lights, so bright I have to look away. I know the saints have led me here, and this is their way of showing me we're almost there. Unlike the other times I saw them, they don't give me any directions to follow. They're just cheering me on, I think.

"I see you," I whisper under my breath. Then, to Uncle Donny, I say, "Go ahead, open it."

So Uncle Donny pushes the glass door open and we go inside together.

As soon as we step inside, the colors are all normal again and even the quiet singing stops. I guess because we're here. The room is just an ordinary place, like one of the classrooms at school or Dr. Pearlman's office. There's a table and chairs, and a window behind the table, except you can't see out of it because the glass is thick and there's wire mesh inside. Everything has that same cleaning smell, only even stronger.

It's hard to see because of the window, and my eyes are still adjusting, but I realize there's a boy sitting at the table. We walk further into the room, and I can see him properly. He looks kind of like the last picture in our hallway, and kind of not. He got a little fatter. His face is round and his hair is short. His skin is red and splotchy across his nose and his cheeks. He's wearing soft fabric pants like pajamas and a soft gray shirt.

"Hello, Theo," says Uncle Donny.

And just like that, it's a *miracle*—my brother, who was dead, has been brought back to life.

"Hi," he says, and his voice is low, not like—not at all like I pictured it.

"It's been a while, I know. You remember your sister?"

His eyes, just like Mama's, leave Uncle Donny and turn to me.

I can't tell if I really remember him, or if I've just looked at his photographs so many times that I feel like I do. I've always known my whole life that I had a brother, but I don't really have too many memories of all the things we must have done together. He's just been the boy in the picture for so long.

"Aoife." He says it just perfect, like only Mama can say it.

"Well, it's been a long time since you two were together," says Uncle Donny. "Aoife, do you want to sit down?"

I take the seat that he pulled out for me, barely looking down at it. I can't stop staring at my brother. It's like looking at a dinosaur or the tooth fairy—those seem about as likely as seeing Theo again.

His hands, on the table, are big, with little hairs on the knuckles. My brother.

"I can't believe you're real life," I say.

"Yes, I feel that way too sometimes," he agrees softly. He looks back at Uncle Donny. "Are you here to talk about the hearing? They were supposed to call Ma about it, but I never heard what she said."

"The hearing of what?" I say.

"Do you mean another assessment?" says Uncle Donny. "Because that . . . didn't go so well last time."

"No, they already did the assessment. This is the real thing. They're going to decide if I can stay here, or if they can punt me over to juvenile court."

"What?—okay, okay, let me, ah, let me get back to you on that," says Uncle Donny. He looks upset.

I'm still not sure what we're hearing about.

"Thanks," says Theo quietly. He plays with his fingers just like I do, and then looks up at me.

We have the same nose, the same eyes.

I remember—

"So, you've grown," he says.

"I have?"

"A little, anyway. But I would still know you if I saw you."

That is a good feeling. I want him to know me.

"Do you remember once, when we went to the beach and I got lost?" I say. That is my first, best memory of Theo. "And you came and found me."

Theo squinted. "A beach? Are you sure it was me?"

I remember his hand reaching for me. His red swimsuit, his face. It must have been him.

I try to think of something else. "Do you remember when we were hiding from the shouting man downstairs? And we ran to a closet to hide."

Uncle Donny clears his throat. "Maybe we can think of some happier memories," he says.

"It wasn't a closet," says Theo. "It was the bathroom."

"You do remember!" I remember how Theo put his arm over my shoulder because I was scared, and then I felt safe. I was scared that the shouting man would come upstairs and find us. "We hid until it was quiet, and the man went away."

And I remember two boys, standing on a rock in the rain . . .

"That was Uncle Mac downstairs," says Theo.

What? It wasn't Mac who was so loud and scary. Was it?

But I remember the sound of that plate shattering into a thousand pieces, too many to ever glue together, and I remember Mama crying on the floor with her face in her hands . . . and I remember . . . Theo—

Two boys, standing on a rock in the rain . . .

"They were fighting about me. I guess you don't remember. Mac and I never got along too well."

"Why not?"

"Mostly because he wasn't my father, I guess."

"I knew that!" I'm excited to know things. "Before Mac, Mama used to have a different special friend. And his name was Ben and he was a Marine."

"Where did you hear that?" Uncle Donny asks me.

I make a face and don't answer.

"My father was a *hero*," says Theo. "Mac is half the man he was."

"Mac is my father," I say.

"All right, let's just try to have an easy visit, okay? Who has something nice to say?" says Uncle Donny.

I can't think of anything nice to say.

"I thought you died," I say, even though it may not be the nicest thing ever. "I thought you were dead, all this time."

Uncle Donny groans.

Theo rubs his face just like Uncle Donny. "Not dead, just gone," he says. "I guess it's almost the same sometimes."

"But Mr. Rutledge told me that you were alive, and I asked Uncle Donny, and he said it was true. So I wanted to see you myself and see if it was real, and it was."

"Wait, what? When the hell did you talk to Mr. Rutledge?" asks Uncle Donny. "You didn't tell me that."

But I don't look away from Theo.

"Mr. Rutledge, eh," says Theo quietly.

"Let's not start this," says Uncle Donny. "We are not here to get into the past today, right?"

"What do you mean?" I ask.

"He's talking about Neddy," says Theo. "That's Mr. Rutledge's grandson. You must have heard a lot about Ned by now."

Ned . . . Slater?

Suddenly I remember the sound of the apple candle, the hollow clunk of it when it hit the rocks and shattered.

"This not why we're here," says Uncle Donny.

But I think that's why I'm here.

"Didn't they tell you?" asks Theo. "Surely someone told you what I did?"

Two boys standing on the rock in the rain. A bigger one and a smaller one . . .

"I remember you fighting," I say. "At the Secret Place, the big rock in the park."

"Okay, I think maybe we should try this again another day," says Uncle Donny, getting up.

Theo is staring at me. "How did you know we called it that? You were too little to remember."

"I remember," I say.

"Theo, stop," says Uncle Donny.

"It's true," says Theo. "We went to the creek, and Ma was having one of her bad days; she made me take Aoife. I didn't want to. I was angry at Mac. We were fighting that morning. And Ned was being a jerk about it. He kept saying I should give Mac a chance."

"And it started to rain," I say. "I remember."

"You started to cry and—and Neddy laughed, and I—I lost my temper. I just—"

"You pushed him," I say.

His arms make circles in the air as he falls back, and I watch his sneakers—red, with a white stripe around the edge and white laces—as they slide backwards, the toes lifting up, and he—falls.

"I killed him," says Theo.

There's a crack that sounds like a watermelon hitting the ground at the church picnic.

Stay right there, Aoife. Don't look.

"Aoife, we're going to have to leave," says Uncle Donny. He puts his hand on my shoulder.

But I am only looking at Theo, who is only looking at me. His face is wet. "I didn't mean to, Aoife," he says. "I just—I was just blowing off steam, but he was so close to the edge, I didn't—I didn't realize how close he was to the edge. The rock was wet. I tried to catch him. But he—he fell."

"What?" says Uncle Donny.

Theo puts his face in his hands.

This is why Mama hasn't been able to come home, because of this secret, sitting right on her chest. I just know it.

"Theo, you told everyone you *killed him*," says Uncle Donny. "You never told anyone any of this. You told the police you were angry, that you shoved him off the rock."

"I did," says Theo softly. "I pushed him, and he fell. It was my fault. It's my fault he's dead."

"But you didn't—Theo, if it was an accident, that's different," says Uncle Donny. He walks around and kneels down next to Theo and puts his hand over his. "That's not the same as murder."

"It was still my fault," says Theo. "Teddy deserved a better friend than me."

But . . . "I thought you said his name was Ned," I say. "Why are you calling him Teddy?"

"His name was Edward," Theo explains, wiping his eyes. "Ned can be a nickname for Edward, but so is Teddy. It was an inside joke, because Teddy can be a nickname for Theodore, too."

That's what Dr. Pearlman said, that Teddy can be short for Theodore. But we never called him Teddy.

Teddy. The boy with the rocket ship.

"Theo, if there's a hearing, we'll be there with you," says Uncle Donny, who has taken his phone out. "But you have to tell them what you told us. And whether it's good or bad, we'll get through it together."

And that's true. He means it *literally*. I can tell.

* * *

When we have to leave, we cross the parking lot without a word. Uncle Donny is walking almost too fast for me to keep up. He unlocks the door with the button. I get in the front seat instead of the back and I do up the buckle myself. He doesn't stop me, just starts up the car.

For a long time we drive without a word. I know I solved the whole mystery at last—and that means Mama is coming home now. I close my eyes and say an extra-special thank-you to Blessed Saint Margaret and the archangel Michael, because they helped me be brave just like Joan of Arc.

"He's never talked about it, ever," says Uncle Donny. "He never said what happened, other than he killed Neddy. Never gave any explanation." He shakes his head. "We all believed he had some kind of break. The doctors said he was—that he was dangerous, that he didn't know what he was doing. And all this time . . ."

I think about pushing Hannah down on the grass. I don't want to think about it anymore. "What's a hearing?" I ask.

Uncle Donny sighs. "That's when people get together in a room and make an official decision together," he says. "You see, last time they assessed Theo, it—it didn't go so well. There are people who wanted to try Theo in criminal court, as an adult."

"For pushing Ned Slater?"

"Yes, for pushing him so that he died. If he did that on purpose because he was angry, that would have been murder. That didn't happen last time, but it came close, and it was very upsetting to your ma. But this is . . . this is good news. What Theo said today. If he can say that again when the people are making their official decision, that would be great."

"And Mama would be happy too?"

"Yes, your ma would be . . . very happy. Very, very happy."

That would make all of us happy.

"I can't wait for Mama to come home," I say. "This time it's going to be soon, for real."

I don't tell him how I know. But I do.

DCF Form 2-1, Investigation Summary—CPP-X-A-1-2.1

List of Interviews—see attachment 2-1A Subject: Scott, Aoife (mother, Siobhan Scott) Current Guardian: Donovan Scott—See Attachment 2-1B		
Determination of the preparer:		
	Yes	**No**
Appropriate resources and social support available to the family. Adequate time/resources to complete thorough investigation.	✓	
Family had history of referrals to CPS. *Notes: Related to past incident, 4 years prior.* *Child removed from home.*	✓	
Caregiver cooperative with investigation.	✓	
Basic needs appeared to be met.	✓	
Satisfactory condition of home.	✓	
Collaterals gave relatively positive reports about family.	✓	
Current issues of domestic violence in family.		✓
A preponderance of evidence of child abuse or neglect is found. *Notes: The level of care provided seems to currently be adequate despite documented limitations.*		✓

Notes: Caretakers are willing to participate in parenting skills program or other services to improve parenting or initiate appropriate services for parenting without referral by the department.

Outcome: Assist in voluntary participation in community-based services commensurate with low risk level.

This report is considered closed.

Chapter Sixteen

⌒

When we get home, I run right up the sidewalk in case Mama is already home. I don't want to miss her for a second longer, and now that we solved the mystery, I know she's coming home.

I look through all the rooms, but she's not here yet. That's okay. I know she'll be here soon.

Uncle Donny comes in behind me and sits on the couch, staring at the wall. "I need to make some phone calls," he says. "Can you play down here? Uh, within sight."

So that's how we spend the next day. And the day after.

I lure the cat from next door right up onto the front steps so she can have tea with me, and Uncle Donny asks the neighbors if they mind and they say it's okay. She's more friendly now that she knows I can be nice, and because Uncle Donny gave me the can of tuna to give her. Uncle Donny says sometimes cats take a while to warm up but that a bribe doesn't hurt.

You know what I have been thinking? Is that Mr. Rutledge must miss Neddy just as much as I have missed Mama all this time. That is the most terrible thing I can think of.

Then finally one morning I wake up and hear voices downstairs. At first I think it might be the radio, because Uncle Donny likes to watch the news in the mornings, but it doesn't sound like news and there's no music playing. I get up and go down the hall in my pajamas, and from the top of the stairs I peep down into the doorway to see who it is.

"Aoife, come on, I've got someone who has been waiting a long time to see you again," says Uncle Donny. He thinks I don't know who it is already, but I do. I walk down the stairs real slow, just in case I'm wrong.

She looks different than the last time I saw her. Her face is thinner and she has droopy skin under her eyes. She looks tired. But then she looks up from the bottom of the stairs and sees me, and she smiles. "Who's this grown-up girl?" she says, and she looks just the same as always.

"Mama!" I say, and I take a flying leap off the landing to run straight into her arms.

"There's my jumping bean," says Mama. I put my arms around her neck just like I always do. She doesn't smell quite right, too much hospital, but underneath it I can almost smell her normal smell. She feels the right shape though, and I hug her and bury my face in her shoulder and feel her silky hair brushing against my cheek.

She starts swaying with me in her arms, back and forth, just like she always does, like we're dancing. I put my head on her neck and listen to her breathing. I hold on so tight that my fingers hurt.

"Aoife, baby, I missed you so much," says Mama, rocking back and forth. And I'd almost forgotten how good it sounds when she says my name. "I'm really sorry I had to leave you alone like that."

"Are you crying, Mama?"

Uncle Donny leans over so we're eye to eye and brushes my hair out of my face. "Your ma's just happy, Aoife, that's all."

"I just missed you so much," Mama whispers.

"I missed you too, Mama! But don't cry. Uncle Donny and I had lots of fun, and I was real well behaved. Wasn't I?"

"Ah, sure, kiddo. I guess you could've been worse."

We walk into the kitchen together, where Uncle Donny has made breakfast. I thought Mama might ask about home base being gone, but she doesn't say anything about it. Maybe Uncle Donny already told her that he took it down. I wonder what she'll think when she sees all the food in the fridge. The boxed milk is gone—Uncle Donny tossed it all away. And there's no dishes in the sink anymore. Plus the tent in the living room is missing, and the TV is back in the TV stand instead of candles, and Uncle Donny's computer is plugged in on the counter.

"I heard you had lots of adventures," says Mama, pulling out a chair so I can sit next to her at the table. She looks a little paler than I remember, but she's smiling, so I smile, too.

"I went all over the neighborhood in the middle of the night! Uncle Donny says I slept walked," I say. By now everybody has said it to me so many times that it feels true, even though I know it isn't. But I also know Mama doesn't want to hear about me and Teddy running around together, or what we learned about Theo. So if Uncle Donny says I slept walked then I'm going to tell everybody that.

"People in this family tend to have that problem," she agrees. "I remember when we were kids, your uncle Donny used to get up at night and walk up and down the stairs."

"He still does!" I say.

Uncle Donny looks surprised. "You didn't say anything," he says.

I shrug.

"We put a special bolt on the door so she can't get outside anymore," says Uncle Donny. I didn't tell him that he's the one who opened it last time. I can keep secrets, too.

"And you got to go see your big brother, huh?"

"Yup," I say. I think I understand now why nobody wanted to talk about Theo. What happened to Neddy was so sad that nobody knew what to say. Nobody even knew how to talk about it, and it turned into a secret. But I'm glad it's not a secret now. I want everything to be right out loud.

And Uncle Donny is going to help with the hearing so it will go better than last time.

Uncle Donny says we'll put up the Slip 'n Slide in the lawn and get the hose out. And Hannah can come over and we'll play all day. But first we have to eat breakfast. I don't want to lose sight of Mama for even a second, so she promises to play with us.

I think it is the best day of my life so far.

* * *

Late that night Mama lies in bed with me and hums "Ave Maria" while I try to fall asleep. She's afraid I'm going to walk in my sleep, which is funny because I wasn't even asleep last time. But I don't tell her that because I like having her lie with me and sing to me. Maybe I'm a little afraid that she's going to leave again, too.

"Aoife, you're not even trying to sleep," she says. Which is true. My eyes are open and everything.

"I'm not sleepy," I tell her.

Mama sighs. "I guess you've got a lot on your mind, too," she says.

"I know you were upset about Theo's hearing," I say. "Are you less upset now?"

"I'm getting there," she says. "I'm sorry I didn't explain to you better about Theo. "Having to send him away—that was the hardest thing I've ever done. But it seemed like our only choice. There were people who wanted to put him in jail, and the doctors said it was his best chance to get better. I guess the thought of going through it all again, now—I couldn't, it was too much. But I'm feeling better now."

"I'm glad," I say. "I don't want you to be confused."

"Baby, I know you're probably thinking that it's not fair that you were born into this family."

I wasn't thinking that at all.

"Maybe there's some truth to it. But let me tell you, this family, we may fall down sometimes, but we always get back up. We are clever and brave and strong. We can get through anything. And you're going to be proud to be one of us someday."

"Pride is a sin," I remind her. Mama always says that. Pride, and wrath, and sorrow.

"Yes, well . . . even Our Lord Jesus was pretty proud of his family tree," she teases. I never heard Mama make a joke about Lord Jesus before.

I'm glad Mama is my mom, because she is the best, and I'm glad Uncle Donny is my uncle. I think I'm even glad Mac is my dad. And I'm glad Theo is my miraculous, real-life brother.

I'm not sure why I'm crying, but it doesn't feel bad.

Mama leans over to kiss the top of my head.

"Now, close your eyes and go to sleep. Tomorrow's another big day."

That night I dream of playing rocket ships at the Secret Place.

Dear Theo,

I got Uncle Donny to help me write this, which he says is called dictatoring. So Uncle Donny is typing on his laptop and I am looking out the window at the cat outside while I talk. Uncle

241

Donny says I can draw you pictures at the end if I want to, after we print it. I think I will draw cats.

I asked Mama if you were going to come home soon and she said maybe. I said what does Maybe *mean and she said it means,* Maybe, Aoife. *So I think that means she doesn't know either. I asked Mama if you are going to pass your hearing and she said that's not how it works. She says some things are not all pass or all fail. Then I asked Uncle Donny and he said yes. [ED—that is not exactly what happened, but she is the dictator.]*

I think I understand why you didn't tell everyone the real story about what happened to Neddy all this time. I am sorry that you were sad, but I hope that you are happier now. I don't think Neddy would want you to be sad forever.

I told Hannah that we solved the mystery and she said that she doesn't want to solve mysteries anymore. I said why and she said because real life is more interesting. She is trying to make the junior dance squad at school now. But I think solving a mystery is much better than junior dance squad, even if Sacred Heart had one, which they don't. And her cartwheels are still wobbly.

I asked Uncle Donny if you were going to come home and he said, he will if we have anything to do with it. I said will that make us a family? And he said we already are a family.

I miss you. When you come, we can go show Dr. Pearlman that I was right all along. And we can go light candles in church and maybe we will see another miracle.

Love Your Real-Life Sister,
Aoife Joan

Epilogue

We're out away from all the houses, and it's getting dark except for a line of pink right at the edge of the sky. By the time me, Mama, and Uncle Donny park in the parking lot, the sun has gone all the way down. After this just the three of us are going to go out to dinner—even though we're on a budget!—to meet Uncle Donny's special friend, Simon. But first we are going to the lake.

Mac is waiting for us in front of the beach, leaning against his beat-up truck.

"Hi, Mac!" I say, running towards him.

"Hey there, Alfie!" He picks me up under the armpits and swings me around in a circle before setting me back on my feet.

He walks over to Mama, who gives him a kiss. I notice he doesn't say anything to Uncle Donny, who clears his throat and looks away. Mac coughs into his sleeve.

"Well, what do you think, Alfie, you want to try these here sparklers?" he says. He holds out a pack of something in his hand, and I squeal and spin round and round in circles because I'm so excited. I've never had a sparkler of my own before.

He offers me what looks like a skinny gray cattail, the kind that grow around the other side of the lake. I don't see how this is going to be a firework you can hold, like Uncle Donny said, but I take one, and so does Mama, who gives one to Uncle

Donny, who mutters something to her under his breath but then takes it. Mac takes out his lighter—it's a new one, I notice, but I don't ask where his other one went.

"Hold the far end, Alfie," he tells me. "Watch your fingers."

"Be careful," says Uncle Donny.

Then Mac strikes the lighter—*tick tick, snick*—and he holds the flame up to the end. Nothing happens at first. Then the sparkler hisses, and all at once I see the little mini firework.

"Whee!" I turn around and around, and the firework glows on the end like Tinkerbell.

"Watch out, Aoife," says Mama. "It's hot; it can burn you. Maybe this wasn't a good idea," she adds, to Mac. I don't care because I'm twirling in circles and the sparkler is twirling with me.

"Look, Aoife," says Uncle Donny, and when I turn around, he's got one lit up, too. He writes with it like it's a pen, D-O-N-O-V-A-N. The light stays in the air for a second so you can read the letters. Mine is white, but his is kind of blueish, and when Mama lights hers, it's pink.

"We should always do this after the Fourth," says Mac, lighting his own until it pops and hisses and lights up the same color as mine. "Less crowded, and cheaper, too."

Mama comes to stand next to me and puts her arm around my shoulders. We watch our sparklers burn down, looking out over the lake. The sky is full of stars, and you can hardly tell a star from a sparkler.

"Happy eighth of July, Aoife," says Mama.

Just then Mac shoots off a bottle rocket, and we all turn to watch it streak out straight up, making a high-pitched noise. Then it explodes with a *bang* that makes us all jump. Then the firework turns into smoke and disappears.

"Someone's probably calling the cops right now," says Uncle Donny. I hope not, because it was scary when Mr. Rutledge called them on me last time.

"Just one more," says Mac. He aims it out over the water this time, winking at me. "For Teddy."

Mama doesn't say anything, and neither does Uncle Donny. But I stand next to Mac and watch him light the fuse.

At the edge of the lake, I can see a shape in the darkness. At first it's a blob, then it's round and on all fours, with a big head.

"Here we go," says Mac.

But I am looking at the outline as it turns into a bear. I think—I think it's *Teddy*.

"Here we go!"

I cover my ears and the firework jumps out of the bottle and zips out across the sky.

Teddy doesn't wave, or come any closer. All the fur is standing up along his arms, but as I watch, it starts to sink into his skin. His legs get longer and the fur disappears.

I take my hands away just in time to hear the *pop* of the rocket as it lights up in a shower of sparks. You can see the reflection in the lake, just like Mama said. It looks like a dream.

I watch Teddy's ears sink into his head and he grows thick, dark hair that curls around his head. He's wearing jeans and a sweatshirt and bright-red sneakers. He's a little boy again. He is glowing, so bright that I can barely look at him.

I wish Mr. Rutledge could see him again.

Then Teddy turns into a cloud of fireflies, around the edges first, and then all the way through. And the fireflies fly away.

"Beautiful," says Mama, stroking my hair.

Then I run and get another sparkler, and spin and spin until I think I'm going to throw up.

Acknowledgments

It takes a village to raise a book. I want to first extend my love and gratitude to my parents, who patiently believed in me all these years. A huge shout-out to all the members of the Metro Wriders, and particularly to Jeff West and Kellie Small—a thousand thank-yous! To Chris Bucci, the kindest and best of agents, without whom this book would never have been published. To the wonderful folks of the Bethesda Writer's Center, particularly Zach Powers, who took time to coach me on my next steps. To my editor Chelsey Emmelhainz, for all her patience with a first-time author. And to Maisy, who had to listen to me read the same chapters out loud over and over again every night for six months straight.